A SCOUNDREL'S KISS

"Come Arabella, there is no need to pretend with me," Neville said as he pulled her back into his arms.

She twisted, now desperate to get away from this sinfully tempting man, or she would be no better than the weak-willed female her father always claimed she was. "Do not touch me again, or I shall rouse the entire household."

His brown furrowed. "Why, I do believe you're in earnest."

"I am. Everybody is right. You are only interested in your base desires."

"And yet you are pure as the driven snow?" He teased her. As if to prove that she was as wicked as he, Neville reached out and pulled her into his embrace. He kissed her with a fierce passion, and his hips slowly gyrated against hers, making her body weak and her heart race. "Or is *this* what you truly want?"

MARGARET MOORE

A SCOUNDREL'S KISS

AVON BOOKS  NEW YORK

AVON BOOKS, INC.
1350 Avenue of the Americas
New York, New York 10019

Copyright © 1999 by Margaret Wilkins
Inside cover author photo by Towne Portraits
Published by arrangement with the author
Library of Congress Catalog Card Number: 98-93544
ISBN: 0-380-80266-X
www.avonbooks.com/romance

First Avon Books Printing: March 1999

Printed in the U.S.A.

WCD   10 9 8 7 6 5 4 3 2 1

To Karen Solem,
with much appreciation
for her expertise and sage advice

Chapter 1

ﹾﹾ⟨◦◦⟩ﹾﹾ

Continuously, loudly and in a manner completely uncivilized, some lout pounded on the door of Lord Farrington's townhouse.

"I'faith, I'll have that fellow's head displayed upon London Bridge!" the heir to the earldom of Barrsettshire muttered as he very slowly eased his six-foot frame to an upright position and scratched his chest through his untied shirt.

Then, not a little disgusted by the dry, dead taste in his mouth, he rubbed his bleary eyes and bellowed for the only servant he retained.

What hour of the day was it? Neville wondered as he got to his feet. It could be any time between dawn and the middle of the afternoon, for all he knew.

He staggered to the diamond-paned second-floor window and peered into the street. A group of obviously curious, well-dressed peo-

1

ple had gathered in the cobbled street, pointing and sniggering at—

A curse flew from Neville's lips at the sight of the familiar coach outside his door. He reeled backward, for a moment entangled in the draperies.

"Jarvis!" he shouted again, this time with urgency and what sounded suspiciously like desperation as he surveyed the paneled withdrawing room littered with empty wine bottles and goblets containing dark-red dregs.

The knocking waned a moment, and Neville held his breath.

Then, to his considerable chagrin, the pounding began anew.

Muttering more curses, he grabbed all the empty bottles he could see and shoved them into the fireplace under the ashes.

"My lord?"

In answer to the Irishman's interrogative mutter, Neville turned to see Jarvis standing in the doorway, his disheveled state not unlike that of his master. His jacket was undone, his breeches half tied and his red hair tousled to a condition of brilliant messiness.

He also looked as stunned as Neville felt.

"Do up your jacket and answer the door!" Neville commanded. "The earl is on the threshold!"

"The earl?" Jarvis asked stupidly, by his foggy tone not yet fully awake.

"Yes," Neville hissed. "The Earl of Barrsettshire. Your master! My father!"

The words were no sooner out of his mouth than the obviously irate earl began shouting Neville's name in the street, an event which would no doubt provide the neighbors with a choice bit of gossip. Jarvis, meanwhile, had at last come to comprehension, for now he stared as if hearing the Trump of God.

"Answer the door," Neville repeated deliberately.

"Oh, yes, at once, my lord!"

Jarvis bowed and hurried away.

What in the name of God was his father doing in London? Neville wondered as he raked his hand through his unkempt, shoulder-length curls. The room was a shambles, and he little better.

In addition to the dirty goblets, bread crumbs dotted the threadbare Turkey carpet where last night Sir Richard Blythe had brandished a loaf while enacting a scene from his newest play. Neville's jacket lay tossed upon a chair on the other side of the room like half of a corpse, and his proudly plumed hat sat on the floor beside it. His baldric, sheath and sword leaned against the door frame.

Where the devil were his boots?

As he heard his father's familiar, heavy tread approaching the withdrawing room, Neville grabbed the wine goblets by their stems, shoved them into an open writing desk and pushed the lid shut.

"Neville!"

His back still to the door, Neville winced at the sound of his father's stern voice. Subduing his mortification and dismay at this unexpected visitation as best he could, he assumed a pleasant expression as he turned to face his parent.

Who stood just as Neville might have expected, dressed all in black like a carrion crow, his hands on his hips, his countenance condemning, his pointed goatee quivering like an accusing finger, while his nostrils flared as if he were a stallion about to bolt.

"This room is a disgrace," the earl declared by way of greeting, growing red in the face so that his narrow mustache and trimmed, V-shaped beard seemed all the whiter.

He ran a displeased gaze over Neville, who made no move to tie his gaping shirt or tuck it into his partially unbuttoned breeches. "So are you."

"Good day to you, too, Father," Neville drawled languidly, stifling any faint hope he had harbored that his father would express some pleasure at seeing his only child. "I confess you come upon me unawares."

Rather mysteriously remaining on the threshold of the room, his father scowled. "Have you just awakened? It is the middle of the day! And look at this place! How can you let the servants be so remiss in their duties?"

"The servant, Father. I can afford but one."

His father's frown deepened. "Because you drink and gamble and whore too much!"

Neville did not trouble himself to deny the accusation.

"I perceive you continue to abuse my household by living like a pig wallowing in the mud," the earl said.

"If you choose to think so, but I am a very happy swine."

"Until the day you get slaughtered by those around you!"

Neville leaned back against the mantel and folded his arms over his chest. "I am no worse than my fellows."

"No, nor no better, either! I suppose I should be grateful I don't find you wearing those ridiculous petticoat breeches," his father growled. "What would prompt a man to wear anything so ridiculously like a skirt?"

"I am surprised you know anything of fashion, living so out of the way as you do."

"I have seen enough on the journey to expect to find you in something similar."

"I understand they are quite comfortable. I've ordered ten pair from my tailor."

This was an outrageous lie, for even if he had

been able to afford them, Neville detested the hideously baggy new fashion nearly as much as his father could.

Besides, his legs were nothing to hide, and he knew it.

Again Lord Barrsettshire scanned the room, his lip curling with displeasure. "Did you not receive my letter telling you of my visit?" he demanded. "Or have you neglected to read it, as you neglect my instructions regarding your duties as the heir to my estate?"

"Now that you remind me, I do seem to recall some mention of a proposed sojourn in your last delightful epistle. Unfortunately, your hand is so poor, I could not make out a date for the happy occasion. To what do I owe the honor of your company? I know it cannot be to see me, and it is no secret that you despise the City."

"I have brought a friend of the family to London."

"I would be charmed to meet the fellow who could patiently listen to your complaints all the way from Lincolnshire," Neville replied truthfully. "I am sure the roads were terrible, the accommodations at the inns repulsive and the food indigestible."

His father did not respond except to glower before he turned and held out his hand.

Neville almost fell over when a woman appeared beside him. She wore a plain cloak with a large hood, so he could not see her face in its shadow.

"Is there an eclipse of the sun?" he asked, suppressing his shock beneath a mask of calm composure.

"Are you drunk? Or is this what passes for wit in these degenerate days?"

"I thought some sort of celestial cataclysm might explain this unusual occurrence," he replied, wondering what he would see when the lady in question threw back her hood.

"You are as much a fool as ever," his father growled. "And you wanted to see him," he muttered to his companion.

Who finally, and with fluid grace, pushed back her hood to reveal her features.

Neville had not seen such a fresh-faced, pretty country lass in years. Soft, brown, natural curls framed a dewy, pink-tinged complexion free of any cosmetic addition. He had a glimpse of large blue eyes before she demurely lowered them to gaze at the floor and thick lashes fanned upon her undoubtedly satin-soft cheeks. Below a fine, delicate nose, she had full lips that could have been fashioned by Eros himself, so made for kissing did they seem.

Immediately, Neville contrasted the genuine loveliness of the fair unknown with that of the ladies of King Charles's court. His conclusions

would not have pleased the women of Whitehall.

Who was she? Where had she come from?
How old was she, and was she married or betrothed?

And more important perhaps, how had she
endured listening to his father complain all the
way from Lincolnshire?

"I doubt you remember Lady Arabella Martin," his father said, his tone implying that Neville, through sheer perverse negligence, could
scarcely be counted upon to remember anything at all.

Arabella? This was little Arabella Martin, all
grown up? So *well* grown up!

Neville remembered that afternoon in the
garden as if it were yesterday: her blushes, her
shy smiles, her admiring eyes.

"She is the daughter of the late Duke of Bellhurst," his father continued.

"Indeed, I do remember her," Neville replied in his most beguiling tones and giving
her his most charming smile as he made a low,
sweeping bow. "I was simply too surprised
and delighted to speak. I am utterly transported to see her again."

"You sound like an imbecile, Neville," his
father grumbled, destroying his son's pleasant
thoughts as effectively as a splash of freezing
water made a man shrivel. "Or a poet."

The earl made the prospect of being a poet

sound infinitely worse than being an imbecile.

"What kind of talk is that? Too delighted to speak! Transported!" The earl sniffed dismissively. "I suppose that is how the fools of the court talk to one another." He pointed at an upholstered chair. "Arabella, sit, if you can find anyplace *clean*."

His father always ordered everybody about as if they were dogs, Neville thought angrily as he watched Arabella glide across the worn and crumb-covered carpet.

Her expression placid, she looked around the room, then perched herself on the edge of the chair. Her cloak fell open slightly to reveal a plain gown of some stiff-looking dark-gray material, high-necked and horrible, that nevertheless could not disguise a shapely figure.

Neville recalled her father, who had converted to Puritanism after the death of his wife some years before, when Arabella had been a little child. He had been very strict in his religious observance. Perhaps he had managed to subdue Arabella completely.

If so, that would be a great pity.

"This is what comes of spending your time with playwrights," Lord Barrsettshire observed, using the same tone for playwrights as he might have used for cutthroats and pirates.

His lordship then proceeded to walk to another chair as daintily as if the floor were covered with hot coals instead of crumbs.

"I have only one friend who writes for a living," Neville amended genially. "Sir Richard Blythe."

"Another member of a fine old family gone to ruin!"

"He has had little choice but to earn his living somehow since Cromwell took his family's estate and sold it."

"But that is not an honorable living!"

Neville shrugged his shoulders. This was an argument he could not win. Indeed, his father never listened to a dissenting opinion, especially from Neville. Therefore, Neville had concluded, the best thing for all concerned was to keep as much distance as possible between himself and his father. In this, at least, and whether his father realized it or not, he had had great success.

Besides, he would rather look at Arabella.

At that moment, Jarvis entered the room with a tray bearing a bottle of wine and three somewhat clean, if streaky, goblets. He had what had once been a linen napkin over his arm. Its current dingy condition made Neville think Jarvis had lately been using it to clean his boots.

Ignoring everybody—although his grave yet blushing face showed that he was well aware of the earl's censorious presence—the Irishman carefully balanced the tray on one hand and with the other took the rag and thrice slapped the top of the table nearest Arabella's chair, sending motes of dust upward like so much chaff. He coughed slightly, then set down the tray, bowed to the earl and slowly backed out of the room.

"That bogtrotter is the only servant you have managed to keep?" the earl asked indignantly.

"I find his hair color amusing."

Neville glanced at Arabella, wondering what she thought of Jarvis—and him. Their gazes met and held briefly, and he saw condemnation in her blue eyes.

Because the room was untidy? Because he was not in any fit state to receive visitors? He could scarcely demand that they wait outside for him to dress.

Typical of a Puritan to condemn without comprehension or sympathy. What did she know of his life since he had left his unhappy home seven years ago?

"I apologize for the state of the house, my dear," the earl said, interrupting Neville's thoughts.

"I am sure she will find it in her charitable heart to excuse it. This is what becomes of men left to their own devices."

Still she said nothing, merely staring at the floor as if she'd never seen a floor before.

He went closer to her. "Tell me, Father, what tragedy has rendered Lady Arabella mute?"

That made her raise her eyes—eyes flashing

with a fiery spark of temper. "I am not mute, my lord," she said in a firm yet delightfully musical voice.

"Ah!" he cried, pleased that he had compelled her to speak. "Then you must forgive me for that mistake."

"You seem to have many faults requiring forgiveness," she replied solemnly.

Surprisingly, her words disturbed him far more than anything his irate father had said.

But then, he quickly reasoned, he was always more susceptible to criticism when it came from such lovely lips.

His father gestured at the wine.

"Neville, what kind of cheap drink is this? Where is the good wine? Or have you and your cronies downed it all during your bacchanalian revels?"

"Your stores are safe below. Mindful of your frugality and regardless of the demands of hospitality, I provide my friends with the cheapest wine I can find."

With a dismissive grunt, the earl again surveyed the dusty, messy room before staring at the ashy grate. "Are those empty bottles I see?" He turned to glare at his son. "You *are* a drunkard!"

Waving his hand dismissively, Lord Farrington strolled toward the dirty window. "Alas, I cannot seem to apply myself to excessive drinking, either."

Arabella watched the young man turn and lean against the windowsill, every movement of his body graceful and elegant yet somehow stifled, as if he were saving his vitality for some other, not quite honorable, purpose.

Lord Farrington was not what Arabella had expected and most certainly not what she remembered. When she had met him seven years ago, the young and handsome Neville had been so kind and sympathetic that she had told him all her woes.

Now the person who had inspired her dreams ever since stood before her disheveled, impertinent and unrepentant, seemingly not at all nonplussed by either his disorderly condition or that of the room. She could easily believe he had slept in his long, fitted black breeches and wrinkled, partially open white shirt, which revealed an astonishing, immodest amount of his muscular chest—perhaps in this very chair. His jacket lay upon another chair, his boots were in the corner behind the door, and she could only hope he was ignorant of the hole in his stocking.

He was still undeniably handsome, his maturity making him even more so, perhaps. The boyish softness of his face was quite gone, replaced by hard angles and planes. The strong line of his jaw was dark with stubble. His thick, curling hair, now to his shoulders, reminded her of the beast she had once seen in a woodcut of Daniel in the lions' den.

As for his eyes . . . Long ago, they had been filled with compassion; now they seemed as hard as coal and just as unfeeling.

And when he spoke, it was with a flippant drawl that was most disconcerting.

Perhaps she had been wrong to discount so much of what Lord Barrsettshire had said regarding his son since she had come to live with him, instead relying on her own fond memory of a single afternoon.

"Pray tell, Lady Arabella, how is your good father?" Neville inquired.

The earl answered for her. "He's dead. Three months past."

Arabella winced to hear the event spoken of so bluntly. Looking at Neville, she thought she saw some flicker of emotion pass in his eyes, but if it was commiseration, it was quickly gone.

"My sympathies," he drawled with a languid bow of his handsome head and absolutely no sincerity.

"I am Arabella's guardian now," the earl announced.

Neville raised an aristocratic eyebrow. "I am certain you will take your responsibility to heart, Father. I know how you enjoy having someone to command, and she seems so amenable to obeying." He sighed. "Alas, I fear no one would have the goodness to pass away and leave such a beauty in my tender care." His rich, deep voice lowered to an intimate whisper. "For I assure you, Lady Arabella, while I could never be a good commander, I can be very tender."

Arabella swallowed hard, unable to think of anything to say. Even if he was right about his father seeming to enjoy commanding people like so many animals, it was very wrong and disrespectful of him to say so.

And as for his other comment . . .

"Neville," the earl snapped, "your disgusting innuendo tells me that what I have long suspected is true. You have been completely corrupted by living in this cesspool."

"The Thames could certainly be considered a cesspool, given what can be found floating in it," Neville responded, apparently not a whit upset by his father's condemnation. "Tell me, Lady Arabella, what do *you* think of London?"

"We have only just arrived, yet already there is much here that is not what I expected," she replied, wondering if he would understand her or care if he did.

He waved his hand in another gesture of dismissal. "No doubt it is vastly different from dull little Grantham."

"London is a hellhole," the earl said, voicing an opinion Arabella had been forced to endure for the whole of their journey. "Cromwell did not improve it, nor has the king, so far as I can tell. I am certain it is still nothing more than a place of vice and waste, which no doubt explains its appeal to *you!*"

Neville Farrington's expression did not alter. "Then I am shocked that you would venture near it, especially with such a companion." He turned his coolly measuring gaze onto her again. "Or perhaps she has a desire to be amused that cannot be satisfied in Grantham? If so, I am at her service."

Arabella gulped as she looked away, her whole body seeming to blush under his scrutiny.

The earl made another sour face. "This sort of talk is what comes of hanging about the court, no doubt. Arabella thought it was necessary for us to come here, and I agreed."

"Indeed?" Neville replied with a raising of his patrician brows. "Arabella thought it necessary? And you agreed?"

With a mocking smile, he made a slight inclination of his head. "I am most impressed. It is no small accomplishment to compel my father to do anything."

Arabella did not reply.

"We come here for a *purpose,*" the earl said, "not idle amusement."

A mildly surprised look appeared on Neville's face. "A purpose? Whatever might that be? I thought you believed there was no reason at all for anybody to ever visit this den of iniquity—unless this is a cautionary excursion, to teach this unspoiled young lady what she is to avoid."

"Fortunately, thanks to her father, Arabella is already a young lady of proper morals and good sense," the earl replied.

"Then for what possible purpose would you journey here?"

"To get her a husband."

Chapter 2

Neville Farrington smiled slowly. "Then, Father, I must applaud your wisdom in coming to the best marriage market in England."

"Do you think I am something to be sold, like a pig or a cow?" Arabella asked, trying very hard to remain calm.

With that infuriating smile, the earl's son raised one eyebrow as he continued to regard her. "Why should you be any different from other women of quality?"

"So are you then a rooster, or a stallion to be brought to stud?"

"Of course." Neville turned to regard his father. "With such beauty, I am sure it will not be too onerous a task to find someone willing to take her, especially since she is the daughter of a duke who, for all his eccentricities, was rather wealthy. I'faith, my lord, you will be so besieged with suitors, you will surely have a devil of a time making a choice. Am I to assume, then, that your stay will be of some duration?" Then the expression in his eyes altered ever so slightly. "Unless there is a need for haste. Is she with child?"

Arabella stared at him in outraged shock. "No, I am not!"

"Pardon me, I'm sure," Neville murmured without one particle of contrition. "Since you are capable of prying my father from his estate and there seems to be some haste in the matter, I naturally assumed a child was in the offing."

Arabella raised her chin defiantly and her lip curled with scorn. She was no longer intimidated by this handsome man's presence and worldly airs. Whatever he had been, he was something vastly different—and inferior—now. "It is not an unnatural thing for a young woman to want to be married. What else would you have me do?"

"I can think of many things a young woman can do that do not require marriage," he drawled meaningfully, another look in his eyes.

A look that made her blush yet again.

The earl shot to his feet. "Neville, that's enough! You and your insinuations disgust me! I am ashamed to call you my son! What you have said only confirms my low opinion of you, though you are my son."

"Because I am your son, I knew it would not take much."

"You are a corrupt, sinful lecher who has no comprehension of responsibility and duty!"

Neville shrugged as if to say he was guilty and did not care that he was.

"I, however, fully understand such things."

"Which?" his son inquired. "Corruption? Or sinful lechery?"

Arabella stepped between the two men, her gaze darting from the calm young one to his red-faced parent, who looked as if he might explode with rage or fall into a fit.

"My lord," she said to the earl, "we have had a long and tiring journey. Perhaps we should rest."

Lord Barrsettshire blinked like a startled owl, or as if he had just remembered her presence. "Rest? If I rest, I am likely to wake to discover that I have lost possession of this house and everything in it because of his debts!"

The memory of her father's unexpected death was fresh enough to put urgency into Arabella's tone. "My lord, please! I am sure a nap will refresh you."

"If he were any more refreshed, he would probably draw that ancient sword of his and attack me," Neville noted, strolling across the room.

"Then you should be glad he is not," she snapped. She turned back to the earl and took his arm. "Come, my lord, I am sure—"

The old man shook off her hand. "This is his grandfather's sword!"

Leaning his weight on one long, lean leg, Neville merely crossed his arms and smiled.

"You go and rest, Arabella," the earl commanded imperiously, "if you can find a suitable bedchamber in the whole of this house."

"At present, the only room suitably prepared for a lady is my bedchamber," Neville remarked. "She is most welcome to avail herself of whatever hospitality it affords."

"Will you keep such vile comments to yourself?" his father snarled.

"Please, my lord, don't upset yourself," Arabella urged gently.

She gave Neville a sidelong glance intended to let him know she was not going to be agitated by his rude impertinence. Regrettably, she could not tell from his mocking smile or his inscrutable eyes if she had succeeded or not.

She turned her attention back to the earl. "If you will excuse me, my lord, I am certain there is a chamber I can make suitable for you. If so, will you rest, for my sake?"

"Oh, very well," the old man muttered.

She smiled at her success, until Neville spoke. "Since Puritans are industrious people, I don't doubt she can scrub and clean with the best of them." He sauntered to the door to open it for her. "Jarvis will take you upstairs. You will find him in the hall, listening to every word we say."

"What—?" his father cried.

"I'faith, sir, as the lady so desperately suggests, calm yourself," Neville said. "I would not have your death of apoplexy cast at my feet along with the multitude of my other sins."

Arabella curtsied to the earl, gave Neville a scornful, sidelong glance, then hurried out of the room.

"Has every courtier in London taken to talking like a whoremonger—or just you?" the earl demanded the moment the door closed behind Arabella.

"I don't know what you mean."

"You could not have been more rude to her if you had believed her to be a harlot."

"Of course I could have."

"You—"

"Disgusting, lascivious scoundrel. Spare me a repetition of my faults, if you please. I will not contradict you."

"Have you no shame?"

"Apparently not."

"Then I shall indeed have no remorse for what I am about to do."

Neville regarded his father with a bemused expression. "Are you intending to attack me with my grandfather's sword after all?" His expression hardened. "I will defend myself."

"I can well believe you would, but what I will do has far more serious consequences, especially for one of your proclivities."

"Go on. I am all ears."

His father sat in the chair nearest the hearth, regarding Neville like St. Peter facing an unrepentant sinner at the gates of heaven. "It has grown increasingly clear to me that you are unwilling or incapable of taking your responsibilities and duties as my son and heir seriously. You waste your days and nights at Whitehall with the courtiers or in other idle pursuits. If and when you choose to marry, you will probably select some creature unworthy of our family who has managed to ensnare you by base or lustful means."

"As long as I enjoy the means, what harm in that?"

"Have you no sense of the honor of our family? Our name?"

"You would tell me to select a woman worthy of us, is that it?"

"You are incapable of that."

Neville's jaw clenched. "Perhaps I should attempt to win the hand of the fair Arabella."

His father sniffed derisively. "She is too intelligent a girl to be swayed by one of your ilk. Nor would I allow it. I have something else in mind. Arabella—"

Neville gasped as a sudden idea assailed

him, filling him with shock and rage and something else. "*You* wish to marry her!"

"Fool!" his father cried, truly aghast. "I will never marry again! I have done with that.

"But Arabella is another matter. I have watched her well and known her long. Unlike the majority of her sex, she is a clever, rational, moral woman. She will be a fine wife for the husband who deserves her—for the husband I will select for her.

"Therefore, when she marries, it is my intention to make her and her spouse the heirs to the bulk of my estate."

Neville stared at him, unbelieving.

"You will have the old manor house on the estate and receive an allowance upon which a *sensible* man might live comfortably, both from now on and after my death. Unfortunately, I cannot strip you of the title."

"You cannot be serious!" Neville gasped at last.

"I assure you, Neville, I have never been more serious in my life. I am determined that the estate of Barrsettshire will not be frittered away on gambling, drinking and whores."

"I'faith, Father, what have *you* been imbibing?"

"You are the one who imbibes to excess, Neville," his father retorted.

"Who says so?" Neville demanded, for the

moment forgetting the wine bottles shoved in the ashes.

"I have it on good authority."

"And is this authority the same source for your belief that I am not worthy of my rightful inheritance?"

"As a matter of fact, yes."

"Who?" Neville asked angrily, all pretext of calm unconcern gone. "Who has convinced you to pass over the son of your body?"

The earl looked away. "That is immaterial."

"Not to me!" Neville cried. Then his eyes narrowed. "Lady Lippet, I dare say."

"And others," the earl declared defiantly. "Would you tell me they are lying? Even you cannot have the gall to deny what so many have said."

"I fear that I have indeed been remiss in not visiting you at the ancestral home," Neville said, fighting to regain his composure. "Then I might have realized you were in your dotage."

"My *dotage*!"

"What else would you call it? Or are you ill?"

"I am in perfect health and my judgment is utterly sound."

"Sound? How can it be, when you would rob your own son?"

"You would have done well to remember that you are my son, with duties and responsibilities, before now," the earl replied. "You are not worthy of your place. This house is nearly falling down from neglect. This room is filthy. You look like a drunken sailor. Add to that all the other things of which I have heard. There is a very multitude of reasons for me to renounce you."

"And I am my mother's son," Neville added grimly, regarding his father steadily.

His father did not answer.

Neville strolled to the chair where his jacket lay. "I confess myself surprised that you would trust a woman with a ha'penny, let alone my inheritance, but then, Lady Arabella is so concerned for you!" He picked up the plain black garment and drew it on. "Tell me, did she promise to look after you in your old age? Did she say that you would always have a home with her and that she would nurse you and fuss over you like a hen with one chick?"

His father scowled. "By your words you again demonstrate both your corruption and your ignorance."

"Oh, I am at fault again, although I am not bestowing a considerable inheritance upon some country-bred female who is no blood relation and who has done nothing to earn such a reward, while your son is to inherit nothing more than a title, a pittance and an old house that has been crumbling since Henry the Eighth ascended the throne. Oh, yes, and for all this, the disinherited son is to be grateful."

"I would rather bestow it on her than see you and your decadent friends waste it! She will put it to good use. *Moral* use. *Virtuous* use. *Christian* use."

"I dare say one's opinion of your decision depends upon how one defines waste."

Neville reached down and swept up his hat. As he placed it on his head, he glared at his father, and for a moment, in their anger, they looked very much alike. "I wonder who first put this ludicrous notion into your head at all? Surely not the moral, virtuous, Christian Arabella Martin. She would not do such a thing. She would not wield winning smiles or pious looks or dedicated prayer, pretending that she didn't know you were listening."

"No, she did not!"

Neville spotted his errant boots and grabbed them before picking up his baldric and sword. "My lord, that is the most astonishing thing you have yet said. You would have me believe you thought of this incredible resolution all on your own?"

"You rude, disgusting, impertinent rascal! You are so corrupt you can no longer recognize a virtuous woman when she stands before you. Leave my house!"

"As you might have guessed when I took up my hat, I am doing just that," Neville said at the door, his boots, baldric and sword held against his chest, his hand on the latch. He gasped dramatically. "Or are you casting me into the streets forever?"

"Don't tempt me—and don't you go near Arabella!"

"If she is as virtuous as you think, she will be impervious to anything I might do. Or am I to assume from this desire to have me gone that you have some doubt of her rectitude? Indeed, Father, given your astonishing announcement, I rather think I have more to fear from her than she from me. Who knows but she might persuade me right out of my clothes?"

"Neville!"

"However, I shall not put her to the test. Instead, I shall take my useless, disgusting presence where it will be appreciated. I bid you good day, Father."

Neville strolled out the door. Then he slammed it hard behind him.

Arabella slowly paced in the dusty, musty upper chamber to which the red-haired Jarvis had reluctantly led her. She did not know if his unwillingness stemmed from his desire to remain where he could hear the earl and his son arguing, or because the earl's bedchamber was in no fit state for anyone's occupation.

Thick, heavy draperies, made of what had once been fine and costly brocade, but now seemed to have the dust of ages upon them,

covered the small mullioned windows over-
looking the street. The dark oak paneling was
likewise dust-covered, as were the table and
worn chair and the very large, heavy bed.
There was a featherbed upon the bed, but no
other coverings of any kind.

Cobwebs hung in the corners, and when Arabella glanced down, she saw that her feet
were leaving patterns on the dusty floor. Apparently mice had also been cavorting about
the room.

Arabella shivered a little and looked around
before laying her cloak over the back of the single chair. She did not fear mice, exactly. Their
wiggling little bodies just bothered her a little.
Rats, however, were another matter entirely.

Muffled sounds drifted up the chimney from
below, for this chamber was directly over the
withdrawing room.

The earl and his son were still quarreling.

She sighed softly, glad to be out of the room
and dismayed, too.

To think she had come to London with such
joyful expectations! For one thing, it was London, where the restored king held court. Where
there were balls and parties and masques and
theaters. Where there would be color and light
and music.

And where Neville Farrington would be.

She should not have been so swift to ration-
alize the earl's opinion of his son, thinking that,

as with many critical men, beneath his harsh words was an abiding love for his child. So it had been with her father, who had often found fault with her. Yet she had never doubted his love.

In this case, however, she saw no evidence of anything other than disappointment and anger in the earl's responses to his son, and a shocking lack of respect and deference and remorse on Neville's part.

Of course, she had expected Neville to be different. It was seven years since the day her father had brought her to the earl's estate, and they had both been little more than children. But she hadn't expected him to have fallen so low.

Unfortunately, what had been sincere, kind and soft-spoken seemed to have disappeared completely, replaced by a cynical, flippant bearing when he was not speaking and looking at her so seductively.

She had attracted men's notice before, yet every attempt by a man to compel her notice paled beside one glance from Neville Farrington.

She looked into the busy street below. Fine coaches rumbled along the cobblestones. Well-dressed couples strolled arm in arm, the women cloaked against the cool spring air, many of the men wearing the new fashion of

petticoat breeches, which looked like beribboned skirts.

Neville had yet to adopt this somewhat ef-
feminate apparel. He had been wearing tight-
fitting breeches that were intended to be tucked
into boots. Given that his legs were long and
muscular, it could be that he was too vain to
conceal them under folds of fabric.

As if to forcefully demonstrate the difference
in clothing, a horseman trotted past, his dress
a model of fashionable extravagance. His
breeches looked so voluminous that they might
have utilized enough fabric to make a dress for
her. His waist-length jacket was of scarlet velvet trimmed with gold, like the breeches. His
broad-brimmed hat had such a large feather,
she wondered if it doubled as a quill pen.

As the stranger rode out of sight, she was
reminded of something else: no matter what
happened between Lord Barrsettshire and his
son, she was in London at last. With the earl
as her guardian, she could move in the first
circle of society. If she was very lucky, she
might even see the king!

With that comforting thought, she turned
away from the window and again surveyed the
room. This could yet be a lovely chamber, with
some cleaning. Deciding it would be better to
work than muse upon recent, unsettling events,
she searched about for anything she might use
as a rag.

A door slammed below. Curious as to what that heralded, she hurried to the top of the stairs.

Neville Farrington was at the bottom, his expression an angry scowl, his white-plumed hat perched on his head as he struggled to put on his boots. A leather baldric and sword lay on the floor beside him.

Even now, despite the changes in him, he was still the most attractive man she had ever seen. Moreover, he seemed to emanate virility as the sun did its rays. His broad shoulders and muscular chest added to that impression, as did his lean, strong fingers.

Those same fingers that had clasped her own in warm intimacy that day in the garden.

Before she could go back to the bedchamber, he glanced up. Straightening abruptly, he snatched up his baldric and sword. His intense gaze seemed to bore through her body as he slowly climbed the stairs toward her.

She clenched the banister. "You . . . you are leaving?"

He regarded her with his piercing eyes. "Not yet."

Suddenly, his arm encircled her waist and he tugged her close. His lips captured hers with arrogant confidence.

She had never been kissed before, not even on the cheek, so she was totally unprepared for the incredible sensation of his mouth upon hers.

The incredible, exciting, overwhelming sensation that spread from her lips outward, to encompass and overpower her entire body.

His hand moved slowly up her arm. His touch seemed made of fire, igniting her. The heat of passion melted away everything else but him, including her resistance.

Just as abruptly, he drew back, a mocking smile on his handsome face. "Allow me to give you a bit of advice, beautiful Arabella," he said with quiet yet unmistakable menace. "You are not in sleepy little Grantham anymore. You have come to great and wicked London—*my* realm. It can be a very dangerous place."

"I believe you," she whispered, stumbling back from him. "And I can believe you are the most dangerous thing in it."

His smile broadened. "You would do well to remember that."

Then he turned and left the house. While Arabella put her hands to her slightly swollen lips as if she could wipe his kiss away.

Chapter 3

With an elegant flick of the wrist, the wide-brimmed, white-plumed hat sailed across the coffeehouse to land neatly on a peg near the dispenser's stall. A rousing and welcoming cheer went up from the patrons as a smiling Neville Farrington paused on the threshold and surveyed them with the magnanimity of a benign sovereign.

None of them, including the serving wench leaning against the counter and incidentally displaying more of her wares than her coffee, would believe that he had spent the past few hours striding about the city, attempting to overcome his shock, anger and frustration.

Now, to the amusement of the noble customers and disapproving glances from the few Puritans inside, Neville suddenly groaned pitiably, stumbled forward as if he had been stabbed and staggered toward his friends sitting at their usual table in the corner.

"Alas, my friends!" Neville cried as he reeled close to them, the back of his hand against his aristocratic brow. "A disaster has befallen me!"

Lord Fozbury Cheddersby, not the most discerning of mortals and, as always, beribboned and bedecked in the latest fashionable attire, no matter how ridiculous, obviously expected Neville to drop dead at his feet, for a look of stunned horror came to his round face.

"Odd's fish, Farrington!" he cried, jumping up and spilling his coffee onto his scarlet velvet breeches.

"Have a care, Foz!" Sir Richard Blythe snarled, his expression as severe as his dark woolen clothing, which made him look more like a Puritan than the cavalier he had been and the playwright he was. "Can't you see he's only acting—and poorly, too? Zounds, you've burned me!"

"An unfortunate baptism by coffee, Richard," Neville said with a sympathetic sigh as he moved his sword out of the way and lifted his leg over the bench to sit. "But that is what you get for criticizing my acting. Besides, what is a little singed flesh compared to my current dilemma?"

"You look as if you have not slept all night or washed, either," Foz noted worriedly, absently mopping up the spilled coffee with his handkerchief of linen and lace, then just as absently shoving the damp cloth into his cuff.

"Oh, I dare say it cannot be so bad that Neville would neglect to wash, although he does need to shave if he's going to persist in going beardless as a boy," Richard remarked.

"Please, my friends, speak softly and give me your pity, for I am in agony," Neville pleaded as he covered his ears with his palms, shaking his head mournfully.

"Let me hazard a guess as to the cause of this agony," Richard answered coolly. "Minette Sommerall still refuses to consider your addresses."

"Ah!" Neville gasped, doubling over. He raised his mirthful eyes. "Another blow I had forgotten!"

As he spoke, he forced away any mental connection between mistresses and the astonishingly provocative kiss he had stolen from the lovely, shapely Arabella. "But this is not the time for idle chitchat," he continued. "I assure you, my trouble is very serious."

Lord Cheddersby scratched his head beneath his peruke. Unlike the other gentlemen seated at the long tables, he had quickly adopted this new fashion, too, perhaps because his natural hair lacked the fullness of Neville's locks.

"Can you not surmise from whence disaster comes, at least?" Neville asked.

"Your father?" Richard suggested.

"You are waking up at last, I see!" Neville cried triumphantly. "Exactly. My esteemed parent."

"He's not sent you any money."

"No, I should say not."

"You lost a considerable sum at Whitehall last night," the playwright noted calmly. "You ought not to gamble."

"Are you quite certain you are not a Puritan in disguise," Neville asked, "or an agent of my father? Besides, I usually win."

"It is easy to take such a lax view if one can afford it," retorted the former Royalist soldier.

"But I gamble only what I can afford to lose—well, most of the time," Neville replied with a wry grin even as he gave his friend a shrewd look. "Granted you lost Blythe Hall in the Interregnum, but not everything, and you make a pretty penny from your plays and poetry. You are not nearly as poor as you pretend, and I think you do that only so that you can borrow gambling money from me without risking your own."

Richard's eyes widened in genuine surprise.

"Ah, you knew not that I was on to you?" Neville inquired with a sly smile. Then he frowned. "Unfortunately, Richard, those days are over. I fear I shall have to be borrowing of you in the time to come."

Foz, who had been immersed in grave and silent contemplation, suddenly exclaimed,

"Your father has cut you off without another penny!"

"Foz, I shall offer to knock down the next person who claims you are a dunderhead, for you have reasoned it out."

Cheddersby's mouth fell open in surprise. "I . . . I have?"

"As close to it as makes no difference," Neville confirmed.

"He . . . he can't do that," Foz whispered, stunned, "can he?"

"It is most unfortunately true. My father arrived in London today to tell me, in his own delightful way, that I will not be seeing any more money from him except an allowance *he* considers sufficient."

"Until he dies. Then you will inherit."

Neville slowly shook his head. "No, Richard, upon that melancholy event, the inheritance is to go to his ward and her spouse, whoever he may be. I suppose I should be grateful he does not give it to her directly."

"What ward?" Richard demanded. "We have heard no talk of any ward."

"Perhaps if I could make out his writing, I might have."

"But you are his son!" Foz protested.

"True. And so I have my title and the old, decrepit family manor."

"Who is this ward?"

"Her name is Lady Arabella Martin, and she

is the daughter of the late Duke of Bellhurst."

"The Duke of Bellhurst? Isn't he the fellow who became a hermit or a Quaker or some such monstrosity after his wife died?" Foz asked.

"A Puritan," Neville replied.

Neville could still remember how Arabella had spoken of the few memories she had of her mother and how he had wanted to offer her some kind of comfort.

"Then why would he leave his daughter in your father's care?"

"Because my father always had certain Puritan sympathies." Neville's tone turned slightly bitter. "For all his condemnation of me, he could not renounce the more luxurious aspects of lordly life and convert completely."

"When did he become her guardian?"

"Three months ago, I understand."

"And she has managed to usurp your place in so short a time?" Richard asked.

"Apparently."

"How?"

"Yes, how?" Foz seconded him. "Is he quite right in the head? Perhaps he should see a doctor."

"I confess the same thought occurred to me, my friend. He claims to be sane. He also claims Lady Arabella is the most virtuous person he has ever met."

Richard's response was a scornful snort.

"I agree absolutely," Neville said. "No woman is truly virtuous."

He thought of Arabella's demure manner in the drawing room and the shy girl she had been in the garden.

Then he commanded himself not to be so naïve. He had learned much of the ways of the world since he had come to London, including the true nature of beautiful women, all of whom used their beauty to advantage. Surely she was no different.

"However," he clarified, "she does possess an air of innocence aided by a certain countrified prettiness."

"An air of innocence, eh?" Richard observed. "I gather that, contrary to your father, you do not think she actually possesses that quality?"

As he recalled her response to his passionate kiss, Neville wondered if what seemed innocent surprise really could have been. Perhaps she was simply a good actress, which might explain his own surprisingly intense reaction—and the reaction he was experiencing now, just from the memory.

"How can she, when she would take what is rightfully mine?" he answered, fighting to dominate his wayward flesh. "My father says she does not know what he intends, but I do not believe that for a moment. She has merely been too clever for him."

Richard nodded pensively.

"She's pretty?" Foz asked, all the gravity of Neville's situation apparently less important to him than this particular point.

"Yes, in a plain sort of way." Neville glanced at Richard. "She is like a lass off a hay cart, so she holds little appeal for me," he lied.

"If she is pretty," Richard said, "perhaps she appeals to your—"

"He will tell you," Neville interrupted, "as he told me, that such thoughts are indicative of a degenerate mind. I would say a worldly-wise mind, myself. Nevertheless, I do believe that there is nothing of *that* sort between them."

"Who does your father think this alleged paragon should marry?"

"I gather he has not decided, except that the fellow must be as unlike me as possible." He gave Foz a pathetic look. "Foz, I truly am expiring for want of coffee. Can you not stand me a cup, given my sudden loss of income?"

"Of course, dear friend!" Foz cried, jumping to his feet and hurrying toward the serving wench as fast as his short legs would take him.

Neville turned to his more discreet companion with a guilty grin. "I shouldn't have done that. He is too genial a fellow."

"He doesn't mind and he can afford it. Besides, no one would give him any notice until you took him under your wing, so I think whatever he does for you is a fair bargain."

Richard's face grew even more grave than usual. "This is all true?"

"Yes."

"And your father came here to tell you, although he hates London?"

Neville nodded.

"And then you quarreled."

It was not a question; it was a statement of fact based upon experience.

Neville sighed wearily. "Of course." He ran his hand through his hair. "I cannot understand it, but whenever I'm with him, I cannot resist the temptation to act in a manner I know will enrage him."

"Did you not tell him that there would be no family fortune at all if you had not taken matters in hand when you arrived in London?"

Neville shook his head. "To what purpose? He would not believe me."

"Then you should have sent him to the bankers and told him to consult with the estate steward. Good God, man, it's time *somebody* told him how you brought him back from the brink of ruin—a ruin his own extravagant ways were fast bringing about. Indeed, you should have told him years ago."

A stern, resolute expression appeared on Neville's face. "A man should do his duty without expecting thanks."

"That does not mean a man has to do it in secret."

"I had to, or he would have interfered." Neville shook his head. "I can scarce believe my cynical, censorious father would ever be taken in so completely by a pair of pretty eyes or a pair of anything else."

And he must not be fooled, either, he warned himself as he watched Foz making his way back to their table, his brow furrowed with concentration and his eyes on the hot brew.

"Thank you," Neville said, wrapping his hands about the steaming cup.

"So let me understand you," Foz said, like a student attempting to comprehend a particularly difficult lesson. "Whoever marries your father's ward will inherit his wealth when he dies?"

"Exactly. You could very well take my inheritance," he noted, glancing over his cup at Cheddersby.

Then Neville's expression changed as he turned to regard his other friend, who desperately wanted to buy back his family's estate. "Or you, Richard."

"You would be certain of a cottage on my land if I did," Richard replied, which was not at all what Neville wanted to hear.

"Richard, you wouldn't!" Foz gasped.

"Maybe he should," Neville replied, once again assuming a mask of light frivolity that was a distinct contrast to his true feelings.

"I'faith, if I am to be replaced like a broken wheel or sick horse, I would far rather have the money go to someone I know than a stranger."

"You are no worse than any other man," Foz offered comfortingly.

Which reminded Neville of his father's admonition that if he was no worse, he was no better, either.

"I doubt there is a man in England capable of meeting my father's expectations," he muttered in his own defense.

Richard put his hand on Neville's shoulder in a rare gesture of sympathy. "He will see your merit one day."

Neville shrugged off Richard's hand. He wished he had kept silent about his father's intentions. Richard was a handsome fellow, and while his manner could be brusque in the extreme, Neville had noticed that many women found the bitter, sardonic cavalier fascinating.

Fortunately, another thought brought comfort and not a little relief: his father would surely never permit his ward to marry a playwright.

Restored to his usual jocund humor, Neville said, "I fear either he or I will expire before he sees me as anything but a complete waste of life and breath."

"Well, whatever you require, you know you have but to ask," Foz replied sympathetically.

"And you must share my lodgings," Richard added.

"Thank you, my friends, but he has not yet thrown me into the streets. It is a comfort to know I shall not starve if he does." Then he grinned. "I tell you, if my father is not proof against beauty, it should be a warning to us all. Anyone might lose their head over a woman."

Foz nodded solemnly. "It is a sad thing when one's father loses his head."

"As I'm sure the king would attest," Richard agreed.

"I never meant anything of that sort!"

"A witty sally, though," Neville said, smiling at poor Foz, whose greatest desire was to be accounted a wit.

"Oh, I say, it was, wasn't it?" Foz replied, his thin chest puffed with pride. "What do you intend to do?"

"Do?"

"Yes. About *her*."

Neville felt as if somebody had upset a bucket of slops on his head. Why, of course he must do something. He could not sit idly by while his hard-won fortune went to another. And that it should be Foz who reminded him of this duty . . . Well, his wits must have truly been addled with shock. Or arousal. "I shall have to show him that he is making a serious mistake."

"Will you challenge him to a duel?"

"He *is* my father, Foz. No matter how he infuriates me, I do not think killing him would be the best solution."

"Then what?" Richard demanded. "What will you do?"

Neville's eyes gleamed with the devilment his friends knew so well. "I shall simply have to prove that Lady Arabella is not as virtuous as he thinks."

Foz looked confused. "How are you going to do that?"

"I shall prove that no one, not even such a paragon, is without fault," Neville replied with a beatific smile, "by seducing her."

And given that kiss, the seduction of Arabella struck him as a most delightful challenge.

"I thought you said she wasn't very pretty," Foz countered dubiously.

"My dear Foz," Neville said with an air of superior wisdom, "she is a woman. That is all that is important to know when my inheritance is at stake."

Besides, if that one kiss was a basis for judgment, she would be worth the pursuit, no matter who she was.

"A very noble sacrifice, my lord," Richard observed sarcastically. "What will you do if you discover she *is* virtuous, and so fail?"

"Can this be Sir Richard Blythe speaking?" Neville demanded of Foz. "Is Sir Richard

Blythe not normally the most cynical of mortals, especially where the fair sex is concerned?" He turned an inquiring eye onto Richard. "Or is it that you would rather attempt the seduction?"

"Oh, not I! Not if you are to be my rival. Zounds, Neville, that would require too much effort. No, no, you shall have that honor all to yourself."

"Yet you think I might fail."

"I merely wondered aloud what you would do if you did."

"I shall not."

"Yet will not seducing her anger your father even more?" Foz questioned. "He might never forgive you."

"He loathes me now, and I can scarce sink lower in his estimation."

"Very well. You are quite certain you will succeed in proving to your father that the woman he thinks superior to you in virtue is not," Richard said. "The only question that remains is, how long will it take?"

"With so much at stake, you can be assured I will be diligent," Neville replied, his tone grave, but his eyes gleaming with the thrill of the hunt.

"Even though you are sure to triumph in the end, I cannot help thinking it will not be as easy as you believe, if she is a Puritan," Richard observed.

"Puritan or no, I'll wager within a fortnight," Foz cried excitedly. "Ten pounds says she will be in Neville's bed in that time!"

Neville regarded his literary friend with a cool smile. "What say you, Richard? Would you care to wager on how long it will take to make the citadel of my Nemesis's virtue fall?"

Richard leaned back and regarded Neville impassively. "Since I have not seen the lady in question, I hardly think that would be wise."

"But you are so knowing in the ways of women. Isn't that what everybody says after they see one of your plays?" Neville replied. "So what need you know but that I am determined and she is not ugly?"

He thought of mentioning the kiss, then decided against it. Let Richard believe this seduction difficult; that would make his eventual triumph even sweeter.

"Very well. I'll wager it will take longer than a fortnight."

"Longer? Are you mad?" Foz cried.

Neville continued to regard his friend, suddenly not quite so certain himself he could succeed with Arabella in a mere fourteen days, despite the passion in her kiss. Yet he would die before he would reveal any lack of confidence to his friends.

"Very well, Richard," he said. "Prepare to lose your money. However, I could use more than ten pounds."

"Then we shall make it more sporting, shall we?" Richard said. "I am willing to wager fifty."

"What?" Foz gasped. "Fifty pounds!"

"Come now, Foz," Richard said calmly. "What is fifty pounds to you?"

"You don't have fifty pounds," Neville charged. He had scarce five pounds in his purse; nor did Richard have much more, he ventured. What, then, was he to make of this astonishing sum? Was Richard that confident he would fail?

"Neither do you, but I could get it," Richard countered. "Are you beginning to doubt your abilities?"

"Not a whit. Fifty pounds, then, that I can get Lady Arabella into my bed in a fortnight."

"What will you give for proof of success?"

"If my word is not enough," Neville brazenly declared, "then she will tell you herself. Will that content you?"

"If you can debauch a Puritan woman and then persuade her to confirm her sinful act to us, I will most certainly be content," Richard agreed.

"Surely debauch is too harsh a term for what I have in mind. Nevertheless, give me your hands, gentlemen," Neville replied, "and we shall seal our wager."

Richard and Foz placed their hands over Neville's and they shook them once.

"I suggest you begin searching for those fifty pounds, Richard," Neville remarked.

Richard got to his feet. "You will forgive me if I do not wish you luck, Neville. Now, I must get to the theater. I fear my actresses are going to do each other injury if I am not there to come between them."

"Perhaps you require some assistance, Richard," Neville proposed, "although really, sir, if you persist in having more than one mistress at a time, I think you have only yourself to blame when war breaks out between them."

The former cavalier bowed courteously. "I learned from a master."

"Yet you bid against me."

Richard continued to smile as he regarded Neville with a steadfast scrutiny that made Neville feel he had just made a terrible blunder. "Even a master may fail occasionally."

"Or succeed where doubt is cast. Well, let us all go and we shall see if either I or Foz can enable a truce."

"Should you not go direct to Lady Arabella?" Foz asked anxiously.

"Oh, I shall see her soon enough," Neville replied with a sly and secretive smile, for he had the beginnings of his siege already mapped within his head.

Chapter 4

Arabella awoke with a start.
Immediately she knew that she was not in her old home, or the ornate bedroom she had been given in Lord Barrsettshire's country house. She was in the earl's townhouse in London in a bedchamber at the opposite end of the corridor from the earl's. For confirmation, several church bells tolled the hour: three of the clock.

However, it was not the sound of the bells that had woken her, she realized. It was another, more local noise: the soft scratching of mice in the wall across from her.

Sitting up, she reached for the bed curtains and pulled them open. Moonlight flooded in through the mullioned window, making diamond-shaped patterns on the bare wooden floor.

She lay down again and told herself there

was nothing to fear. It was only a harmless little mouse burrowing through the wall. Or perhaps a few of them. Surely it was not a rat.

At that more distressing thought, her first instinct was to pull the covers over her head. However, she also knew that if she did not discover what was making that noise, she would never be able to go back to sleep.

Therefore, clad in her thin nightdress, she rose from her bed and with chilly fingers struck flint and steel to kindle the rushlight set in the holder on the table beside her bed. The rushlight burned up brightly, then settled into a fairly steady, if dim, flame.

Before picking up the holder, she wrapped a shawl about her shoulders and found her thick boots in the chest that had arrived that afternoon with the rest of the baggage. She had no desire to be creeping about a strange place in her bare feet looking for small furry creatures.

With her other hand, she lifted the basin Jarvis had set beside the ewer of water on the table. Thus armed, she crept into the hall.

A thin stream of golden light issued from beneath the door of the room that shared a wall with hers. It had been closed when she had come upstairs earlier, and Jarvis had not said to whom it belonged. As she drew near, the scratching noise grew louder. And then she heard a muffled curse.

Moving cautiously forward, she gently

pushed at the door with the basin, opening it wider so that she could peer inside.

A single candle burned upon a table near the head of a bed, aiding the moonlight. At once Arabella realized this room was much cleaner than hers was. The curtained bed sported linen and a brocade coverlet, none of which had been lately disturbed.

She opened the door a little wider, trying to see more of the room.

She stifled a gasp as a half-naked Neville Farrington came into view, his back to her as he washed his face. His powerful arms that had held her upon the stairs were like those of the blacksmith in Grantham, lean and sinewy, and his exposed, unexpectedly muscular back tapered to a thin waist above narrow hips. Thick, black, curling hair brushed his broad, bare shoulders.

It was Neville's own hair, too, she confirmed. No wig accounted for his dark ringlets, but only Nature's hand, as if She had decided to give this mortal man the ultimate finishing touch.

It was not that she had never seen a man without his shirt on before. Living in the country, she had seen farm laborers thus unattired in the warm summer months many times—but she had never seen any man quite like this one, who could have provided a model for Adonis or Apollo, so well formed was he.

Breathing a little faster, she licked her lips, thinking of the pressure of his mouth upon hers when he had kissed her.

And the excitement that had coursed through her. The yearning. The need.

She told herself to go back to her room at once.

As he leaned forward, his black breeches grew snug around his backside and thighs, which showed that every part of his body was well formed and muscular. His skin glowed bronze in the candlelight, adding to her impression that he could be a sculptor's model.

She might have stayed thus, merely watching and remembering, for a long time. But he suddenly turned and stared right at her.

Before she could run away, he crossed the floor, grabbed her arm and pulled her into the room. Dismayed, she twisted out of his grasp, knocking the door shut behind her. Then she accidentally touched the flame of the rushlight to his hand.

With a profane curse—words she had also heard from country laborers—he dashed across the room and shoved his hand into the washbasin.

"I'faith, woman, would you set me on fire?" he demanded under his breath.

"I'm sorry!" She set down the light and basin, and hurried over to him. "Let me see. Is it very bad?"

With a scowl, he disdainfully offered his hand to her as if he were an arrogant king expecting her to kiss it.

Which was a most disconcerting thought.

Nevertheless, the important thing was to see to his wound.

She looked carefully at his proffered appendage. The burn mark was red and surely painful and might leave a scar, but she did not think it overly serious.

Her gaze shifted to the rest of his hand, his undeniably masculine hand, including his slender, artistic fingers that were so surprisingly strong. It was easy to envision them stroking . . . a musical instrument.

She shook her head as if that would curb her wayward thoughts.

"This does not look terribly bad," Arabella said quietly as she examined the burn without touching him for what seemed an inordinately long time, the tip of her tongue resting ever so temptingly against her upper lip.

"Perhaps not to you, but it hurts like the very devil," Neville replied in a low growl, glancing at the red mark the size of a guinea on the back of his hand, which was starting to sting.

In truth, he was considerably less angry than he might have been had she not been so pretty, so remorseful and so scantily attired. She wore only a thin—very thin—nightdress and shawl. Her hair fell loosely over her breasts, which rose and fell in a most enticing manner, her rosy nipples visible beneath.

"You shook your head like a physician whose patient is not expected to recover."

"A bit of hair fell in my eyes."

He had not noticed that, perhaps because he had been wondering what might be seen if someone were to throw a basin of water over that thin nightdress.

"Since your wound does not appear to be life-threatening, my lord, I shall leave you."

He drew on his shirt. He mustn't frighten her with too rapid a pursuit, tempting though it may be. "You cannot go without offering an explanation for wandering about the house. And armed, too."

"I heard a noise and wondered what it was."

"I was as quiet as the proverbial mouse," he said softly, approaching her as cautiously as a hunter stalking a deer.

"Precisely, my lord," she replied with a shiver. "I thought you were one, or a big black rat."

"Hardly a flattering comparison."

"Again, my lord, I apologize. It was an accident. You grabbed me most unexpectedly—again."

"And so you thought to set me alight? Is that

not excessive?'' he asked, noting with great satisfaction that she seemed in no hurry to depart. ''Did it not occur to you that the sight of you spying upon me was just as unexpected?''

''I wasn't spying!''

He was pleased that she was a little flustered. ''No, you were hunting with a basin. Did you intend to capture one of God's little creatures and set him free?''

She shrugged her shoulders and clasped her hands like an errant schoolgirl. ''I don't know what I would have done if it had been a rat. I would have killed a mouse.''

His eyes widened in genuine surprise. ''You sound surprisingly bloodthirsty for a Puritan.''

''Mice are nuisances, and I am not a Puritan.''

''You quite take me aback,'' he said truthfully. ''How could you live with your father all those years and not be a Puritan?''

She flushed, the pink dawning on her cheeks in a most becoming manner. ''I could not accept all the tenets of the faith.''

''How very interesting.''

''I might ask you what you are doing wandering around the house in the middle of the night, my lord.''

''You make it sound as if I were creeping about like a housebreaker. I was in my own chamber, preparing for bed.''

She glanced at the large piece of furniture

not far from her. Suddenly, he had a vision of Arabella naked in his bed, waiting for him.

It almost took his breath away.

He reminded himself that he intended to proceed with caution.

He glanced at her boots peeping out from beneath her nightgown. "I suppose that is the height of fashionable footwear in dear Grantham."

"I didn't want to encounter a furry little animal in my bare feet."

He came yet closer to her, and she did not move away. "It could have been worse than merely a mouse. I might really have been a housebreaker. What would you have done then?"

She did not look away or blush. Instead, she made the most attractive, secretive little smile Neville had ever seen.

"To speak the truth," she confessed with a shiver, again reminding him of her interesting state of undress, "I think I would have been more undone by a rat."

He chuckled softly. "Perhaps I should be glad I escaped with only a minor burn and not a bashed skull."

"I think I know the difference between a man and a mouse, so you were quite safe."

Her shawl slipped slightly off her shoulder, but she didn't seem to notice.

He had seen women wearing considerably

less, and yet never had he seen anything that aroused him in quite the way this did.

"Am I really safe from you, Arabella?" he asked quietly.

"Of course."

"And you must feel safe with me, for you are still here."

She cocked her head to one side as she studied him in a way that made him feel like a specimen about to be dissected. "I do."

Lord Farrington had been flattered, admired and pursued by all sorts and conditions of women, yet never had he felt more gratified.

"My lord, must you quarrel so with your father?"

Any pleasure he felt dissolved. "Yes, I must."

"But he is an old man, and I'm sure—"

"Unless you are his child—and you are not you do not know whereof you speak."

Her blue eyes shone with pity. "You have been from home a long time now, my lord. Perhaps he has changed."

Had this apparently sincerely sorrowful expression been the weapon she had used to pry away his inheritance? Had she listened to his father denounce him with the same sympathetic commiseration in her big blue eyes?

He did not want her sympathy or her compassion. He wanted only what was rightfully his, and he would not let her, or anyone, take it from him.

He strolled closer, transfixing her with his eyes. "Tell me, Arabella, do you believe what my father says of me?"

"I know not what to believe about you, my lord," she answered hesitantly. "You are much changed."

"And although you are not afraid of me, you do not think it is for the better."

Her gaze wavered, and she started to back toward the door.

"You are much changed, too," he said softly as he walked toward her. "You are a very beautiful woman, Arabella. The Devil could scarce have made a better snare for a man's heart than you."

She halted when her back hit the door and she could go no farther.

He came closer still, not stopping until he was mere inches from her. She held her breath, waiting for him to kiss her.

Expecting him to kiss her.

Wanting him to kiss her.

She did not know what was happening here between them. All she could be sure of was that she had never felt this way in her life—so hot, so excited and so troubled.

Then he smiled, a slow, knowing smile that made her think that he could command of her whatever he would and she would obey, even at the cost of her immortal soul.

Taking hold of her shoulders, at last he kissed her—but not with possessive arrogance. This time, his embrace was gentle and almost tentative, as if he were asking permission to continue. Yet lurking below that tenderness was a passionate urgency.

An urgency she felt, too, and a passion that bloomed like the roses in the garden that long-ago day.

Had she not imagined this a thousand times? Was this not one reason she had lingered here?

Surrounded by the strength of him, inhaling the scent of his clean skin, she could not stop him. Not yet.

Not even when she felt his hand upon her breast. Over the flimsy fabric, his thumb gently brushed back and forth across her hardened nipple. Both astonished and aroused by his action, she moaned softly and arched, wordlessly willing him to continue, while her own hands began to explore.

His muscles tensed beneath her fingers, and he pushed her back against the door. In the next instant, his tongue thrust between her lips. Their tongues entwined with feverish desire, tasting, pleasuring.

As he pressed against her, she felt his excitement, while an ardent, unfamiliar throbbing grew between her legs.

A church clock rang out, the sudden somber note like an alarm bell.

Abruptly she pushed Neville away, staring at him with horrified eyes. Shame and guilt rushed to fill the place where desire had been.

What was she doing? her conscience demanded in the voice of her censorious father. How could she be in a man's bedchamber, in his intimate embrace?

This incredible feeling, nearly overwhelming in its strength, had to be lust. Love could not come so quickly, and when she knew so little about the man holding her.

Neville was not that boy in the garden anymore, but a man—and she was a woman who should not be alone with him, or any man, under such circumstances.

He chuckled and tried to pull her back into his arms. "Come, Arabella, there is no need to pretend for me."

She twisted, now desperate to get away from this sinfully tempting man, otherwise she would be no better than the weak-willed female her father had always said she was. "Do not touch me again, or I shall rouse the entire household!"

His brow furrowed as he stepped back. "I do believe you are in earnest."

"I am! Your father is right. You are a loathsome lecher interested only in his own base desires!"

"Yet you are pure as the driven snow?"

Never had she felt less pure.

As if to prove that she was as wicked as he, Neville reached out and yanked her into his embrace. He kissed her again with fierce passion, and his hips slowly gyrated against hers, exerting a pressure that made her legs feel weak and her heart race.

She shoved him away. "Let go of me!" she demanded with all the firmness of purpose she possessed.

For she was good. She was moral.

All those times her father had chastised her— he had been wrong. She would prove that he had *always* been wrong!

"Is that what you truly want, Arabella?"

"Yes!"

"Or what?" A cold, hostile smile came to Neville's face. "Perhaps you could have me thrown in prison for attacking you. How convenient."

"*Convenient?*" she gasped incredulously.

His chilling smile disappeared as anger filled his eyes and voice. "If I were what you think, I would not stop now. I would rip that flimsy nightdress from your body and take you whether you fought or kicked or if I had to keep my hand over that lovely little mouth of yours to smother your screaming." He snatched up his jacket, baldric and hat. "But I am not so evil, no matter what my father might think, so I will let you go even though *you* came to *me*, lingering in your near-nakedness. At least I am not a hypocrite."

Arabella opened her mouth, ready to denounce him, when he held up his hand. "Spare me your protestations of innocence. You only waste your breath."

He strode past her and grabbed the door handle. He turned back to run a scornful gaze over her. "With a body and kisses like that, you should do very well in London. I'faith, your breasts seem made for the palm of a man's hand."

He grinned mockingly. "And no matter how you dissemble, you do like such exciting diversions, don't you, my dear?"

Before she could protest—if she *could* protest—he pushed her away and marched from the room.

She ran after him but halted at the door.

What was she doing? She had nothing to say to him.

"Ho, there! What's afoot!" the earl bellowed querulously from his room at the other end of the corridor.

Quickly she blew out the candle and rushlight, and stood panting in the dark. She must not be found here, not at this hour and in her nightdress, yet she was trapped in Neville's room, for she could not get back to her own without being seen.

She glanced at the high bed. If she was desperate, she could hide beneath it.

"Neville, is that you?" the earl demanded.

"Father, there is no need to wake the entire street," Neville drawled with absolutely no indication that he had been angrily denouncing someone moments before.

"Do you think this is a tavern or a bawdy house that you can come and go as you please, disturbing everybody?"

"It was my understanding, Father, that I could continue to reside under your august roof."

"Not if you are going to behave as if this were a common inn! It is a mercy Arabella did not hear you."

"If she did not hear me, I fear the same cannot be said of your immoderate tones, Father."

"How dare you talk to me like that? Get out! Get out of my house! Go to your bawds and whores and gamesters. They will not care how late you carouse. And they're probably so drunk, you couldn't wake them if you tried."

"Am I to understand you are banishing me from this house?"

"Since you are not fit to live among decent people, yes!"

There was a moment's pause, then Arabella heard Neville turn and start to return to his bedchamber. She held her breath.

"Where are you going?"

"To collect my things. I trust you will allow me that."

"I will have Jarvis bring your clothes to you. Or to your mistress."

"He may bring them to Lincoln's Inn Fields Theatre tomorrow. If I am not there, Richard Blythe will take charge of them."

"That debased rogue!"

"Then he must be a fitting companion for me," Neville replied. "Good-bye, Father."

So calm, so cold! Even her father, usually so reserved, had expressed some tender sentiments toward her on his deathbed when he knew he would not see her again, yet Neville apparently felt nothing at being cast out of his father's house.

Neville's familiar tread sounded on the stairs, then the outer door opened and shut.

So he was gone, and she was glad of it. She would not have to dread his return or a repetition of tonight's shameful episode.

Perhaps she would never see him again, and she told herself that was good. Never again would she be tempted to linger in his presence, trying to discover if some vestige of the Neville she remembered still existed. Never again would she feel this sinful desire to be in his arms or to feel his lips upon hers.

If she should happen to meet Neville Farrington again, she would remember tonight and be on her guard.

Indeed, she doubted she would ever be able to forget.

Chapter 5

Late the next morning, Arabella stared in some surprise at the unknown lady sitting in the earl's withdrawing room.

Arabella had gotten an early start cleaning and had gone to fetch a fresh bucket of water with which to wash the windows. Obviously, at some point during her brief absence, the stranger had arrived, and the earl had been summoned.

Seated by the hearth, the woman appeared to be of an age with the earl. However, the lady also seemed very desirous of giving the impression that she had ceased to age past nineteen years, to judge by her liberal use of paint and powder as well as her garments. The bodice of her dress was cut very low, the waist very pinched, the skirts very full. The overskirt of bright green and yellow striped satin was, in the fashion of the day, drawn back to reveal a petticoat of golden silk. Her green broad-brimmed hat, which threatened to tumble off with every utterance, was trimmed with gold and yellow ribbons that fluttered down so far as to be an obvious nuisance, for she occasionally blew them out of the way as she spoke.

As for the woman herself, her face was thin and her nose long, rather like that of a hunting dog. Indeed, she looked as if she was on the scent, although for what, Arabella couldn't tell.

She also wondered what the wigmaker had used to achieve that particularly flat shade of black that had surely never naturally occurred on a human head.

The earl tore his gaze away from this aged vision to address Arabella. "Come, Arabella, and meet a dear friend of mine, Lady Lippet of Peath. Lady Lippet, my ward, Arabella."

Arabella obediently took a step further into the room and curtsied. Then she waited, not quite certain what to do next or where she should look, tempting though it might be to stare at their visitor, provided her eyes could accommodate themselves to the riotous stripes of Lady Lippet's clothes.

"I trust you were not disturbed by the commotion last night," Lord Barrsettshire said.

"Commotion?" Arabella replied noncommittally.

"Neville was here. Came in the middle of the

night, as if this were a tavern! He was drunk, too."

Arabella didn't think the earl's son had been drunk, but she certainly did not wish to discuss Neville's disturbing nocturnal visit. "He did?"

"You must sleep deeply. He made enough noise to wake the dead."

Or a soundly sleeping elderly man, she thought, glad the earl was such, or else she might have been discovered in Neville Farrington's bedroom, clad only in her nightdress.

She should never have remained alone with him! She should have fled the moment she saw Neville Farrington's naked back. Then he would not have been able to kiss her again and touch her. She would not have experienced the lustful desire his warm, soft lips provoked or the sinful craving engendered by his hands stroking her thinly clad body—

She flushed hotly when she realized the earl was staring at her.

"I do sleep soundly," she said with a silent prayer for forgiveness of this little lie.

"Rest is so important for maintaining one's beauty," Lady Lippet announced in a voice that reminded Arabella of the barn cat when it had gotten its tail caught in the door.

Her tone also implied that this regimen of rest explained her own youthful appearance.

"She is charming, Wattles, simply charming!" the lady continued. "Pretty as can be, and with a form—well, the young men will all go mad for her!"

Wattles? She called Lord Barrsettshire Wattles? Now that she thought about it, Arabella realized, he did look like a turkey.

The earl must have seen her effort not to laugh, for he scowled darkly. Arabella quickly turned her attention to the floor.

As she regarded the worn and wine-stained carpet, suggestive of many bacchanals, she reflected that a nickname indicated a friendship of some intimacy and age, and she wondered what Lady Lippet thought of Neville.

"I don't want them to go mad for her," the earl said petulantly. "I want one of them to marry her."

"I do not see any trouble there!" Lady Lippet cried archly. "Turn around, my dear, and let me get a good look at you."

"Do as she says, Arabella," the earl commanded. "Lady Lippet is here to help you get a husband."

Arabella reluctantly did as she was told.

"Her shape is more than acceptable," Lady Lippet declared when Arabella, blushing, had completed her circle. "But these clothes, Wattles! They are an affront! They simply will not do!"

"I thought they were a little plain," the earl confessed.

"A little plain? She looks like a poor penitent. You were wise to send for me, Wattles, very wise! We must have some new gowns without delay, and I am just the woman to help you buy them."

Arabella's heart beat a little faster. Oh, to have a new dress! And one in the latest fashion!

"Nothing too expensive," Lord Barrsettshire replied warily.

"You do not put a lovely jewel in a setting of tin."

"No, no, I suppose not."

"Therefore, she must have some fine new gowns. Do not worry. I shall ask my dressmaker to do what she can as cheaply as she can."

Her dressmaker? Arabella's heart sank even as it had risen moments before.

"Mademoiselle Juliette is a marvel."

She had to be something extraordinary if she was responsible for Lady Lippet's current ensemble.

"I would be grateful if you would be so good as to importune this Mademoiselle to be quick. I would not be longer in London than I must."

"These things take time, Wattles, if we are to make the best possible match. Unless there is some reason for haste?"

"No, there is not," Arabella said firmly.

Lady Lippet started a little, as if she had forgotten that the subject of the conversation was in the room. She quickly turned her attention back to the earl. "Then there are two ways to proceed. I will be happy to give a dinner party for her, and we can hope other invitations will follow. Or . . ."

"Or?" Lord Barrsettshire demanded.

"Or we could go to the theater and show her off to many at once."

"The theater?" Arabella cried happily.

She had long wished to see a play performed. Her father had denounced plays as works of Satan, yet she thought they sounded harmless enough. As she had been tempted to say to her father, if a person's morals could be harmed by a play, it was likely they were not very sound to begin with.

And what if the king came? King Charles enjoyed the theater. Indeed, he was a patron.

Surely that would be too much to expect.

She realized Lord Barrsettshire was giving her a condemning glance worthy of her late father.

"Perhaps the theater is too wicked," she said, trying to sound more subdued.

"Nonsense! The theater is no more wicked than any other place where courtiers gather," Lady Lippet said, as if Arabella had insulted her personally. "I assure you, Wattles, it will be the best thing if you wish a speedy marriage."

"Must we make such haste, my lord?" Arabella asked. "Would it not be better for me to have some time to learn about the man I am to marry?

"Do you want to be a spinster all your life?"

"No, my lord."

"Then I see no reason for delay. We must find you a nobleman with sense, if there is such a thing in this terrible place."

"A nobleman? I assure you, my lord, I do not aspire to a nobleman," Arabella said. "Indeed, I am most certain one of them will not suit my temperament. I would prefer a more modest man. Perhaps a banker or merchant—"

The earl bolted from his chair as if he had been shot.

"A merchant?" he thundered. "The daughter of the Duke of Bellhurst marry a merchant?"

"My father tried to renounce his title," she reminded him.

"That does not matter!" the earl retorted as he threw himself back into the chair like a cranky child. "To allow you to marry anyone below the rank of viscount would be an abomination! It would be anarchy!"

The earl's son was a viscount, which was utterly unimportant.

"My lord, naturally I would be extremely flattered to have such a man court me. However, I think we must be practical. My father gave the bulk of his estate to his church when he converted to Puritanism."

"You are rich, nonetheless, and of noble rank."

"Rich?" she asked, bewildered.

"Your fortune left by your father is ten thousand pounds."

While Lady Lippet's falsely black eyebrows rose to amazing heights, Arabella stared at him in stunned disbelief. "How . . . can this be?"

Her father had prided himself on his frugality, even though a Puritan was not supposed to be proud. He had counted every penny when she went to market and chastised her for vanity if she so much as bought a ribbon for her hair. He even begrudged candles, always claiming rushlights would do.

"Ten thousand pounds?" she whispered. "He always said he intended to leave what money he had left to the church, too."

"Obviously, he wisely reconsidered," Lady Lippet exclaimed. "Why, with that sort of fortune, a title, and your own loveliness, it should be ease itself to find a good husband!"

"With that sort of fortune, I could perhaps do without one entirely," Arabella noted.

"Don't be a fool," the earl rumbled. "You need someone to look after your money. A noble husband will be used to overseeing a fortune."

"Noblemen are also used to spending a fortune," Arabella mumbled.

Unfortunately, she would have done better to keep that thought to herself, for the earl overheard her.

"Like my son, eh?" he demanded.

Arabella had no desire to get into a discussion about Neville. "Be that as it may, I think—"

"I will be making inquiries and I will insure your husband is a man of good character and morals, and well able to oversee such a vast sum. I will choose someone who has not been indulged and spoiled, someone who will not disappoint me."

He sounded as if the main thing was to replace Neville, not find a good husband for his ward.

Arabella thought of the boy in the garden those years ago. He had not seemed spoiled or arrogant or overindulged. He had seemed lonely, as lonely as she.

Neville Farrington had no place in her life now and should not be in her thoughts, either, she inwardly commanded.

"Do you know, I think we may be in great luck with the gowns, Wattles," Lady Lippet said, leaning forward excitedly. "Dear Lady Spotsford has passed away at last. She's been ailing for ages—since I first met her in the days when those horribly dull Puritans took charge of the country."

"Arabella's father was a Puritan, Lady Lippet," the earl whispered loudly.

"Oh, yes, of course, and quite the scandal that was, too." She gave Arabella a pitying, patronizing look. "That also explains your hair and clothing, my dear. Never mind. I shall fix you. And I have just the maidservant for you, too. I shall send for her to come directly."

"I have never had a maidservant," Arabella said dubiously. "I would hardly know what to do with her."

"But *she* will know what to do with *you*," Lady Lippet said, as if Arabella were in great need of renovation. Her ladyship faced the earl. "What Nancy doesn't know about hair is not worth knowing. I will give your ward the loan of her while you are in town."

"Is this maid responsible for your fascinating coiffure?" Arabella inquired.

Lady Lippet squirmed with pleasure and touched a gloved hand to her brow. "Indeed she is."

"I shall be most intrigued to see what she can do with mine."

Lady Lippet's brow puckered for a brief moment, as if she was trying to decide if she had been criticized or not. However, the matter of gowns proved to be enough to make her forget any possible insult. "Now about poor Lady Spotsford—her new gowns were almost finished when she shuffled off this mortal coil and went to her reward, although why that woman deserves any reward after the scandalous life she led . . . Well, it doesn't do to speak ill of the dead."

Lady Lippet cleared her throat delicately, as if, given the chance, there was much ill she could speak about the dear departed. "However, if I am any judge, she was close enough in size to Arabella for it to be a simple thing for Mademoiselle Juliette to alter the gowns for her.

"And," she added significantly, "we should be able to get them cheap, because Mademoiselle will be anxious to sell them."

"Excellent!" the earl cried, the point apparently decided.

Arabella, however, was considerably less enthusiastic about wearing a dead woman's clothing, even if the woman in question had never actually put them on.

Still, she consoled herself, the clothes would be new, they would be fashionable and, if Lady Lippet guessed right concerning Mademoiselle Juliette's pricing, they would likely be a bargain.

"If they can be ready soon, we can begin to show her about without further delay," Lady Lippet said.

The earl nodded.

"If possible," Lady Lippet said with a hint of sly manipulation, "we should go to the theater as soon as humanly possible. There is an absolutely delightful new play that everyone is talking about and, more important, attending. I believe that is the one we should see."

Arabella tried not to betray too overt an interest in the conversation.

"What is this play?" Lord Barrsettshire asked.

Lady Lippet's brow furrowed, then she smiled. "The name escapes me, I fear. It is by a most fascinating young man, who I believe may be an acquaintance of yours, Sir Richard Blythe."

Richard Blythe—Neville's friend! Of all the plays in London, surely that was the one they should *not* attend, Arabella thought.

Then it occurred to her that Neville would have seen his friend's play already.

"That man should be horsewhipped! He was a fine soldier, and now he's disgraced himself and his family with this writing nonsense!"

Lady Lippet shook her head. "Wattles, you must get over these old-fashioned notions. He is a famous fellow, and justly so, for a more witty playwright does not exist, or so everyone of the first rank declares. Besides, many noblemen will be there. It is simply too good an opportunity to miss. If an appropriate gown can be found for her, we should go tomorrow."

"My lord, I fear I am being too much of a burden to you," Arabella protested, more from a sense that she should than from any true regret.

She did so want to attend a play!

Nevertheless, she continued in the same self-sacrificing vein. "It all sounds like so much hustle and bustle."

"So it must be, if we are to find you a husband without wasting time," Lady Lippet replied, shaking her head decisively to make her point and nearly sending her hat tumbling to the floor.

"You will let me pay for the gowns from my inheritance, won't you?" Arabella asked, and in this she was sincere.

"We shall see, we shall see. The important thing is to do what Nettie says if we are to get you wed," Lord Barrsettshire said. "What time do these infernal things begin?"

"Half past three o'clock," Lady Lippet replied. "I could take her to the dressmaker's today, and surely at least one gown could be made ready for tomorrow.

"And there must be no more scrubbing and mopping as if she were a servant," the lady added with a curl of her falsely ruby lips, glancing at the bucket by the door. "Her hands will be totally ruined."

"But I don't mind—"

"Arabella," the earl growled before he marched to the door, "if I am willing to put myself out for your good, I should think you would be happy to do as Lady Lippet and I say."

"Yes, my lord," Arabella murmured as he bellowed for Jarvis.

"A pox! I don't believe it!" Neville declared as his booted feet, which had been propped on the table, hit the wooden floor with a bang.

"It's true," an affronted Jarvis replied as he set down the bundle of clothing and other items belonging to Neville on the rough floorboards. "I heard 'em meself, my lord, may I be stricken with plague if I'm lyin'."

"When was this decided?"

"This morning, my lord," Jarvis replied absently as he surveyed the small chamber above a cheese shop currently serving as both Richard's withdrawing room and Neville's temporary bedchamber.

In addition to the interesting odors that wafted through the floorboards, Neville and his companion were treated to a cacophony of sound from the street below. Hawkers proclaimed their wares, carters cursed with astonishing imagination, and passersby grumbled about the crowd, the dirt, the soot and everybody but themselves.

Neville noticed that Jarvis's hand had apparently became possessed of the power of levitation, for it slowly rose, palm outstretched.

"Tomorrow?" Neville repeated as he

reached for his slender purse. "You are certain they are going to the theater tomorrow?"

"Aye, my lord. What happened to your hand?"

"Nothing of consequence. A slight burn."

Jarvis glanced down at the coins that had magically appeared in his hand. He closed his fist around them.

"I see they are wasting little time in the pursuit of a husband," Neville remarked.

"No, my lord, they ain't," Jarvis agreed.

"This can hardly be my father's idea."

"No, my lord, it was the lady's."

Neville scowled darkly. What more evidence did he need that Arabella could, and did, exert considerable influence over his father?

Just as he now had ample evidence of Arabella's hypocrisy. What virtuous woman would have remained for so long in his bedchamber, given her state of undress? What innocent maiden kissed with such inflaming passion?

If only he had kept his composure last night! He should have alerted his father to her presence in his bedchamber, and any notion his father harbored that she was morality personified would have been destroyed.

But he had not, because he had been rendered an idiot who was too frustrated to do anything save leave the house entirely.

When he had an opportunity to have her hypocrisy and immorality discovered again, he would not hesitate.

He would win the wager, too.

He prodded the bundle with his toe. "I fear you have forgotten something, Jarvis."

The man frowned. "I don't think so, my lord, although I might have, with all the upset."

"What upset is this?"

"The cleanin' and the washin'. You'd hardly recognize the place," Jarvis said with a touch of nostalgia.

"Pining for days of bachelor disorder gone by, Jarvis? I expect my father's hired several servants to clear away the debris."

"No, sir, he hasn't. It's *her*. Lady Arabella."

"What, all by herself?"

"Until he made her stop."

"Must be the Puritan influence," Neville mused. "Washing away of sin and all that."

"Then she must have thought us all regular pagans, the way she went about it."

"Perhaps, or in need of some cleansing herself," Neville muttered with a sardonic smile.

"Her?" the servant said incredulously.

"Why not?"

Jarvis shrugged.

Neville subdued the urge to scowl. Was there a man in England beside himself who was proof against her fraudulent appearance? "I tell you, Jarvis, you have forgotten something, which will, unfortunately, necessitate my return to the house."

He reached for his purse again.

This time, Jarvis was faster to comprehend.

"Aye, my lord, so I did, so I did," he agreed as his hand once again ascended.

"I don't know quite when I shall discover that something has been overlooked, but when I do, I shall expect to be admitted to the house to retrieve it, whatever the hour of the day. Or night."

"Your father might dismiss me if he finds you there."

Neville added another coin to the pile in Jarvis's palm.

The Irishman glanced down. "O'course, he hates me anyway," he reflected philosophically.

"He hates just about everybody."

"True, true."

"Do you know the name of the play they intend to see?"

"It is Sir Richard Blythe's new one."

"Not *The Country Cuckold*?"

"I didn't hear the name of it, my lord."

"Yet you are certain it is Richard's play they plan to attend?"

"Aye, my lord, you can rip me liver if I'm wrong."

Neville smiled. "Fortunately, I don't think it will come to that."

Chapter 6

❦

"**O**ut of our way, oaf!" the earl thundered as he led Arabella and Lady Lippet through the boisterous crowd in front of Lincoln's Inn Fields Theatre.

The coal smoke, ever present in the city, made Arabella cough, and she held her skirt and cloak close about her as she eased her way forward. She didn't want to tear her lovely new gown or have her elaborate coiffure ruined. It had taken the maid a long time to create the *confidantes*, clusters of curls at the side of her face. Nancy had wanted to do more curls, but there had not been sufficient time, for which Arabella was grateful. It seemed sinful to waste any more effort on her hair.

She felt almost as guilty about her gown. It was an elaborate royal-blue velvet dress in the very latest fashion, or so petite Mademoiselle Juliette, who had better taste than Arabella had

suspected, assured her. The low, rounded bodice was trimmed with gold embroidery, as was
the gathered skirt. The skirt was drawn back
and held by a series of slender gold chains to
reveal a light-blue silk underskirt. Her feet
were clad in thin slippers that made negotiat-
ing the mud and dirt of the street a difficult
task, and she was in perpetual fear that someone around them would tread on her toes.

Her gown was protected from the soot by a
thin cloak of taffeta, whose hood rested lightly
on her elegant hair.

Lady Lippet was attired in a similar gown,
albeit of persimmon and lemon yellow, with a
cloak of the most astonishing shade of brilliant
pink Arabella had ever seen, which made the
earl seem positively subdued in his garments
of indigo blue. Where they had come from, she
could not begin to fathom, unless his absence
from the house this morning meant he had
been to a tailor.

So many surprising things had happened
since their arrival in London that she could believe even this.

"Clear the way, you impudent puppy!" the
earl demanded, speaking to a splendidly attired fellow blocking his way.

The man, who was with a pale, plump, overdressed woman, turned around and ran a disdainful gaze over the earl before slowly
surveying Arabella. As he did so, his scornful

scowl transformed itself into the most insipid smile Arabella had ever seen.

He was dressed in what Arabella knew to be the most extreme example of fashionable male attire, from his curling wig, ruffled lace jabot and bright green jacket, petticoat breeches adorned with so much ribbon and lace that they looked more like a petticoat than her own undergarments, down to his silver-buckled shoes. His powdered face bore so many patches that he looked as though he had a nasty disease.

His companion was likewise dressed in a flamboyant, expensive ensemble of pea green, which had the unfortunate effect of making her look astonishingly bilious in the daylight. Arabella could only hope she looked better by candlelight.

"May I ask who petitions me in this bold manner?" the fashionable male vision inquired. Although he ostensibly addressed the earl, not for a moment did he take his impertinent scrutiny from Arabella.

Neville Farrington had also regarded her with bold impertinence, yet he had not made her feel soiled, as this man did.

The stranger's companion looked at Arabella with hostile eyes, and Arabella wanted to tell her that she thought the man looked utterly ridiculous and totally unattractive.

"I am the Earl of Barrsettshire," the earl declared, running an equally disdainful gaze over the man. "Who the devil are you?"

Lady Lippet shoved her way forward.

"Your Grace!" she cried, as if this stranger's appearance were the answer to all her prayers.

"Madam?"

"It is I, Lady Lippet."

The stranger bowed. "Ah, yes, Lady Lippet. Your servant, ma'am."

Lady Lippet grabbed the earl's arm to pull him forward. "Your Grace, Lord Barrsettshire. Lord Barrsettshire, the Duke of Buckingham."

"The Duke of Buckingham, eh? I knew your father," the earl replied, and it was quite obvious the earl was not impressed.

The duke didn't seem disturbed by the earl's reaction; indeed, Arabella noted with some distress, he hardly seemed to notice her guardian at all. "And this charming young lady is . . . ?"

The duke's smooth tone reminded Arabella of some of the peddlers who came to Grantham, the ones whose goods were particularly shoddy and overpriced.

"Your Grace, may I present Lady Arabella Martin," Lady Lippet gushed. Apparently overcome by the honor of conferring with the duke, she began to fan herself so rapidly that a small cloud of powder rose from the unnaturally white expanse of her bosom. "Arabella, this is the Duke of Buckingham."

Arabella dropped a curtsey and kept her

gaze focused on the large silver buckles on the duke's shoes.

"London has missed your distinguished presence, my lord," the duke said.

"London is missing many things these days," the earl retorted, "like sense and morals."

"It was lacking even more until the arrival of your beautiful and charming companion. A pleasure to have you among us, Lady Arabella," the duke said as he swept the plumed hat from his head and bowed again.

He reached out to take her hand and leaned forward to kiss it.

The last thing Arabella wanted was to have her hand touched by the duke's painted lips, for the man's appearance and insolence disgusted her. Unfortunately, the crowd continued to press around them and look at them with curiosity, so any action on her part would likely have drawn more attention. Therefore she allowed him the liberty.

"Odd's bodikins!" a familiar voice drawled from close by. "George Villiers, as I live! And—can it be? Not my own esteemed parent! With the lovely Lady Lippet, too."

Arabella might have welcomed the Devil himself if he had allowed her to retreat from the decadent duke. Instead, it was Neville Farrington who appeared at her side.

"What are you doing here?" the earl demanded.

"Is this not my natural habitat?" his son replied with an elegant smile and an impudent languor that was a match for the duke's.

In contrast to the duke, however, Neville's plain yet well-fitting black jacket, simple lace jabot, white shirt and black breeches seemed a model of restraint. And he still looked astonishingly splendid, whereas the duke looked more like a court jester than a courtier. "I would say it is you who do not belong here," Neville continued.

"I can go wherever I like!" the earl rumbled.

"Indeed you may," Neville replied carelessly. "No father exists to censure you." He turned to the duke. "I see you are making the acquaintance of my father's ward."

"His ward?" Villiers replied with a knowing smirk that made Arabella flush hotly.

"Yes, his ward. To suppose otherwise would be to insult her and my father, eh, Villiers?" Neville Farrington's tone did not alter, yet there came a hostile look into his eyes that told Arabella that whatever his outward appearance and manner, Neville could indeed be a dangerous man.

"And dear Lady Lippet—how long has it been? How many months since you told the king I cheated him at piquet? Fortunately, we had been playing cribbage. An honest mistake, I'm sure."

"Yes, yes, it was," Lady Lippet said, blushing beneath her face paint. "Someone told me you had, and of course I thought only to warn the king—"

"Of course, of course. Duty and honor and all that. I quite understand," he replied, but the expression in his eyes was not a pardoning one.

"Your charming and esteemed father was so good as to address himself to me," the duke said.

"Really? I'm sure he was all civility." Neville gestured at the woman standing beside the duke. "Who is this lovely creature we are all ignoring?"

"That is Mrs. Hankerton, my particular friend," Villiers replied.

"Delighted, Mrs. Hankerton, the duke's particular friend!" Neville said, making an elegant bow, amply demonstrating his virile grace.

The woman, whose face bore a heavy coat of cosmetics and whose hair was as false as the duke's, made no attempt to hide her pleasure at Neville's notice. She actually preened, laying a hand to her rather astonishing cleavage as she curtsied in acknowledgement.

"I trust the duke is usually more attentive," Neville said sympathetically. "Now you really must meet Lady Arabella, my dear. I am quite sure you will find you have much in common with her."

Arabella, who could easily guess the nature of the woman's friendship with the duke, wanted to slap Neville Farrington's handsome, audacious face.

Her wits must have been addled to take any comfort at all from his presence!

The duke made a slight bow. "Good day to you all," he said. He turned and proceeded into the theater with his coquettish courtesan, causing Arabella to breathe a sigh of relief, but then the aggravating Neville swiveled on his booted heel and faced them, smiling with complete composure. "We shall miss the beginning of the play if we do not enter soon. I shall be most delighted to offer you the hospitality of my regular box."

"Your regular box," his father sneered. "I should have known. We will sit where I say we will sit."

"It will have to be the pit then, for I think there will be no other available seats."

"Not the pit!" Lady Lippet cried, as if the pit would be filled with snakes instead of those who could not afford box seats.

"No, you ought not sit in the pit," Neville seconded. "Lady Arabella's gown might be damaged. Or her fine cloak. Or her splendid little shoes."

"I think the pit will be acceptable," Arabella replied with a hint of defiance.

"Amongst the rabble? Surely not! How will you find a husband there?"

Arabella flushed and did not answer.

"It would have been quite a coup to be invited to the Duke of Buckingham's box," Lady Lippet noted in a whine, giving Neville a peevish look.

"Since he made no effort to do so, you will have to wait for another time."

"He might invite us to sup with him after the play," Lady Lippet proposed hopefully.

"I should remind your ladyship that the duke already has a wife."

"He is an influential man," Lady Lippet declared defensively.

"He was, until even Charles could not overlook certain . . . how shall I put this so that it is fit for women's delicate ears? Until the king could not overlook Buckingham's proclivities."

"That whole family is a disgrace," the earl announced. "His father was the most disgusting sodomite—"

"Now there is one sin that has never been laid at my door," Neville interjected, "but really, Father, I believe discussing the late duke is upsetting Lady Arabella."

In truth, Arabella was finding the entire situation distressing.

"I should point out that if you intend to see

this play today," Neville continued, "we should go inside without further ado."

"If it's so late, perhaps we should return home," Arabella murmured, trying to decide what would be worse: missing the play or sitting near Neville Farrington.

"After going to all the trouble to get here?" the earl demanded, his goatee quivering. "I should think not!"

Neville suddenly stepped close to Arabella. "Come along, then, my dear."

Before she could protest, he took her hand in his strong grasp and placed it over his arm; then he pulled her along beside him through the doors and into the theater itself, leaving the earl and Lady Lippet to follow behind.

As he led Arabella into the building, Neville told himself he had had little choice but to intercept his father, Lady Lippet and Arabella as they spoke with George Villiers.

The duke hadn't gotten where he was because he was completely without some attractive points. He was handsome, he was rich and he could be charming, especially to women.

Yet it was Villiers, it was said, who had instructed the king in various vices during the long years of exile. It was also rumored that the duke was familiar with more decadent practices than most men knew existed.

Now this infamous debaucher of women,

notorious libertine and reputed royal pander
had discovered Arabella.

Neville realized that if his goal was merely
to engineer Arabella's fall from her virtuous
pedestal, an intimate relationship with Villiers
would accomplish that. But Villiers was a disgusting lecher, and Neville would see no
woman, not even his rival, sacrificed to that
man's depravity.

And besides, he would lose the bet with
Richard and Foz if Buckingham seduced her.

As they moved toward the boxes on the second level of the theater, they were crowded on
all sides, the pressure of the mob forcing them
together. The hood of Arabella's cloak caught
on a tall man's shoulder. She emitted a little
shriek of dismay as it fell back, while he took
the opportunity to study her.

Her glossy brown hair was dressed and
curled in the latest fashionable style, so that
teasing little *confidantes* grazed her pink-tinged
cheeks in a most becoming manner.

As yet, her face bore no cosmetics, and she
had not adopted patches. Given that Lady Lippet was now involved in this hunt for a husband, it was probably only a matter of time
before she did.

A plump gentleman squeezed past them,
and they pressed against the wall that formed
one side of the corridor. On the other was a

partition, with entrances every few feet leading into the separate boxes.

Arabella clutched Neville's arm so that she wouldn't stumble.

He would never have guessed that so simple a thing could be so arousing, yet so it was.

It was as if he were an inexperienced, virginal youth again, but one with a detailed and extensive knowledge of what a couple might do in bed together.

At that notion, a hundred different things he would like to do with and for Arabella leaped into his brain with astonishingly vivid clarity.

Then he noticed that Arabella's cloak had slipped back even more, giving him a most tantalizing glimpse of cleavage as her body was forced against his.

It would appear her breasts were as naturally wonderful as her face.

The memory of their soft weight in his palm immediately proved even more distracting than any imaginary activity.

What would she have done that night if he had slipped the nightgown from her shoulders and put his lips where his thumb had been, flicking his tongue until she cried for mercy, or more—

"Is it always so crowded?" she asked with obvious frustration.

She was not the only frustrated person here.

A pox on such ruminations in so public a place! Any person looking at him would know which way his thoughts were tending.

He forced himself to regard his companion with all the dispassion he could muster—and suddenly took note of the fine cloak over the even finer gown. How had she come by such garments? More important, who had paid for them?

Any lingering pleasure he felt from her proximity and his graphic imaginings disappeared. He would do better to remember that she could disinherit him.

"Richard's plays are always popular," he replied quietly, giving her his most seductive smile. "And then, this building was not designed to be a theater. It used to be a tennis court."

She made no effort to move on. Neither did he, especially when he realized that his father and Lady Lippet were nowhere nearby.

"Perhaps we should wait for this crowd to thin," he said.

"If you think so."

"I do."

She nodded, setting those delightful little curls to dancing.

"I must confess myself surprised to meet you here," Neville remarked. "I never would have expected my father or you to choose *The Country Cuckold*."

Arabella started and stared at him. "The country *what*?"

"Cuckold. You know, a fellow whose wife takes a lover."

"I know what a cuckold is."

"Ah, but do you know the circumstances likely to produce one?"

"I am sure you are well versed in that knowledge, my lord, and will be delighted to tell me."

The nobleman raised his eyebrows in an exaggerated gesture of innocent incomprehension. "I only meant that Richard's play should prove instructive on the true nature of women."

"To you, too?"

"I had that lesson long ago," he replied evenly.

Her brow furrowed slightly, then she looked back the way they had come. "I do not see the earl or Lady Lippet."

"Perhaps they have gone astray in this den of vice and iniquity."

Arabella pursed her lips. "I think we may continue toward your box now."

"Very well," he said, for in truth, the crowd had thinned out considerably.

"Ah, here we are," he said after a few moments, indicating where she was to enter.

He followed her inside, to find her regarding the interior of the theater with wide-eyed wonder. Her face glowed, her eyes shone and her perfect breasts rose and fell with her excited breathing.

She looked as he must have looked the first time he had been in a theater, although his attendance at his first play had also come with an element of risk. Theatrical performances had been against the law in Cromwell's England.

Still, he remembered the excitement and the fun, the banter and the boos when an actor missed his cue, the insolent remarks of the orange girls, who sold their fruit at the foot of the stage during the play, and themselves afterward.

Even now, the theater filled him with a curious mixture of anticipation, excitement and dread.

Rather like the way he felt being with Arabella, although why he should feel dread he didn't stop to consider.

He realized that several men in the crowded pit and boxes seemed to find her fascinating, the Duke of Buckingham in particular.

It was all Neville could do to keep a scowl from his face. "I suppose it was the bewitching Lady Lippet's idea to come to the theater. She is a great patron of the arts."

He moved in front of her, screening her from other men's prying eyes.

It would be difficult for any spectators to

know exactly how close he was to her or what they might be doing. Given some of the performances he had seen in this very building—and not upon the stage—it could be almost anything.

He must and would stake his claim on her tonight, so that all gentlemen of rank would understand that if they pursued her, they would have to compete with him.

"Your father agreed."

"But you did not?" he suggested, waiting for her to say something about the base nature of the theater or to condemn such harmless entertainment in the very best Puritan manner.

"I have long wanted to see a play, my lord."

"A shocking confession, Lady Arabella."

"As Lady Lippet also thought it necessary, I did not object."

"Sitting in the dark surrounded by strangers is hardly conducive to finding a husband, I should think."

Her eyes seemed to sparkle, but that could only be a trick of the light. "Since you have yet to engage in finding a spouse, I think your opinions on the subject are not necessarily valid."

"If I did want a wife, I would not seek her in a theater."

"Where would you go?"

"To the country. Grantham, perhaps."

"Surely not," she protested gravely, "for it

is such a dull little place, only bumpkins must live there, and I am certain your lordship would never be happy with a bumpkin for a wife."

"That is quite true," he said softly. "Yet you come from Grantham, and I would never call you a bumpkin."

She deftly side-stepped him. "Nor will you ever call me wife."

Suddenly, as if a signal had been given, the whole audience rose to its feet and turned away from the stage to face the middle of the gallery.

"What is it?" Arabella asked as Neville bowed in the direction of the elegantly dressed group who were entering a previously empty box in the center.

"The question you should be asking, my dear," Neville replied, "is, *who* is it?"

"Very well. *Who* is it?"

"The king."

Chapter 7

Like a ripple upon the surface of a calm pond, the entire audience bowed toward its ruler.

"The king!" Arabella murmured excitedly as she performed a low curtsy, all the while keeping her eyes on the dark-haired, mustached man in the center of the box.

His Majesty's clothing was of a deep and lustrous purple embroidered with silver thread, and his hair was long, dark and curling. He turned this way and that addressing the beautiful woman and magnificently attired courtiers who attended him, yet she could see that his features were as comely as people said, although he was not nearly as handsome as the man at her side.

As King Charles gestured grandly in acknowledgment, Arabella smiled to think that she was seeing him so soon after her arrival in

London. This stroke of luck almost made up for every other discomfiting thing that had happened since they had come.

Then she realized the king was looking directly at her.

Nonplussed, Arabella instinctively curtsied again. When she rose, she saw that the king had turned his attention to the beautiful, bejeweled woman beside him, wearing a luxurious gown of peacock blue.

"Here you are," the earl growled.

Arabella and Neville both turned to face the irate nobleman and a panting Lady Lippet as they entered the box. "What the devil did you mean by taking off like a fox at a hunt?"

"Hush, Father. The king " Neville eyed the royal box significantly.

"Oh!"

Immediately, the earl bowed low, while Lady Lippet curtsied with an alarming cracking of joints.

As they straightened, Arabella glanced at the royal box, to encounter again the disconcerting gaze of the sovereign.

"A royal conquest perhaps," Neville noted.

"Don't be an idiot, Neville," Lord Barrsettshire reprimanded him in what Arabella supposed he meant for a whisper, although he was audible to anyone within twenty feet. "He was looking at me. No doubt he recalls that I once held the stirrup of his father's horse."

"He was looking at *me*," Lady Lippet gushed, waving gaily at the royal box. "We are on the most intimate of terms."

"You and the king?" Neville muttered. "If that is true, I fear for the royal eyesight."

Arabella stifled a smile, while Lord Barrsettshire gave his son a sour look. "Why don't you join your cronies and leave us in peace?"

Arabella flushed at the earl's rudeness, for they were in this box by Neville's invitation.

"I wouldn't dream of deserting you," he replied. "Besides, while this is not the best of boxes, I have a very fine view of the stage from here."

"You mean the women who parade upon it."

"Perhaps," Neville replied lightly.

Arabella suddenly found the building, which was crowded and lit by smoking candles, unbearably stuffy and hot. But she would not leave without seeing the play. Otherwise, she might seem a country bumpkin. "Shall we take our seats?"

"Indeed," Lady Lippet seconded. "Arabella must sit in the front beside me, and you men at the back."

The earl looked displeased, but he grudgingly obeyed, while Lady Lippet scanned the theater. "An excellent crowd," she murmured. "More gentlemen than ladies."

"I am sure your ladyship is the soul of generosity, for I suspect many of these are not gentlemen or ladies," Neville said behind them.

"You would know," the earl grumbled. "This place is probably full of pickpockets and whores, and the inmates of Bedlam would be more entertaining than the immoral twitterings we are going to have to sit through."

"Ah, ladies, are my father's words not the epitome of gracious speech?"

"Oh, look! We are in luck!" Lady Lippet exclaimed, ignoring them. "There is Lord Denshaw and the young Earl of Westlorne and— oh, my dear!—that young nobleman with the wart on his nose. Oh, what is his name? Whatever it is, he has a huge fortune!"

"Arabella, you will get overheated if you keep your cloak on," the earl admonished her.

Arabella obediently slipped her cloak off her shoulders. As she did, she hoped the play would commence shortly. Then everyone would have to be quiet.

Someone in the pit applauded, and people began to stare at her. The women frowned, and the men . . .

To her chagrin, Arabella realized the men were regarding her with leering, speculative curiosity, as if she had suddenly appeared stark naked before them. She quickly pulled up her cloak a little.

"Have you ever considered a career upon the stage, Lady Arabella?" Neville whispered behind her, his breath hot on the back of her neck. "You would undoubtedly cause a sensation."

She stiffened. She would not respond. She would ignore him and his warm breath on her skin. She would not compare him to the other men around her, overdressed and impertinent rascals the lot of them, especially the Duke of Buckingham. She would sit and enjoy the play.

Somehow.

"I wonder if Lord Rochester will be here," Lady Lippet mused. "And dear Sedley."

"If Buckingham is come, I think his dogs must not be far behind, provided they could rouse themselves at all," Neville remarked.

"This whole country is going to the dogs," the earl rumbled. "The dogs!"

"Smile, Arabella," Lady Lippet ordered. "This is a glorious opportunity!"

"I am quite sure she never misses an opportunity."

"Pay him no heed, Arabella!" Lady Lippet commanded. "Smile!"

"Do you see that pretty girl there who is also smiling?" Neville asked, his arm reaching past Arabella's shoulder to point to a lovely young woman giggling with female companions in the box beside the king. "That is La Belle Stewart. Charles is quite infatuated, they say. She resists his advances, however. Some say it is her morality, others that she is simply too stupid to understand what the king wants of her."

"Neville, keep your disgusting observations to yourself or I will have you thrown out!" the earl admonished.

"Do not tempt me to seek fame by being forced from both my home and a theater in so short a time, Father," his son replied calmly.

"The queen is much prettier than I expected," Arabella observed quietly.

"Oh, my dear!" Lady Lippet cried. "That is not the queen. That is Lady Castlemaine."

"Egad, is she really?" the earl said. "She is indeed a beautiful woman."

"Quiet, Father, lest you hurt Lady Arabella's tender feelings," Neville whispered loudly. "Surely you do not think the king's *grand amour* prettier than your charming ward. You do understand French, do you not, Lady Arabella?"

"I know what that means, my lord," she replied stonily, resisting the urge to turn around and glare at him.

She did not appreciate being compared to the king's mistress, even favorably.

Mercifully, the stage curtains parted, signaling the beginning of the performance.

A pretty young woman stepped forth. She was gorgeously attired in a rich and elaborate gown of surprising immodesty, which exposed nearly as much as it covered.

And so the play began.

As *The Country Cuckold* progressed, Arabella knew she should disapprove of what was being enacted, and in her rational mind, she did. Much of the tale concerned an adulterous wife and her lovers' attempts to dupe her dullard of a husband. The wife, much younger than her spouse, had married for wealth, he because he believed the woman loved him. For the duration of the play, the wife and her several lovers came up with a variety of improbable and increasingly ridiculous methods of disguising themselves and their true relationships from the husband.

Unfortunately, the wife and her lovers were so witty and clever, their schemes so outrageous, the husband so dim-witted, that Arabella had to laugh in spite of herself.

In addition to the actual performance, the rowdy, unruly behavior of the audience was a spectacle in itself. Members of the audience talked, joked and sauntered about the theater, so much so that at times Arabella could scarcely hear the actors for their clever banter.

Also distracting was the notion that the king kept looking at her. As tempting as it was to try to confirm that impression, the Duke of Buckingham and Mrs. Hankerton, as well as several other men, were in a box directly beside the sovereign. Every time she looked in that direction, she encountered the duke's leering smile.

As if all this were not enough, she had to contend with the knowledge that Neville was sitting directly behind her.

Her only recourse was to keep her gaze firmly fastened on the stage, no matter what unbelievable and immoral activities were being represented.

In spite of her resolve, however, she completely forgot to watch the play when she saw Neville standing at the side of the stage, apparently entertaining a group of young women.

She had no idea that he had even left the box.

"What in the name of God is Neville doing?" the earl muttered behind her, telling Arabella he had not noticed his son decamping, either. "Look at him with those creatures!"

"Who are they? Actresses?" Arabella asked Lady Lippet.

"No, those saucy wenches sell oranges," Lady Lippet replied with a sneer. "Bold hussies, the lot of them, and none more so than that Nell Gwynn! Look at her, the baggage!"

Arabella could not help looking at the pretty girl who seemed so amused by whatever Neville was saying that she had to hang onto his shoulder for support.

He certainly seemed to take this familiar behavior in stride.

Arabella tried to turn her attention back to

the play, which was not at all facilitated by Neville's ensuing stroll across the stage, providing her an unavoidable opportunity to study his athletic grace.

By the time the final curtain came down, to the boisterous applause of the audience, Arabella could see why her father and the earl always spoke of the theater in disparaging terms and why the Puritans had declared actors immoral rogues.

She could also understand why the theater was filled to capacity.

The players took their bows and curtsies, and the immodestly dressed actress playing the wife received thunderous applause. A veritable garden of flowers appeared at her feet, composed of bouquets tossed by several men. Finally, with much kissing of her hands to the audience, the actress left the stage.

Only then did the king rise and hold out his hand for Lady Castlemaine, who, Arabella thought, appeared to be decidedly out of sorts. Despite her expression, however, she meekly allowed the king to lead her from the box, while the audience stood in respect.

A general hubbub ensued as the patrons began heading for the exits.

Arabella turned toward the earl and discovered that he was acknowledging a woman of middle years across the pit.

"If you will excuse me a moment, ladies," he

said, getting to his feet, "I really must pay my respects to the Viscountess Bradley. Her late husband was a very dear friend of mine."

As he left the box, Lady Lippet pushed past Arabella. "That charming young Rochester is here after all, in the Duke of Buckingham's box. I will fetch him if I can, for he is not married. Perhaps I can manage an invitation to a late supper."

Arabella rose reluctantly. She had absolutely no wish to go the duke's box.

Lady Lippet gave her a studied look. "I think it would be better if you stay here. I'll be back before you even know I'm gone."

As tempting as it was to avoid the duke, Arabella knew she should not be left alone in so public a place. "Surely I should—"

"You will be perfectly safe here, my dear," Lady Lippet said decisively as she marched from the box.

Feeling far less convinced of that than Lady Lippet, yet unable to resist the evasion Lady Lippet offered, Arabella moved to the back bench, where she would be less noticeable.

She scanned the pit and the stage, relieved to note that no one seemed to be looking her way. Instead, the boisterous orange sellers commanded the attention of the men near them, and everyone else seemed in a hurry to leave, perhaps for parties or dinners.

With a sigh, she began to relax and think

about the play. Truly, it was a scandalous story, and yet she could scarcely remember laughing so hard in her life.

"By the world, have they left the wolves' bait all alone?"

Arabella jumped to her feet and turned to see Neville leaning against the door frame, effectively blocking her exit, his arms crossed over his chest as he regarded her, and with that devilishly seductive smile on his handsome face.

Neville continued to smile, even though he was shocked that his father would do something so careless and foolish as to leave Arabella alone.

Almost every man in the place, virtuous or not, had looked at her throughout the performance, and it did not take a seer to guess what they were thinking—including the king, for Neville had watched him closely.

Charles rarely confined his attentions to one woman at a time and had learned to disguise any overt interest in another woman while with the fiery-tempered Lady Castlemaine; nevertheless, Neville knew the Merry Monarch had taken note of Arabella. She was easily the most beautiful, enticing woman in the theater, whether on the stage or in the audience, surpassing even Lady Castlemaine.

Neville told himself he was concerned because he did not relish any competition, and certainly not from the king.

Therefore, as Arabella faced him, flushed and surprised, he was grateful he was the first to reach the box and for this golden opportunity to be alone with her. Better yet, he never should have left in the first place. However, it had taken every ounce of inner strength he possessed to keep from placing a finger on the smooth bare skin at the back of her neck as she had sat in front of him. Or from pressing a kiss there. It had been such a temptation to touch her that he had all but fled rather than risk ruining his seduction with an injudicious gesture in his father's presence.

"Your father saw an old friend, and Lady Lippet went to effect an invitation to supper, I believe," Arabella said with a gleam of defiance in her bright blue eyes.

"That woman would speak to the Devil himself if she thought it would get her an invitation to dine."

"Some people would think it is I who am conversing with the Devil, my lord, or at least one of his minions."

Neville chuckled as he came further into the box. "I have been called worse things in my time. Tell me, did you find the play entertaining?" He waited for a Puritan-inspired, sanctimonious denunciation.

"I found it quite amusing."

Neville hoped he did not look as taken aback as he felt. "I would have thought you would condemn it from the first word."

"Obviously you do not know me well."

"No, and I would improve our acquaintance."

Her eyes narrowed, and she backed away slightly. "As you did the other night?"

"I was a sinful wretch driven to disgraceful behavior by your beauty."

"You were certainly sinful, although I am not so vain as to believe my looks had much to do with it."

"Oh, I assure you they did."

"You should not have kissed me."

"You enjoyed it."

Her expression was frustratingly inscrutable in a way he had never encountered in a woman before. "I may have. I am but human, after all, which means I can be as weak as anyone. But I have learned my lesson, my lord, both with you and tonight."

"Indeed? What have you learned?" he asked, feeling a most unusual and utterly ridiculous anxiety.

"To beware of rascals who think of only one thing when it comes to women, and who treat honorable vows as inconsequential."

"I agree *The Country Cuckold* is one of Richard's more witty cautionary plays. However, I thought the lesson it taught was to beware falling in love."

"I cannot disagree, for I gather we were to consider the poor honest husband a buffoon who deserved to be hoodwinked because he had the misfortune to love his wife."

"There are many who would say that to be in love at all is to be a fool."

"Are you of that pathetic, cynical sort, my lord?" she asked, giving him a shrewd and pointed look that he did not care for.

"I wonder, am I cynical—or wise to the ways of the world?" he mused aloud. "Pathetic—or simply unromantic? Or could it be that I have never been in love?"

"Your many lovers would surely feel cheated if they knew that."

"I do not think they would complain."

"Maybe they did not love you, either."

His jaw clenched. "King Charles seemed to find the performance enjoyable," he noted after a moment, watching her face to see her response to the mention of the king.

"Did he?" she replied, apparently not impressed with the king's approval.

"Yes, just as he enjoyed looking at Minette Sommerall. Rumor has it she is his latest lover."

An expression of disgust flew across Arabella Martin's face. Or maybe it was dismay. "He must be very energetic."

"Oh, he is."

"If what you say is true, I am not surprised the king liked the play. The characters cared as little for fidelity as he apparently does."

"Or perhaps he saw them as honest creatures, not hypocrites."

"You would say it is ethical to betray a spouse, then? Next you will likely tell me that it is human nature to be fickle and disloyal."

"It is a woman's nature."

"It is only women who disregard sacred vows made before God?" she inquired in a sardonic tone that would have done credit to Richard himself. "All the men who have lovers are not married? I must be deluded, for I understood the king to be married."

"Would you claim the opposite, that no women betray their vows?"

She shook her head, setting her charming curls dancing. "In all honesty, my lord," she replied with a gravity that was even more confounding than her sarcasm, "I cannot. Yet would you not agree that if any person, man or woman, makes a sacred vow before God, they have a duty to obey it? If they would rather not adhere to their vows, they should not make them."

"You preach very prettily. However, you would do better to save your sermons for my father."

Her eyes narrowed. "He seems a model of morality."

"Men are not always what they seem."

"I like to think I do not judge by appearances."

"I wonder, should I be pleased or not by that remark?" he mused, moving closer to her.

Her response was a little smile that was at once challenging and mocking. "I leave that to your determination, my lord."

"I can be very determined, Arabella."

With his free hand he gently brushed back the curls at the side of her face, letting his fingers caress her soft-as-goose-down cheek.

She made no sound of protest, nor did she draw back, resistant, as he gently pulled her into his embrace.

The rosy scent of her perfume sent him back in time to when he had been an innocent youth discovering love.

"A woman should marry a man who is her match in vitality and passion, Arabella," he whispered.

With gentleness, he lightly touched his mouth to hers, half expecting her to protest, fearing that she would, when all he wanted was to taste her sweet lips.

Truly, he told himself, it was his intention to tease, to hint, to promise what tender passion they could share.

That intention lasted no more than an instant, for it seemed that here, in the shadows of the theater box, she was willing—very willing. He had found her kiss exciting before, but he quickly discovered it was but a foreshadowing of the passionate desire that suddenly burst into being now.

With a low growl, he gave himself over to the pleasure of sensuous delight, her taste and perfume mingling in voluptuous enticement that held him as sure as any spell. The sound of the departing audience, all but forgotten, seemed far away, and like the rustle of leaves. He could almost believe they were standing in a garden, about to experience all the joy and passion of love for the very first time.

Like Adam and Eve before the fall.

"Ah!" came a drunken cry from the corridor. "There she is!"

Chapter 8

Neville spun around, not at all pleased to see the Duke of Buckingham leaning against the door frame as if he had scarcely any spine to speak of. The wine bottle dangling from his hand no doubt explained his disheveled, red-faced limpness.

"Bu' na' alone," the duke slurred.

"Your servant, Your Grace," Neville said with the slightest of bows.

"Your shervan', my lord. Mos' def . . . mos' defininin . . . mos' certainly your slave, Lady Arabella."

The duke attempted to bow but lost his balance and staggered forward, colliding with Neville, who fell back, inadvertently shoving Arabella. She stumbled and would have fallen into the pit if Neville had not lunged forward and caught her in his arms, pulling her forward into the shadowed corner of the box.

He could feel the rapid rising and falling of her breasts against his chest and the soft exhalation of her breath against his chin.

She did not push herself away from him this time, either.

"Good night, Villiers," he said firmly, and without so much as a glance at the duke.

Villiers squinted as he tried to focus. "Wha's tha' you say?"

"Good night!"

"I leave the field for now," the duke mumbled grumpily, "to return an' figh' another day. Mrs. Hankerton, my shylph!" he cried as he noisily staggered away.

Neville looked down at Arabella, searching her face in the dim light as he tried to read her expression.

"Let me go," she said softly.

Very softly.

"You do not mean that," he replied in low, husky tones, cursing the fullness of her skirts and wishing she was wearing that thin night-dress again. Or nothing at all.

He took her hand and gently kissed the cleavage between her fingers, his tongue lightly licking, giving a promise of other delights he wanted to share with her.

"Let me go!" she repeated, somewhat breathlessly, but with sternness.

He felt as if she had slapped him full in the face. Had he been so wrong?

He let go of her hand as if it were a burning rushlight.

"Good night, my lord," Arabella said firmly.

It had taken all her will to keep from kissing him again. She had nearly swooned when he kissed and *licked* her hand, but she had not swooned, and now he had to go. Before she weakened again.

"Beg pardon, old friend, if I'm interrupting."

As before, when the duke had arrived, Arabella wasn't sure what to do or say as a tall man simply dressed entered the box, followed by another fellow for whom the word "fop" had probably been invented. Unlike Neville Farrington and the tall man, the fop wore garments nearly as extreme as those of the Duke of Buckingham, only on him, they seemed to hang like costly sacks.

The tall man was definitely the better looking of the two, with dark hair as natural as Neville's drawn back into a tail, a firm jaw and fine nose. He was not as handsome as Neville, of course, and his dark, sardonic eyes made her feel as if he were coldly measuring her against some standard only he understood.

That was not a pleasant sensation.

"Ah, Richard," Neville said jovially as he faced these unknown persons, "I thought you would be backstage with the actresses."

This must be the playwright, Arabella reasoned. He looked far more like a soldier than a man of letters.

"Foz told me he had seen your father with an older lady and a very charming and lovely young lady," Sir Richard Blythe replied. "This is the charming and lovely young lady, obviously. Do you not intend to introduce us to your fair companion?"

The fop cleared his throat loudly and smiled expectantly.

"Lady Arabella," Neville said, nodding toward the fop, "Lord Cheddersby."

"Your . . . your servant, Lady Arabella," Lord Cheddersby stammered.

He attempted to remove his hat in what she assumed was imitation of Neville's élan. Unfortunately, the poor man's wig went up with his hat, revealing limp brown hair before he replaced both hat and hair.

Lord Cheddersby would have been completely ridiculous, but there was a simple sweetness to his plain features that had been distinctly lacking upon many faces she had seen at the theater, so she smiled kindly.

"I am pleased to make your acquaintance, my lord," she said as she curtsied.

Lord Cheddersby blushed and looked at the other men with evident delight.

"And this grim fellow is the playwright, Sir Richard Blythe, of whose play you did not approve."

Sir Richard's brow puckered. "You did not like it? It did not amuse you?"

Arabella straightened her shoulders. "Your work *was* amusing, sir, but I must protest against the lack of morals in your characters."

Lord Cheddersby sighed with relief. "Oh, nothing so very serious then."

Arabella turned to look at him. "I consider that a serious fault indeed."

"If I write of immorality, it is because I write what I see," Sir Richard observed with slight hostility.

"Since she has only recently arrived from the fens of Lincolnshire, Richard, I think we may consider her opinion uninformed criticism."

"Obviously, we poor country bumpkins are incapable of understanding the higher intelligence of adulterers and coquettes," she concurred mournfully.

"Oh, Neville, come! You are too harsh!" Lord Cheddersby cried.

"I'faith, Neville, that was unkind," the playwright muttered.

Neville himself was feeling he had gone too far when Arabella glanced at him, her eyes sparkling with devilment and a little smile lurking about the corners of her delectable lips.

Gad, she was a sly creature—and he had fallen right into her trap!

"Neville, what the devil are you doing accosting Arabella?" Lord Barrsettshire demanded, appearing at the entrance to the box and glaring at them, arms akimbo. "Who are these fellows?"

"If you leave a lovely flower untended, bees are bound to swarm about it. I do not consider that accosting. And, sir, this is my box."

The earl glanced over his shoulder at Lady Lippet, who was trying to see what was happening. "Where have you been?"

"Trying to effect some suitable introductions," Lady Lippet replied defensively, all the while regarding Neville with undisguised scorn. "You should have better control over your wayward son."

"Lord Farrington came to my aid, my lord, when a man who was most rude and insolent tried to speak with me," Arabella said, deciding she could not stand to see Neville disparaged by Lady Lippet, who had not behaved in a manner befitting a chaperon. "I do not think I should have been left by myself."

"Well!" exclaimed Lady Lippet. "I was only trying—"

Neville quite calmly interrupted. "Father, you remember Sir Richard Blythe. And may I have the honor to present Lord Cheddersby?"

Both men bowed toward Lord Barrsettshire, who did not acknowledge the introduction save with a scowl.

"Come, Arabella," he barked. "We are leaving!"

Arabella's smile was loveliness personified. "If you gentlemen will excuse me, I am summoned."

With that, she glided past Foz, who stared after her as if he had just been told he was really the King of France, and the sardonic Richard, who seemed curiously pensive.

"I didn't think the play was that immoral," Richard reflected after she had disappeared from view. "Did you?"

"She is so beautiful!" Foz said dreamily. He looked accusingly at Neville. "You didn't say she was beautiful. You said pretty. And she championed you most excellently, don't you think?"

"Yes, she is lovely, but I am not in need of any championing from Lady Arabella or anyone else," Neville replied coolly, even as he wondered what had possessed Arabella to do that.

Maybe she was the kind of woman who was not happy until she had every man's approval. Or maybe he was truly on his way to winning his wager.

"I thought your play was the best yet," he continued.

Richard shook his head ruefully. "Zounds, man, although I perceive you have settled upon the gallant protector role in your plan for conquest, you are going to be out fifty pounds."

"You think so?" Neville replied as he sat upon the bench.

"A fortnight? She will never succumb in that time. For all her fine clothes and undeniable beauty, I think beneath those perfect breasts beats a puritanical heart. That is, of course, unfortunate, as it is unfortunate she has not better taste in plays."

Neville smiled. Richard would never forgive her criticism of his work, so she was safe from him. "If you think she is immune to me, you should have arrived a little sooner."

Foz gave Neville a look that was at once avidly curious and trepidatiously critical. "What do you mean?"

"She is not completely impervious to my attentions."

"Nevertheless, I would not count my fifty pounds yet," Richard said. "Buckingham could scarce take his eyes off her."

"That disgusting lecher!" Foz cried. "If he so much as speaks to her, I'll . . . I'll . . ."

"Challenge him to a duel?"

Foz flushed.

"Let me worry about Buckingham," Neville said.

"Why worry about him?" Richard asked. "If he despoils her, will that not solve your problem?"

"The thought of her—or any woman—despoiled by Buckingham does not sit well with me. Besides, the wager has been made."

"Do you think she liked me?" Foz suddenly asked with more intensity than Neville recalled him ever displaying before.

"No," Richard replied sardonically. "I don't think she likes any of us particularly, not even Neville."

Foz's face fell.

"Do not trouble yourself with her, Foz," Neville said, deciding that Richard was seeing only what he wanted to see in this instance. Arabella had criticized his play, therefore she must not like Richard, and so then she would not like his friends.

"Truly, she's too ignorant for men of our sophistication," he continued. "Come, let us retire to a tavern to tell Richard what the people in the pit were saying about his *magnum opus*."

"It was all good," Foz said eagerly.

"I had a moment's doubt when I saw the king frown during the first speech," Richard confessed. "I had to threaten Minette with dismissal before she would consent to say the opening just as I wanted, and then I feared I had offended His Majesty."

"She's the most beautiful creature I've ever beheld," Foz said with a sigh as they exited the box.

Neither Neville nor Richard realized he was not talking about the actress.

* * *

Very early the next morning, George Villiers stifled a yawn as he watched the king play tennis in the newly built court at Whitehall Palace. Charles had decided he was growing stout and thought exercise would make him thinner. To see if in this was successful, he weighed himself before and after every game.

Now, clad in a white shirt and petticoat breeches, the king ran about after the ball like a madman, his pack of spaniels yipping and barking and tussling among themselves on the sidelines. There was also a gaggle of courtiers watching the game, and they were only slightly more quiet than the dogs.

The king's partner was Lord Belmaris, also called Croesus because of his vast wealth. The fellow was dull in the extreme, stocky, had a wart on his nose and snorted like a pig when he ran, but he was a good enough tennis player, Villiers supposed.

Better Croesus Belmaris than Neville Farrington, the one man at court Villiers saw as a rival in intelligence, wit and looks.

The crowd of fawning courtiers cheered as the king made a fine hit. They always cheered heartily, the hypocrites. Some of these had even cheered when Charles's father lost his head.

If Charles could forgive them, Villiers thought angrily, why could he not forgive his oldest friend and ignore the straitlaced Puritans who presumed to condemn the man who had been with Charles all those years in exile? They blamed *him* for the monarch's excesses, as if there was something wrong with a man satisfying his appetites.

Villiers did not believe that, and neither, he was sure, did Charles—especially with regard to the appetite for women.

Besides, the execution of his father and the constant conflict within his own government could never be far from the king's mind. A man with such concerns must be forever in need of diversion, and it was in this need that Villiers knew the path to his own restoration lay. As of yesterday's attendance at *The Country Cuckold*, he was sure he had found that path.

Finally, the game ended. As Charles wiped his face with a towel and strolled toward the scales, Villiers hurried to join him, ignoring the questioning looks and outright scorn of the other courtiers.

Fools. Did they think he would forget?

It took great effort to keep smiling when he saw the peevish look that came to the monarch's face as he realized who stood beside him.

"Well played, Your Majesty."

"Thank you, Buckingham," the king said with apparent good humor, while Villiers noticed that he used the more formal term of address. "What brings you to Whitehall so early?"

"I wanted to know how you liked *The Country Cuckold*."

"We thought it very clever." With a broad grin, the king regarded the measure of his weight. "Look here—we have lost three pounds!"

"Excellent, Your Majesty! With God's blessing, you shall live to a fine old age."

"With God's blessing and treading very carefully," Charles muttered, a dark shadow passing over the usually cheerful face.

"Did you notice the Earl of Barrsettshire at the theater, Majesty?"

The king gestured for a liveried servant to give him his jacket. "Who?"

"The Earl of Barrsettshire." Villiers maneuvered his way closer to the king and dropped his voice to a conspiratorial whisper. "He was in a box to the right of the stage and had an astonishingly pretty girl with him, even more lovely than La Belle Stewart."

"We didn't notice."

Liar, Villiers thought. He knew the king too well to be fooled by his apparent lack of interest.

"I think she seems a good deal more intelligent than Frances Stewart, too," Villiers added significantly before raising his voice slightly as he stepped back. "It has been many, many years since the good earl has been in London, Majesty. Would it not be a kind gesture to invite him to Whitehall?"

"A fine idea, Buckingham. We must make sure all our nobles feel welcome when they visit London." Charles turned as if to go, then glanced back. "We thank you for suggesting it."

As the king strolled toward the palace, trailed by his courtiers and his spaniels, Villiers made a sweeping bow.

His head lowered, no one saw his sly, triumphant smile.

"Oh, my dear! Oh, Wattles!" Lady Lippet exclaimed as she entered the earl's withdrawing room later that day in a flutter of ribbons, lace and feathers.

Today, her gown was mauve, her underskirt orange, her hat more precariously perched than ever and her powder spotty, evincing some haste in dressing. "Is it true? That red-haired varlet wasn't lying?"

The earl rose and gestured at the chair beside Arabella, who was in dutiful attendance. "Indeed it is. We have been invited to Whitehall this evening."

"Oh, this is marvelous!"

As Lady Lippet lowered herself onto the chair and proceeded to fan herself briskly, the earl handed her the note he had received from the palace.

Arabella regarded all three with something less than complete delight. After meeting the Duke of Buckingham and enduring Neville Farrington's attentions, she was coming to realize that life among the upper class in London was not quite what she had imagined it would be.

Parts of it were as different as Neville was from the boy she remembered.

But not everything had been a disappointment, she reminded herself. Despite the subject of the play, she had enjoyed the theater. Perhaps the court would be enjoyable, too, if Neville and the Duke of Buckingham were not there.

Lady Lippet held the note from Whitehall to her bosom as if it were a message from her true love. "An invitation to the palace so soon! What a triumph!" She waved the letter at the earl. "Did I not tell you we should go to the theater? Was that not a brilliant plan? And now the court! Oh, Arabella, you are the most fortunate of women!"

"I knew the king would remember me," the earl said proudly.

Lady Lippet's eyes narrowed as she considered Arabella. "You do not seem to appreciate the honor, Arabella, or the opportunity."

"Indeed, Lady Lippet, I am sensible of the

honor to Lord Barrsettshire, for the invitation was extended to him."

"And us, surely!" the lady cried in horror as she scanned the letter again.

"We are not mentioned."

"It does not say we are *not* invited," Lady Lippet said, once again grinning with joy. "Besides, the Banqueting House is always so crowded, you and I will hardly be noticed."

If she wore another such gown, Arabella thought, Lady Lippet could hardly escape notice.

The lady rose as fast as her constrictive bodice would allow. "Now I had better return home to prepare. I shall come here in plenty of time so that we can journey to the palace together."

The earl nodded as Lady Lippet, with a sigh as if abandoning her lover, handed him the note. "Until later, Wattles. Look for me at seven o'clock."

She bustled out of the room, her ribbons streaming out behind her like pennants in the breeze. Leaving Arabella to wonder if it might not have been a better idea to look for her husband in Lincolnshire, after all.

Chapter 9

"Arabella, take care of your skirt,"
Lady Lippet commanded. "Water
will surely stain it."

As Arabella stepped carefully into the boat
rocking on the Thames, she obediently checked
to make sure she wasn't inadvertently sitting
in a puddle, despite the canopied covering, or
dragging her skirts in bilge water.

Going to Whitehall by river, Lady Lippet
had explained, was faster and easier than being
jostled about in a coach in the narrow, cobble-
stone streets of the city.

It certainly offered a different view of London, Arabella reflected, looking at the buildings crowding the banks of the Thames. In the
distance she could make out the bulk of St.
Paul's and Parliament.

Unfortunately, the odor of the Thames was
decidedly unpleasant, so after taking her seat,

Arabella held her handkerchief to her nose.

As for the river being less crowded than the streets, that was only slightly true. Many vessels of all shapes, sizes and conditions plied the river.

The earl got aboard and then Lady Lippet, whose advent caused the ten-foot-long boat to rock precariously.

Having an immediate vision of being dumped in the Thames, Arabella gripped the thwart tightly while the boatman made a grab for Lady Lippet's arm.

"Take care, my lady, we wouldn't want you to drown," he muttered.

"Nonsense!" Lady Lippet cried, sitting down heavily so that her full skirts half-covered the earl. "You are not holding it steady, you oaf!"

Arabella shifted further toward the stern to allow the earl more room and glanced at the burly boatman.

She thought that Lady Lippet had better watch her tongue. Otherwise, she might wind up in the Thames, and not by accident. Since her gown of bright yellow and red must weigh at least ten pounds, she would surely sink directly to the muddy bottom.

Once everyone was settled, the boatman guided the vessel away from the wharf to join the many others on the river. Some, like theirs, were intended for passengers, with canopied seats in the bow. Others were clearly for transporting goods. The boatmen, all of whom seemed to have a similarly brawny build, called out to each other as they passed, sometimes good-naturedly, at other times distinctly the opposite.

"What is on that side of the river?" Arabella asked, gesturing to the south.

"Oh, my dear!" Lady Lippet exclaimed as she looked where Arabella had pointed. "Bankside is a place for men, sailors and other such blackguards. No one of good repute goes there!"

"Unless they want to see a decent cockfight," the boatman muttered. "Or other sport that requires a cock."

"What other sport requires a cock?" Arabella asked.

"I beg your pardon?" the earl demanded.

"I was asking the boatman—"

"About Bankside, my lord," the man answered quickly. He gave Arabella a somewhat disgusted look. "I was telling the young lady about the cockfights."

"Never, never go to Bankside, my dear!" Lady Lippet cautioned, as if Arabella had suddenly announced a burning desire to do so.

"That's for poorer folk," the boatman noted gravely. "Them as has money goes to Covent Garden and the theaters thereabouts."

"They prefer the theater?"

The waterman's lips turned up in a knowing

smile. "They prefer the buildings behind the theater."

"The taverns?"

"I think we have had quite enough of this discussion," Lady Lippet declared. "If this fellow will apply himself, we should be at the palace shortly."

"I told you the king recognized me," Lord Barrsettshire said in the smugly satisfied manner that he had used all day. "Perhaps he's not the fool I thought he was."

"Wattles!" Lady Lippet cried, aghast. "Do not call the king a fool! He will not appreciate it! Besides, now that he has finally been restored, all men and women of rank should do their best to support him."

"Of course we must support the king," the earl replied. "However, he is a young man in serious need of guidance."

The earl's tone made it clear he intended to impart that necessary guidance.

"My lord," Arabella said delicately, "perhaps he will not want to be given advice."

"Nevertheless, it must be done."

"By you?"

"Since no other man has the backbone for it, I must."

"Wattles, this is no time to speak to the king of political matters. Our first object is to get Arabella married. And I should warn you, your advice might be considered traitorous."

"I do not call warning King Charles of the error of his ways traitorous," the earl grumbled.

"*He* might."

"I am not a coward!" Lord Barrsettshire cried. "I will say what I think."

Lady Lippet's smile was rather strained as she turned to Arabella and left his lordship to scowl in peace. "Now, here are some things to remember. If Lady Castlemaine appears, do not say anything about her husband. Or Sir Charles Berkeley. Or Lord Chesterfield. And I would not speak of the Duke of Monmouth, either."

"I do not know these men," Arabella reminded her.

"Well, *she* does. And of all of them, be sure to say nothing of Monmouth."

"Who is he?" Arabella asked, quite mystified.

Lady Lippet spoke as if the water around them were filled with spies. "The king's natural son by Lucy Walter, who thankfully died. Such a nuisance she was! Anyway, Lady Castlemaine was very attentive to the dear boy when he arrived last year. Too attentive, if you understand me, though he was but thirteen. They say that is why the king was so quick to marry him off to the Countess of Buccleuch. Of course, the countess was very wealthy, too."

"I shall do my best," Arabella assured her.

In what was probably a short time, although Lady Lippet's continuous gossipy monologue concerning liaisons among the courtiers made it seem like an hour, they reached a series of stone steps leading up to a jumble of buildings.

"Is all this the palace?" Arabella asked in wonder.

"What an untidy mess," the earl declared.

"It *is* rather spread out," Lady Lippet agreed. "The king is doing his best to repair the damage done by those tasteless Puritans."

"It should all be torn down and built new."

"But that would cost money, Wattles," Lady Lippet replied.

"He would be able to afford it if he didn't spend so much on his whores."

The boatman held out a grimy hand to help Arabella out of the boat. "I'll try and hold 'er steady. Watch it now."

With only a few grumbles, the earl managed to get onto the wharf, and then he assisted Lady Lippet. He pulled two small coins from his purse and gave them to the boatman. "If you come back at midnight, you may take us home."

The boatman's expression led Arabella to believe he would be otherwise occupied at midnight.

Meanwhile, the earl took Lady Lippet's arm to lead the way up the slick steps, and as they went, Arabella reminded herself that she wasn't going to anticipate anything but a delightful time. She would hope that neither Neville nor the disgusting duke would be in attendance and look forward to meeting the king.

Despite this resolve, the moment Arabella entered the gilded splendor of the Banqueting House with its high, ornate ceiling decorated by Rubens, the enormous pillars and the hearth taller than most men, she felt very much the country bumpkin.

All around her were people splendidly attired in brightly colored satins and velvets, flowing wigs and numerous patches. Her own lovely gown of rose-colored silk suddenly seemed plain, her hair not curled enough and she almost wished she had agreed to wear a patch or two.

"It is not his father's court," the earl muttered, looking around as if he felt as uncomfortable as she did.

Then he started like a deer hearing the huntsman's horn.

"Good God, isn't that Thomas Taddleslop?" he cried happily. "It's been twenty years!"

With that, he pushed his away through the crowd.

"Oh, there is Croesus Belmaris!" Lady Lippet exclaimed, ignoring the earl's defection. "A most eligible young man!"

Arabella followed her gaze and then wanted

to groan with dismay, for the man Lady Lippet was referring to was pale and somewhat plump, with heavy features and a protruding lower lip. He also had the most disconcertingly large wart on his nose that Arabella had ever seen.

Even more disturbing, he was talking to the Duke of Buckingham.

"I fear I feel somewhat faint," Arabella said, not exactly untruthfully. "I would like to sit down."

"Sit down?" Lady Lippet cried as if Arabella had asked to be anointed goddess of the universe.

Arabella looked at Lady Lippet sorrowfully. "Yes, please."

The older woman's brows puckered peevishly. "I suppose this might be overwhelming for you. There are some chairs here."

She gestured at the area behind a pillar near the door. "Why do you not rest there, and I will bring the gentleman to you?"

Arabella nodded, and Lady Lippet headed for the two men.

As soon as Lady Lippet was gone, Arabella began to move away, slowly sidling around the outskirts of the huge room. She was not as afraid of being in this company unchaperoned as she was of encountering the Duke of Buckingham again.

She came to a halt in a dimly-lit corner. From

here, she could watch the magnificent gathering, and no one could see her, unless they chose to hide in the shadows, too.

Relaxing somewhat, she observed the finely dressed courtiers, beautiful women and servants mingling together.

She caught interesting little snatches of conversations, too. If someone had asked her what she expected the talk at Whitehall to be about, she would have said Charles's new laws or the renovation of the palace or the difficulties with the Dutch. Instead, the only topics people seemed to be discussing were the king, Lady Castlemaine, Frances Stewart, the latest fashions from France and, if she heard aright, who was sleeping with whose wife.

These people were very much like a country fair full of gossiping villagers, albeit better dressed.

Thinking that, she relaxed even more. What were these nobles but people, after all? And for all their finery, they were not so very different from others she knew.

The middle-aged fellow in the tightly fitting velvet jacket reminded her of the butcher at Grantham, who always tied his apron too tight because he was under the mistaken impression that it made him look thinner.

And that young woman over there, preening in a gilded mirror and pretending not to, was as vain and self-deluding as the milliner.

Arabella moved out of her sanctuary a little. A few men, more sensibly dressed than the others, caught her eye. They looked to be of a more conservative bent, if the disgust on their faces as they regarded some of the more ludicrously attired could be taken as evidence. One or two of them were of an age with Neville Farrington. Perhaps these were the kind of men the earl and Lady Lippet wanted her to meet.

That thought did not excite her, just as they did not. They looked so . . . ordinary.

Not that she wanted the extraordinary, she reminded herself. She wanted steadiness and kindness, not flippancy or quick, sardonic wit. She wanted love, not passion or the dangerous sort of man that could make her confuse the two.

Then she noticed a group of young courtiers who seemed the epitome of sartorial excess. One, who was apparently the leader, had on an elaborate black wig, which contrasted with his falsely pale face. A black patch had been placed at the corner of his left eye and another on his cheek. His burgundy clothing was very much embroidered, and his shoe buckles were of gold. He had been at the theater, she thought, in the box with the Duke of Buckingham.

The two other men attending him were similarly attired, albeit with less embroidery. One wore a shade of blue like nothing in nature at all. The next, in a brown wig of extreme curl, wore a bright shade of green.

Then she caught sight of another familiar face, one that made her smile. Lord Cheddersby wandered about the hall as if he were lost or in some strange foreign land—feelings with which she could sympathize. Indeed, she was sorely tempted to come out and commiserate with him, until the black-bewigged courtier spoke.

"Bodikins, will you look at him?" he said, staring at Lord Cheddersby with open scorn. "Have you ever seen such a pudding? He makes La Belle Stewart seem an intellectual."

The other men chuckled in agreement, and the blue-clad fellow, who did not look any wiser than Lord Cheddersby, said, "What is the aristocracy coming to? Could we not petition the king to pass a law requiring some sort of basic wit before one can attend the court?"

If King Charles agreed to do so, Arabella thought, that fellow would likely fail it. And if Lord Cheddersby seemed rather lacking in intelligence, at least there was a kindness in his manner that these three did not possess.

"Look at that hat, those breeches," the man in green lisped. "His tailor should be put in the stocks for letting him go about like that."

Arabella looked again at Lord Cheddersby, and she could not see any difference at all between the clothing of the speaker and the object of his disdainful criticism.

"I think Sedley should find an excuse to fight a duel with him," the blue-clad man proposed. "That would rid the court of the fellow."

Sedley, the leader, looked at his companions with a mixture of superiority and disgust. "I have no desire to have anything to do with that fop-noodle. He's not worth dulling my blade. I wonder where his keeper has got to? Farrington usually sticks to him like a burr."

"Only to catch the loose coins falling from Cheddersby's purse," the blue-clad man replied. "There's likely a woman in the case. I heard Farrington was pursuing that new actress in Blythe's latest play. Say what you will about Farrington and his choice of friends, his taste in women in exquisite."

"I am so delighted to have your approval."

Arabella started nearly as much as the courtiers when she heard Neville Farrington's sardonic response. She was even more surprised to realize he was standing not ten feet away, leaning against the wall, his arms crossed.

He wore his black jacket with a full, dazzlingly white shirt underneath. The cuffs of it were three inches deep in lace, and his black breeches were tucked into the wide cuffs of shining black boots. More impressive than his clothing, however, was the cool confidence he exuded. He looked as if he could duel all three at once and defeat them without even starting to sweat.

But must he always keep appearing like some kind of spirit? Was he spying on her, that he must always be where she was?

Then she realized he had not so much as glanced at her, and considering where she was, he must not have seen her.

Which pleased her, naturally.

With a smile that seemed distinctly menacing, Neville pushed himself off the wall and strolled toward the group of courtiers.

She was very, very glad he was not coming toward her with that particular look on his face.

"Farrington," Sedley said with an insipid drawl and a slight bow. "What a charming surprise. I thought you would be at the theater this evening, watching Minette Summerall."

"I had better things to do."

Then Arabella nearly swooned, for he suddenly turned and looked directly at her—or at the least into the corner where she was hiding. "Come, my dear Lady Arabella, and meet three ornaments of the king's court."

She had no more desire to meet those men than she had to be near Neville Farrington!

She desperately tried to think of a way out of this predicament; unfortunately, there was no way to flee, for it was too crowded and she didn't want to make a spectacle of herself.

"She is a shy little thing," Neville said condescendingly as he walked toward her.

His dark eyes regarded her with an intensity that seemed calculated to remind her of every moment she had spent in his arms.

Even though he had not so much as touched her, her breathing quickened, her heart raced and her legs weakened—with dread, surely!

When he came close enough to kiss her, she backed as far away as she could and whispered, "Please, let me stay here! I do not want to meet them!"

His expression seemed merciless. "Where is my father? Has he abandoned you to your fate again? And dear Lady Lippet—she is being as remiss as I could ever be."

"Your father thought he saw a friend, and Lady Lippet . . ."

"Well, what of Lady Lippet?"

Now truly desperate, Arabella said, "She went to fetch Lord Belmaris, who was with the Duke of Buckingham. I—"

His eyes lit up with genuine pleasure as he smiled. "You fled."

"Come, Farrington, enough flirting in the corner!" Sedley called. "Bring her out!"

"Yes, my lord, I did," she said rather desperately, "as I would flee these men, too."

"I don't think he's going to," the blue-clad fellow jeered. "Wants to keep her all to himself, the selfish cad."

"T'faith, Lady Arabella, this is scarcely the way to find a husband!" Neville noted softly. "Of course, I would rather hide here with you, away from curious eyes."

Arabella suddenly felt as if she had just asked a snake to nestle in her bosom like Cleopatra's asp. "Can you not make them go away?" *And take your disconcertingly attractive self with them?* she added to herself.

"Are you asking for my help?"

"If you are a gentleman, yes!"

"Even if I am not, no doubt you will be grateful if I succeed. That is a most tempting lure to do good, I must say. Much better than anything my father has suggested."

Arabella had had enough—of him, of those men, of feeling like a baited bear. She took a step forward, silently challenging him to try to block her way. "If you will not help me—"

He neatly intercepted her, taking hold of her hand. He raised it to his lips and kissed it in an elegant fashion. "I merely note I shall have to take some responsibility at last."

Unfortunately, her internal response to the sensation of his lips on her skin could only be called primitive. Now she wished she had stayed away from Whitehall entirely, especially when he coolly led her forth as if he encountered young ladies hiding from courtiers with some frequency.

"Demme, Farrington, this is the beauty from

the theater! I thought she belonged to your father," Sedley said as he ran a most insolent gaze over Arabella. "Or does he share?"

"Lady Arabella, this rude fellow is Sir Charles Sedley, who will, I trust, eventually learn the value of keeping his sordid opinions to himself."

Before Sedley could answer, Neville turned to the man in blue. "This is Lord Buckhurst, and this," he continued, facing the other man, "is Henry Jermyn, a great favorite of my lady Castlemaine these days."

Jermyn seemed not to know whether to smile or scowl at this introduction and finally settled upon looking at Arabella with the most disgusting leer she had ever seen. He made the Duke of Buckingham look subtle.

"What a pretty little friend," Jermyn observed.

Thinking of Mrs. Hankerton at the theater, the duke's "friend," Arabella bristled. Before she could reply, however, Neville spoke. "She is not my friend."

Then he took hold of her hand and pressed a long, lingering kiss upon her palm. His gaze seemed to burn into hers before he glanced at the others. "Yet."

The men chortled knowingly, and Arabella was tempted to wipe her hand on her skirt, as if that could erase the burning desire that his touch always created within her.

"Come, Arabella, these are men of the world!" Neville cried. "There is no need to feign maidenly modesty." Grinning slyly, he looked at the others. "Privacy, gentlemen, if you please, for wooing in a mob is never successful."

Arabella wanted to denounce Neville, his words, and his insolent intention. She would have done so, had Buckhurst and Jermyn not moved away, chuckling in a manner obviously intended to indicate that they were men of the world and they did understand.

Sedley, however, remained.

With a barely perceptible glance at the courtier, Neville suddenly pulled her to him and in full view of Sedley—and anybody else who happened to be looking—kissed her on the mouth.

Not tenderly. Not gently.

Possessively.

As if he were her master and she his slave.

Chapter 10

Her chest heaving with anger, Arabella pushed Neville away and glared at him. "Are you mad?"

He held a finger to his lips and glanced over his shoulder. "He has gone."

"I don't care about him! You impudent, disgusting scoundrel!"

"Do not go into hysterics, Arabella. That kiss was merely a tactic to rid you of the attention of those coxcombs. Now I shall escort you back to your charming little sanctuary."

Sanctuary? As long as Neville was anywhere near her, she could not feel safe, and not just from his lascivious attention.

Her own rebellious desire gave her as much discomfort as he did—perhaps more. She had to admit that, but only to herself. "Surely a clever man could have thought of a better tactic!"

Frowning gravely, he said, "That demonstrates how little you know of the men of the court. Those three are cronies of Buckingham and the worst knaves in all of London. They require strong evidence."

"No doubt you know them so well because you frequent the same places of debauchery in . . . in Bankside!"

His lips jerked. "I see you have been learning about London. Frequent is, perhaps, too strong a word for my occasional visits there, but if that will lend credence to what I say of them, so be it," he said with a little bow. His tone grew serious again. "As long as you do believe it."

"Nevertheless, your behavior is unacceptable. You must stop kissing me!"

His eyes narrowed. "Are you upset because I kissed you again or because I kissed you in Whitehall?"

She crossed her arms over her chest. "It was surely not a necessity to choose so extreme a method and in so public a place."

He lowered his voice to a husky, seductive tone. "Naturally there are more private places I would rather kiss you."

"You are incorrigible," she said disdainfully, leaving him to return to her place in the corner, only to realize he had followed when she turned and found him directly in front of her, his body mere inches away.

Why did he have to have such fascinating lips, neither too thin, nor too full, and with a perfect shape?

How was it that simply by moving the corners of his mouth ever so slightly, he could make her want to laugh or frown or sigh with desire?

Or hide.

With him. Preferably in a bed with the curtains drawn.

Clearly, being in London was addling her wits.

"I thought you might not want to be the object of their pursuit," he remarked, smiling in a way that made her resolve to curb her outlandish imaginings once and for all.

"I do not wish to be anyone's object. Please go away."

"Except a potential husband's, I assume. Is that why you are here, to cast your net for a suitable candidate?"

"The king himself invited us," she replied haughtily.

Neville's expression altered for the blink of an eye, then returned to its usual cool nonchalance. "The king himself. How thrilling for you."

"It was, until—"

"Until a most terrible scoundrel kissed you in front of a debased rogue." His smile was annoyingly condescending. "But if those other terrible scoundrels believe *I* intend to seduce you, they will stay away from you, at least for a little while."

Although she was appalled by his explanation, she could believe that might be so, while a tiny portion of her mind simultaneously envisioned allowing herself to be seduced by Neville Farrington.

She could almost feel the pressure of his mouth upon her lips, his arousing caresses, the weight of his body, the thrust of his hips—

She must not give in to the sinful lust coursing through her body. She must be honorable. She must be good.

Or else she would be no more than a weak, wicked female full of original sin, as her father always claimed.

As if reading her mind and finding her fevered thoughts amusing, Neville smiled his devilish little smile.

"I can think of many a worse fate than sharing my bed," he murmured softly, reaching out to cup her chin in his hand.

She was powerless to resist as he eased his mouth over hers in a slow and leisurely kiss. His gentle touch proved as thrilling as his most impassioned embrace, and this unexpected tenderness even more compelling.

How easy it would be to allow him to continue. How simple to let him do whatever he wanted. How tempting to respond without restraint.

And how very wrong.

She shook her head, making him stop and let go of her. "I can think of nothing worse than being in your bed!" she lied, desperate to regain some measure of self-control.

His jaw clenched. "I can. You could be dispossessed or forced into a loveless marriage with a man who sees you only as a fat purse and pleasing bedmate."

"I will not be *forced* into marriage!"

His expression changed. "I can believe you mean that." Then he smiled. "But calm yourself, my dear. My action is unlikely to cause a scandal."

He made a great show of looking about the assembly.

"Let me see," he began pensively. "Over there I see Sir Daniel Templeton and his third favorite mistress doing somewhat more than kissing."

Arabella commanded herself not to follow his gaze.

Neville gestured languidly in the other direction. "And over there, by the second column, is old Sir Douglas Whattley with his young wife—his fourth, she is, the others having perished from a surfeit of Sir Douglas.

"By the world," he cried with mock horror,

"I do believe that is his hand disappearing down her bodice."

Then his tone grew studiously concerned. "Perhaps she has lost something and he only seeks to retrieve it."

Arabella would not look at what had to be a disgusting spectacle and she assuredly would not smile, no matter how merry his reportage.

"There is something that is sure to shock your delicate sensibilities," he continued in a loud whisper. "Mrs. Hermione Fotheringham— or so she calls herself, when everybody knows her name is really Polly Jones—has let her bodice slip far too low." He glanced at Arabella's bodice. "With none of the charms of certain young ladies to show."

Arabella blushed and told herself to walk away, despite the enthralling allure of his rich voice.

"Now watch as she laughs and pretends the display was all an accident."

Finally, Arabella could not resist the temptation to look at the woman across the room, who was now in the company of Sedley and his cronies. She was not unattractive, from what Arabella could see, yet there was a faded, desperate air in her smiles and posing, and her loose bodice was truly cut scandalously low.

Perhaps, at one time, she, too, had come to London from the country. Maybe she had met a man she found attractive and exciting, who had seemed to promise bliss if she would but surrender to her passionate desire, only to find herself abandoned, save as an amusement for ignoble courtiers with cruel eyes, like those of the men cheering her efforts.

"Look how she smiles as if her action was not calculated to get the attention of her former lover, the Earl of Easterbough, who is doing his best to ignore her. Poor Mrs. Fotheringham. He is not playing the game tonight."

"Poor Mrs. Fotheringham indeed," Arabella affirmed, pitying the faded beauty despite her vulgar behavior.

"You are sorry for her?"

"Who would not be sorry to see any woman reduced to such a sorry state that she feels it necessary to behave so?"

"Indeed," he said softly and with genuine sympathy.

His dark eyes held hers for a long moment, and in that moment her heart leaped, for she saw again the compassionate eyes of the youth in the garden.

Did Neville feel a tie that bound them yet? Did he sense that she cared about him and regretted the changes life in London had wrought in him?

Unfortunately, in the next moment, she felt sure she must have been mistaken, for he struck a courtly pose and coolly drawled, "I'faith, Lady Arabella, I confess myself shocked that a woman raised in a Puritan household would rush to the defense of so obvious a sinner."

Arabella told herself she was a fool to imagine that any vestige of the youth remained in the fellow before her. "We are all sinners, Lord Farrington, only unlike some, Puritans admit it and do not claim that since sin is the way of the world, there is no reason to attempt to rise above it."

"My father thinks you are not a sinner. He considers you the very model of womanly virtue."

Even though she flushed under his sardonic scrutiny, she raised her chin defiantly. "I am pleased that he thinks so highly of me. I shall endeavor to maintain that good opinion, even here."

Without another word, he turned away to look again across the room, then straightened abruptly.

"What ho!" he cried softly. "I was premature! Hoorah for spurned mistresses everywhere! Lo, the errant lover comes!"

He pointed triumphantly to a middle-aged man who was charging toward Mrs. Fotheringham like a mad bull.

"No doubt he fears she will strip naked next if he does not speak with her. So you see, Lady Arabella, one hasty embrace is hardly worth a glance to these people."

If he could think of the kiss they had shared as nothing more than a hasty embrace, so could she.

And so she would, she vowed, no matter what she had felt at the time.

Lord Cheddersby suddenly came bustling into view, a beaming smile on his face.

"Lady Arabella, a delight! An absolute delight! I was *thrilled* when Neville told me you might be here. I have been searching for you everywhere, haven't I, Neville?"

"Indeed, he has," his lordship replied evenly.

Arabella sought to emulate Lord Farrington's cool composure.

"I had nearly given up in absolute wretchedness, but Charles Sedley was so kind as to point me this way."

"Sedley is the soul of generosity."

"I did not think so before, but he was certainly all amiability this evening." Lord Cheddersby looked at Arabella like an adoring puppy. "How lovely you look this evening, Lady Arabella! That color suits you to perfection. And your hair! You are as lovely as . . . as lovely as Lady Castlemaine!"

While Arabella could not get used to hearing herself compared to the king's *grand amour*, she responded to the sincere approval behind Cheddersby's compliment with a warm smile. "Thank you very much, my lord."

"Foz, Lady Lippet seems to have gotten herself lost," Neville said. "Would you be so good as to try and find her and tell her Lady Arabella has been left alone again?"

"Absolutely! Delighted to be of service! Stay where you are, and I shall bring her here." He glanced at the far end of the room. "I trust I shall have time to find her before the king arrives."

With that, the kind-hearted fellow hurried off.

Arabella regarded Neville steadily. "Does he always do whatever you say?"

Neville frowned. "Foz is free to do whatever he wishes."

"Truly?" she replied skeptically. "He seems to live to do as you suggest."

"Or as you might, or any pretty young lady. Or any gentleman Foz believes to be his friend. He is an accommodating, innocent soul and needs protecting from people who would exploit him."

"Ah!"

Neville's eyes narrowed suspiciously. "What do you mean, 'ah'?"

"I understand how it is between you, that's all."

"And how is that?"

"That it is well and good for you exploit him because you claim to protect him, too."

"I don't exploit him!"

"Order him about then. And does he not pay for any dinners or wine?"

"He can afford it better than I."

"I see," she replied pertly.

His lips pressed together slightly. "No, you don't."

"Then perhaps Sir Richard Blythe could write a play that will explain such things to a country bumpkin like myself."

"It might be rather amusing."

"As amusing as all the activities of the courtiers to which I have so recently been a witness, perhaps. He must ask your advice, for you seem very familiar with the doings here at Whitehall, my lord. You are invited often, I assume."

"I do not need a special invitation."

"You are that intimate with the king?"

He smiled. "I am not intimate with any man."

She flushed and commanded herself not to be embarrassed because of something *he* said. "You are on good terms with him, then."

"He likes to play tennis with me. And pallmall."

"You are good at sport," she said, wondering what he meant. Perhaps tennis and pallmall were card games.

"I am better at another," he said quietly, the gleam in his eyes no longer one of amusement.

She had had quite enough of his easy,

shameful banter and seductive looks. "No doubt, since you have spent so much time in such pursuits, to the detriment of your duty to your father."

His expression hardened and he took hold of her hand firmly. This time, his touch did not kindle desire. The fierceness of his grip made her remember her first impression of him in London—that there was much more to Neville Farrington than he chose to reveal. "Who do you think you are to presume to criticise me?" he demanded. "Are you prescient, that you know all that has passed over the years between my father and me?"

As the tension stretched between them, and Arabella continued to regard him with her shrewd, sparkling eyes, Neville was tempted as he had never been before to tell someone of his secret activities on behalf of his father. He wanted Arabella to understand that his father did not know his own son, and that he was not the lax wastrel the earl thought he was.

He wanted to tell her of his most recent interview with Messrs. Pettigrew and Hutchins at the bank. It had taken him nearly half the day to persuade them to advance his father whatever monies he required while in London without mentioning Neville's involvement in the family finances. Finally, after many pointed reminders of how things had been before he had gotten involved, the bankers had agreed.

Suddenly, there was a commotion at the far end of the hall. Neville glanced over his shoulder to see what was happening.

"Has some other spurned mistress decided to get her lover's attention by some shocking, immodest, undignified display?" Arabella asked, tugging her hand away.

"Nothing nearly so disgusting, Lady Arabella. The king approaches." Arabella gasped as she looked past him, and Neville permitted himself a small smile at her discomfort while they both made their obeisance to the approaching monarch. Let her be uncomfortable, for she seemed to have an ability to make him feel more upset and uneasy than he had been in many a year.

Determined to act as if nothing were amiss, he turned his attention to the king, who was, for once, accompanied by his queen.

The petite Catherine had been the Infanta of Portugal, and had brought with her the greatest dowry ever given to an English king. In person, she was a dark-haired, dark-complected lady who was not unattractive; however, against the brilliant beauty of Lady Castlemaine, she could never shine.

But Neville preferred her to the famous beauty, because she was an honorable woman who seemed to genuinely love her royal husband.

Neville glanced down at the curtsying Arabella—and nearly forgot all about his dismay and the approaching royalty, for her action brought the swelling tops of her breasts and enticing cleavage into his view.

If she had done what Mrs. Fotheringham had done, the entire male population of Whitehall would have been at her feet, slavering like dogs.

Someone cleared his throat. Neville looked up, startled, to see that the eyes of the Merry Monarch himself were upon him, twinkling with laughter.

Then Buckingham swooped in between Neville and Arabella.

"Your Majesties, may I present Lady Arabella Martin," he said, as if he had every right to do so.

The king smiled warmly and extended his hand to Arabella, taking hers to indicate that she was to rise. "Lady Arabella, you are a most welcome addition to our court."

Queen Catherine glanced at her husband, and Neville knew she was of the same mind as he. They both guessed what that smile presaged, and neither one of them was glad to see it.

Neville elbowed Buckingham out of the way.

"Your Majesty," he said with a bow.

The king's smile grew. "Ah, Farrington! We might have known you would be close by a young lady of such obvious charms."

"Lady Arabella is my father's ward."

"Indeed?" His Majesty replied, and it struck Arabella that he seemed more amused than anything else. "Then your father is here?"

Neville looked surprised. "Yes, sire, he is."

"We recall him from our father's court. No doubt he wishes to give us some advice."

Arabella saw the laughter in the king's eyes and suspected he knew exactly the sort of thing the earl was likely to say.

She could now understand why King Charles was held in high esteem despite his moral lapses. If everyone in the country could have seen their ruler at this moment, they would have thought themselves very lucky. He did not behave pompously or proudly; he might have been any well-to-do man of middle years, and one with a particularly friendly address.

"We would have you join us for tennis tomorrow morning, Farrington."

"I would be honored, Your Majesty."

Charles turned to Arabella. "And Lady Arabella must watch, of course. We enjoy having company when we play. Inquire of the royal dogs if you do not believe us."

Arabella, momentarily robbed of the power of speech by the king's invitation, could only curtsy again in reply.

"We shall expect you at the new tennis court at six o'clock." The king glanced over his shoulder, then leaned closer and lowered his voice to a conspiratorial whisper. "Now we must speak with the ambassador from France. Odd's fish, the fellow's a bore, but we owe Louis too much to insult anyone he sends here."

Charles straightened, and as he did so, Arabella suddenly sensed that he was attempting to look down her bodice.

She was seeing shameful behavior everywhere, thanks in no small part, she was sure, to Neville and Buckingham and those others.

"Adieu, then, until tomorrow, Farrington," the king said with a pleasant smile. "We are delighted to meet you, Lady Arabella. Buckingham," he finished dismissively, barely glancing at the duke. The king strolled away, the queen at his side.

"I beg your pardon," a young male voice said from somewhere nearby.

Arabella, Neville and Buckingham turned to see a very good-looking liveried servant approaching. "Lady Castlemaine requests your presence in her apartments, Lord Farrington."

"Summoned by Lady Castlemaine, eh?" Buckingham said with a mocking grin. "Whatever does this mean?"

Arabella glanced at Neville sharply, but his expression betrayed nothing—not anger, not pleasure, not surprise, not shame.

"She says it is urgent, my lord," the servant

said with slightly more emphasis and not a little arrogance.

"You had better go," the duke said. "Have no fear that your entrancing companion will pine for you. I will see that she is kept amused."

As Arabella took a step away from the duke, Neville nodded at something behind her.

"There will be no need to exert yourself, Your Grace," he said with a wry smile. "I believe I see Lord Cheddersby bringing Lady Lippet along right now—and the wealthy, unmarried Croesus with her."

Arabella glanced over her shoulder. Bustling toward them, Lady Lippet led the wart-nosed nobleman by the arm in a grip that would not have been inappropriate for one of the king's men taking a traitor into custody. Lord Cheddersby brought up the rear.

Arabella smiled with genuine relief—until she turned back and realized Neville was already walking away, following the beautiful Lady Castlemaine's servant.

Chapter 11

Barely controlling an urge to turn back, Neville marched behind the young man, whose duties probably included a certain intimacy with his mistress. Much as Arabella confused and disturbed him, he hated leaving her with Buckingham.

What did the king's mistress want with *him*, anyway? That she often looked at him he knew; it was even a little flattering. But he had been friends with her husband, Roger, a cuckolded laughingstock who had taken himself to his estate in Ireland rather than see the mocking faces at court and hear the snickering laughter behind his back. For that, Neville would never forgive his wife.

Nor was she loyal to her royal lover. Indeed, her infidelities were legendary—just as the reasons for her continued hold over the king were cause for much speculation. It was said she knew more ways to bring a man satisfaction than a hundred whores.

And what a whore she was, Neville thought with no small disgust as he was brought right into the bedchamber of the opulent apartments next to the king's own.

Lady Castlemaine reclined on a tall, canopied, gilded bed covered with satin sheets and a multitude of pillows. The furnishings were costly in the extreme, as were her clothing and jewelry.

It was also extremely obvious that the king's mistress was expecting her second child. The babe could not be Roger's; they had not lived together for over a year. Rumor had it that this time the father was not the king, either, but Sir Charles Berkeley. Sometimes empowered to act as ambassador between the king and his mistress, it seemed Berkeley and Lady Castlemaine had a rather interesting notion of the extent of his duties.

"I trust you do not mind meeting with me under these circumstances," she said coyly as Neville bowed, "but I fear I am easily fatigued these days."

Even in her present condition, she was one of the most beautiful women in England, but in her eyes, there was a hard, cold calculation that destroyed her beauty for him.

How very different was the expression in Barbara Castlemaine's eyes from Arabella's.

Lady Castlemaine plucked at the sleeve of her gown while he continued to stand. "I hear your father has a ward, a pretty little thing."

"He has a ward, my lady."

"And she is young?"

"Young, and in search of a husband."

"A husband?"

"A husband," he confirmed.

"Has she any fortune?"

Neville's jaw tightened. "Some."

"Ah. I have heard another rumor, Farrington," Lady Castlemaine said, languidly raising herself on her elbow and leaning toward him, her full breasts straining at the fabric above her rounded belly. "Is it true that your father plans to will his money to her and not to you?"

How the devil—?

Cheddersby! He never should have let Foz know about that! He should have waited until he was more in mastery of his feelings. Still, there was no point in dissembling. "He threatens to do so, my lady."

"Then you should wed her."

"As delighted as I am to know that you take my concerns to heart, my lady, you must know my father would never approve."

"Wed her anyway," Lady Castlemaine replied in a tone that was very nearly a command. "Wed her in secret, if you must. Or bed her first and get her with child. Do whatever is necessary. Surely it will not be a hardship."

Neville regarded the beautiful courtesan. She must consider Arabella a threat, and judging by what he himself had witnessed when the king had spoken to Arabella, this feeling was not without merit.

He also realized that becoming the king's mistress would certainly prevent Arabella from stealing his inheritance. So would marrying her himself—and of the two, he knew which he would prefer. Nevertheless, he did not think either a likely occurrence. "She is quite adamant that she wishes to marry for love."

Lady Castlemaine laughed raucously. "Marry for love? Is she a fool?"

"No," he replied gravely, attempting to hide his own disgust at her callous response. "Naive, perhaps, and moral, but not a fool. Therefore, I doubt the lady would ever agree to become my wife."

Barbara stretched out like a contented cat, raising her shapely arms over her head and regarding him with a playful smile. "You will forgive me, Farrington, if I do not concur. Any woman would be delighted by your attentions. I am sure you could make her fall in love with you with very little effort."

He acknowledged her compliment with a bow. "Unfortunately, I fear she shares my father's opinion of me, something not unexpected considering she has spent some weeks in his company."

"You can overcome any poor opinion, surely."

"You do not know the lady."

"I am glad I do not. She sounds frightful."

"You need have no fear of her, my lady. She may be flattered by the king's attention, but it will go no further with her."

Her eyes flashing, Lady Castlemaine climbed from the bed. "I fear no woman. I have ways of ensuring that the king remembers me."

"So I understand."

She sauntered close to Neville, and her heavy, musky perfume surrounded him. "How is it you have never come here before, Farrington?" she asked in a low, sultry voice.

He stood as stiffly as a soldier, knowing that no matter how debased he felt by her perusal— as Arabella must have felt at the theater, perhaps—it would not be wise to insult her. "I have never been invited, my lady."

She walked behind him. "I have been most remiss."

"The king no doubt occupies your thoughts constantly. And perhaps, occasionally, your husband."

From behind him, a lilting trill of a laugh echoed through the vast chamber. "Roger? He is happy in his Irish bog."

He is surely happy to be away from you and the shame you bring to his name, Neville thought coldly.

Then he jumped as she reached around to caress his manhood. "Most remiss," she murmured in his ear, her breath hot on his cheek.

Absolutely disgusted, he stepped away and turned to face her. "If that is all you wish to speak to me about, Lady Castlemaine, I beg to be excused."

She regarded him steadily, and with not one hint of contrition. "This Arabella displeases me, Farrington," she said in a cold, business-like tone. "I would have her gone from court. If you marry her, so much the better for us both. But if you cannot or will not do what is necessary, I will see that someone does."

She smiled sweetly, reminding Neville of what she might have been had she been pure and good. "Since she is pretty and stands to come into a considerable fortune, I dare say some will not be overly fastidious about gaining her consent."

Neville suddenly felt ill. He knew what she was really saying: that there were those among her friends who would be willing—nay, eager—to force Arabella to marry them, even to the point of raping her to make her bend to their will.

Never in his life had he hated anyone as much as he hated Barbara Castlemaine at this moment. "Good night, my lady."

"Must you leave?"

"Yes, my lady."

"Then adieu, Lord Farrington, and good luck."

Congratulating herself on managing to escape Lady Lippet, the eager Lord Cheddersby, and Lord Belmaris—who was surely the most boring man she had ever had the misfortune to meet—Arabella slipped through a pair of doors leading to what she thought must be the king's Privy Garden.

She had guessed aright. The garden itself was nearly bright as day from the full moon, which made the statuary cast odd shadows. The moist scent of the river reached her nostrils, while in other parts of the garden, soft voices murmured, their owners hidden by trees and shrubbery.

She was very glad to be out of the hustle and bustle of the Banqueting House. Here she could find some peace, she thought with a weary sigh.

A male shape appeared on the path, and she tried to slip into the shadows.

"Arabella? Is that you?"

She didn't respond to Neville Farrington's query.

"I do believe it is," he drawled as he sauntered closer, "or a statue very like her. I shall have to touch, perhaps, to see if this is a woman made of flesh or only a statue made of stone."

She stepped onto the path.

He halted and regarded her. "You are in the Privy Garden alone? Where are your many admirers? I'faith, you seem unable to keep any company about you."

"I came for some quiet. I am not used to the crowd. Surely there is nothing wrong with that."

His low chuckle filled the air between them. "Men and women do not come here at such an hour to be alone."

Suddenly, the soft sounds from nearby took on a completely different meaning, and Arabella blushed hotly. "I . . . I had no idea."

"I thought not."

Then she straightened her shoulders. "Where is your companion, then, my lord?"

"Mine?"

"I understand that men and women do not come to the Privy Garden at such an hour to be alone."

"Perhaps I, too, desired some quiet."

"Yet I was given to understand you thrived in the atmosphere of the court."

"That would be my father's opinion."

"You would deny it?"

"Would you believe me if I did?"

She could make no reply to that, since she could not be sure what to believe about him. "You are finished with Lady Castlemaine, then?"

"Indeed, I am."

He sounded very sincere about that, but she told herself she didn't care what he had been doing with that woman.

"Run along, Lady Arabella. You have a mighty task, and hiding in the garden will not prove conducive to its accomplishment."

"I am not hiding."

He smiled mockingly as he inclined his head. "Very well, you are not hiding. You are standing in the darkest corner of the king's garden because you enjoy the smell of the Thames."

She ignored his sarcasm. "What is this mighty task you speak of?"

"Why, the selection of your husband, of course. So many fine courtiers to choose from!"

"So many like you, I fear."

"Perhaps you would have been wiser to stay in Grantham."

"Given what I have seen of life in London, I cannot disagree, but since I have come to London, what would you have me do? Huddle in the corner like a mouse? Never venture outside at all?"

"That would be the safest thing."

"I must stay in the house like a prisoner when I have done nothing wrong except to be a young woman who desires to be married?"

She could not see his face clearly, and when he spoke, his voice sounded completely without emotion. "Except to be a beautiful young woman who stands to come into a great deal of money.''

''So I am to blame? It is my fault that I am pretty and that my father left me ten thousand pounds?''

Neville started. If she had ten thousand pounds, she most certainly did not need his father's money, too!

Arabella folded her arms indignantly. ''My father was right. Money is a curse!''

''When you marry, you may be cursed even more,'' he observed, attempting to discover how much she knew of his father's plans.

''If I do not marry for love, I will be cursed. I would rather be poor and happy.''

''You have no need to marry if you have ten thousand pounds.''

''I . . . I want to be married. I want to be a wife and a mother.''

''You sound most sincere.''

''I am. Therefore I will not hide in your father's house. I have been a prisoner long enough, since I was twelve years old and the men in Grantham started to look at me differently. I had to beg my father to allow me to go to the market, and then I had to worry all the time that he would accuse me of sinning with some boy—as if I would have taken that chance, knowing how he would punish me if I had. Perhaps I should have, for I was punished nonetheless.''

"So you have been falsely accused."

"Yes."

"I know very well how that feels," he murmured.

"So do I," she reminded him.

"How did your father punish you?" he asked, his hands balling into fists at the thought than anyone would hurt her.

"He did . . . nothing."

Neville felt as if he had tripped unexpectedly. "Nothing?"

"My father never said a word when he thought I had done something wrong. He simply meditated in endless silence until I thought I would go mad trying to figure out how I had erred and if I could do anything to correct it."

"That is better than being constantly berated."

She cocked her head as she looked at him. "While that is surely unpleasant, my lord, at least you knew of what you stood accused and could amend your behavior if you would."

"Familial harmony can be as easy as that?" he asked sarcastically.

"Constant criticism would be easier to bear than stony silence, I think. But my father also believed in a certain amount of mortification of the flesh. Fasting was his preferred method."

"My father would say it has done you good."

"Perhaps it has. I cannot say."

"Maybe I should try fasting. You would no doubt agree I am in need of improvement."

She hesitated a moment. "Yes."

"By the world, you don't sound very sure. Am I improving upon acquaintance?"

"Perhaps. Would you say that your father's accusations about you are *all* unjustified?"

"I pay no heed to them. I have not for years, since I left his estate."

"That isn't true," she declared, fixing a gaze of absolute conviction upon him. "You care very much what he thinks, and it disturbs you greatly that he has such a low opinion of you, especially since you feel it unjustified."

"Upon what do you base this incredible conclusion?"

"What I see," she answered honestly. "I, too, have tried to please an intolerant parent."

Neville met her steadfast gaze. "I wish I knew the truth about you."

"What do you care to know? I have nothing to hide."

"Truly?"

"Ask of me what you will, my lord, and I shall answer as best I can," she said, straightening her shoulders as if bracing herself for his interrogation.

"Why do you want to marry if you are rich?"

"Because I want a husband and children,

and an honorable woman has few other choices when it comes to her future."

"How do you feel about my father?"

"I respect him and am grateful for his guardianship."

"So you think him a fine man?"

"I think he is a man who can be fine but also stubborn. He holds his own opinions dear and will not allow dissent."

Neville laughed softly and stepped closer to her. "I credit your perception. What do you think of me?"

"That you are not as you pretend to be."

"What is that?"

"Unfeeling. Uncaring. Unconcerned."

"You would tear all my masks off, is that it?"

"Yes, for they do not become you."

"You had best take care, Arabella. Say much more, and I shall believe you care about me."

"Should I not?"

"My father would tell you I am unfeeling, uncaring and unconcerned about anybody but myself."

"That is not so."

"Perhaps," he whispered as he reached for her and pulled her gently into his arms.

He felt her initial resistance and drew back slightly. "I would change for you," he whispered.

Her gaze searched his face, and then she smiled.

Once more he kissed her, struggling to control his fierce desire so that she wouldn't run away. Embracing him tightly as if she longed to stay in his arms forever, she laid her cheek against his rapidly rising and falling chest.

Then, to his infinite joy, she raised herself on her toes and kissed him fervently. Her mouth took his with all the passion he could ever hope for and with a boldness all the more exciting because this was not a woman who would ever do such a thing merely for a moment's fleeting excitement.

Here and now, hers was a willing, seemingly selfless surrender, as if she was giving not just her lips or her body to him but something of her self. Her soul.

As if she found him worthy of so great a gift.

Then he knew that no matter what his father planned, he respected and cherished Arabella as he had no other woman.

And he wanted her more than he had wanted any other woman.

His arms tightened about her as if he would never let her go. With an urgency that was tender yet imperative, his tongue probed, and she yielded.

Their kiss deepened as he guided her further into the shadows, until her back met the garden wall.

He never wanted to stop kissing her.

And he wanted to give her all the pleasure he could.

His mouth still upon hers, his hand slipped inside her bodice and found her soft, rounded breast. How perfect, and how arousing to note the hardened nub beneath his fingers.

Moaning softly, she arched as if offering him whatever he chose. With her, there would be no giving and taking as if their bodies and passion were goods to be exchanged or bartered, or a competition to prove skill.

They would share freely, as true lovers should.

Her hands stole inside his jacket. Eagerly, she lifted his shirt. His breath caught when he felt the palms of her hands hot on his bare back.

His mouth left hers to trail feather-light kisses along her satin-soft cheek, down her neck toward the tender flesh exposed above her bodice.

Softer than satin was her skin and lightly scented, like the first hint of blossoms on a spring breeze.

Then he felt her hands upon his chest, and in the next moment, she had found his nipples. With tentative yet exciting motions she touched him there, but she seemed uncertain as to the effect her gentle caresses had upon him.

"Yes," he whispered huskily, encouraging

her as he insinuated his knee between her legs. "Again, dear, sweet Arabella. Touch me again. There and"—he took hold of her arm and moved it lower, gently positioning her hand— "here."

A woman's laughter trilled close by.

With a gasp, Arabella jumped back. She quickly looked around, but no one was close by. Except *him*, this man whose touch and kiss seemed to make her lose all reason.

Still afraid they had been seen, she could not bring herself to look at him. Indeed, she half expected he would have his breeches open and his—

Instead, she took a deep breath, trying to calm herself and still the thudding of her heart. "We should go back inside. We have been . . . impetuous."

Neville chuckled softly, apparently not the least upset that someone might have witnessed their intimacy. "I am quite certain there has been *impetuous* behavior in this garden since it was built."

"Why, what have we here?"

Arabella cringed as Buckingham appeared, a polite smile on his face and a very shrewd look in his evil eyes.

"A lover's tryst? Egad, and right under the king's very nose, as it were. And here I was just saying to Sedley that neither of us stand a chance if Farrington and the king both desire you, Lady Arabella."

As embarrassed and dismayed as she was to be found in such a situation by anyone, Arabella thought the man must be mad to think the king desired her. Then she risked a glance at Neville's face and knew that he was not so skeptical.

The king? Wanted *her*?

She did not want *him*! There was only one man she wanted, and he was standing beside her.

"Come, Arabella, let us go back inside," Neville said. "I fear the air here is fetid." He inclined his head very slightly to the duke. "Your servant, Your Grace."

He took her hand, and she gratefully let him lead her away from the duke and into the Banqueting House, even as she tried not to think about his hand or his arms or his lips or any other part of his body.

Why, if that woman hadn't laughed—

No, she would have stopped Neville if he had tried to do anything more. She would have left him if he had lifted her skirt, running his strong, slender fingers up her stockinged leg until he reached—

They entered the Banqueting House. Before Arabella could subdue her fantasy, Lady Lippet hurried toward them.

"You should take better care of her," Neville said evenly before that estimable lady could open her mouth. "As you can see, there is no telling what disreputable fellow might come upon her." He made a brief bow and sauntered away through the crowd.

With a scornful sneer, Lady Lippet watched Neville go before turning to Arabella. "You really must stop disappearing in this astonishing manner."

Feeling bereft as she watched Neville wend his way through the mob of courtiers like a royal prince among the rabble, Arabella thought she was not the only person given to astonishing departures.

"But still—such wonderful news!"

Raising her eyebrows questioningly, Arabella faced Lady Lippet, who regarded her as if she thought her young charge a dullard. "An invitation to the king's tennis match! And so soon! Your beauty has had a most marvelous effect!"

Arabella thought of Buckingham's remarks and Neville's response. Perhaps this invitation was not the cause for happiness that Lady Lippet so obviously believed it to be.

Much later that night, Buckingham waited by the Privy Stair on the Thames, a private entrance to Whitehall Palace solely for the king's use. He had been summoned there by Chaffinch, the king's confidential page.

Charles obviously did not intend to spend the rest of the night with either Lady Castlemaine or his queen.

"Ah, George!" Charles cried softly as he appeared at the top of the steps.

"Sire," Villiers acknowledged with a bow.

"She pleases us greatly, George," the king said as he continued down the steps, and Villiers happily noted that the king had used his Christian name. "There is a country purity about her we greatly admire."

"You speak of Lady Arabella?" Villiers replied, keeping any sign of satisfaction from his face.

"Of course. She is quite lovely. What exactly is her relationship with Farrington?"

"I believe he has designs on her, Majesty, but has yet to succeed."

Charles smiled broadly. "Ah. We thought he had a most possessive look in his eye when we spoke with her. He rarely fails in such endeavors, or so we understand."

"He does possess a facility for charming women, sire, but his skills are nothing compared to your own."

"Nor is he a king," Charles added ruefully.

"You were a favorite of the ladies before you were a king."

"True enough," Charles replied with a satisfied chuckle. "Well, given that, and we are now a king, perhaps Farrington will realize he should quit the field."

"If he has any sense at all, he will," Buckingham agreed. "She seemed very gratified by your attention, Majesty."

Charles struck Villiers on the shoulder good-naturedly. "What is all this 'majesty' nonsense, my friend? Charles will do, especially at this hour."

The duke did not hide his pleasure at this remark, but then he frowned. "Her father was a most strict Puritan, Charles. She may have some ridiculous scruples."

"So she might, and they do her credit if she has," the king replied as he glanced at the waiting boatman. "It may take a little time and some persuasion. We are willing to be patient." He eyed his companion. "You would not be unwilling to be our ambassador, would you, George?"

"I would be delighted to speak for you, sire," Villiers answered, thinking happily of the benefits Berkeley enjoyed in a similar situation. "Not that she will take a great deal of persuading, I'm sure," he added.

"Good, good!" The king started down the steps, then glanced over his shoulder. "We are seeking a little sport in Bankside tonight, George. Would you care to come along? It will be like old times."

"I would be honored," the Duke of Buckingham replied gratefully as he followed the king to the boat.

Honor, however, was something that man had not possessed in quite some time.

Chapter 12

Very early the next morning, after a night of fitful sleep, Arabella followed the earl and Lady Lippet toward the king's new tennis court.

She could not remember a time when she had felt less confident of herself, in any situation, even when her father had been at his most unresponsive.

She had come to London hoping to meet Neville, then decided she never wanted to be near him again—and now, certain she had misjudged him, she was anticipating seeing him more than ever before.

Unfortunately, there was also the problem of the king's alleged interest in her. To believe in that interest might be sinfully vain, yet did not the Duke of Buckingham and Neville know their monarch better than she?

If the king did have an interest in her, what exactly did that presage?

Also, what was she to do about the lascivious behavior of the other men at court? She had very little real experience in dealing with the opposite sex. Her father had seen to that.

And there was the troubling business of the hunt for her husband, something she wished she could call off. She hated being paraded about like a horse for sale.

Not that she did not want to be married. She wanted a husband and a family. She had been virtually alone for so long!

All in all, Arabella was in no very contented mood as she followed the older couple.

Although it was very early in the day, the continually yawning Lady Lippet wore a gown of brown satin and orange velvet; her expression upon seeing Arabella's much plainer gown had made it obvious that she did not approve of the younger woman's subdued selection. Remarkably, however, she had said nothing, a restraint Arabella gratefully attributed to her obvious fatigue.

The earl, unfortunately, had apparently decided to step into the breach, for he had been quite loquacious regarding what he intended to say to the king. Arabella had kept her sighs to herself, yet if the earl managed to say even a portion of what he wished, he would surely need at least an hour of His Majesty's undivided attention.

She was also quite sure that King Charles would not appreciate hearing that every single thing he had done since his restoration was a mistake.

They reached the new court. Most of the spacious interior was a large, bare rectangle. A tasseled rope stretched across the middle between the outer wall and what seemed to be a long, covered stall, for a waist-high wooden partition separated the many spectators from the rectangle where the game was played.

She noted with relief that the Duke of Buckingham was not there, nor Sedley, Buckhurst and Jermyn. This was quite a different group of people.

The king was on the far side of the tasseled rope; the man on the nearer side was Neville.

Attired in an open white shirt, dark breeches, low boots and with his shoulder-length hair tied in a tail, he was all lithe, swift action as he batted a small ball with some kind of paddle over the rope toward the king.

As she watched the king hit it back, she decided the idea was to keep hitting the ball from one person to the other until somebody missed it.

"Now, this is the penthouse," Lady Lippet explained in a loud whisper as she led them into the long covered area. "We can stand or sit here and watch the game."

Lady Lippet maneuvered her way through the spectators, tugging Arabella and the earl along like horses on a lead. Finally she came to a halt in the center of the penthouse. "Now we shall see everything," she declared.

"More laxity when he should be attending to matters of state!" the earl grumbled, albeit softly. "Who are these men? If they are courtiers, they should be about the business of government."

"It is surely a compliment to your son that the king wishes him to be his partner in this game," Arabella said to the earl, keeping her voice low and carefully dispassionate.

"A compliment? To play some childish sport?" the earl retorted with a sniff.

"If he lived a truly decadent life, I doubt he would be able to move about so quickly. Would he not be slow and sluggish?"

"The king has little trouble keeping up with my son. Would you say he is a model of decency?"

Unfortunately, Arabella could not disagree, so she turned her attention to the spectators.

The number of people with the king this early in the morning was rather startling, until she considered that of course the king would have many friends and servants to attend him. Although the spectators kept a portion of their attention on the game, clapping at certain times and cheering at others, it seemed to her that they were far more interested in their own concerns—especially the servant who was holding onto the leashes of several straining, barking, tussling spaniels.

Ignoring the earl's complaints, Lady Lippet continued to scan the gathering. "Well, this is a disappointment, I must say. These men are certainly not courtiers. They all look like clerks."

Arabella silently agreed. This was a much more sombre, respectable-looking group than she had seen last night at Whitehall.

"There is that fellow Pepys," Lady Lippet said, gesturing toward a slightly plump man in plain clothing at the far end of the penthouse. "He fancies himself a musician, I hear, although my friends say he has little talent. No doubt he believes he will be a famous fellow one day. The poor man is going to be disappointed."

The earl followed her gaze. "Does he not have something to do with the navy?"

"I believe so, yes," Lady Lippet replied.

"Ah! Then I have much to discuss with him, too," the earl declared, marching off toward the pleasant-looking man, who was, as yet, unaware of the fate that was about to befall him.

Paying little heed to the earl or Lady Lippet, Arabella decided the king must have done something rather special with one hit, for Neville started to laugh deprecatingly and called out that His Majesty was getting much too good for him.

Neville's laugh was really most attractive, free and natural, very much reminding her of his youthful self. This morning, his manner also seemed unrestrained and easy, utterly natural in a way it had not been in the Banqueting House. She could watch him for a long time when he was like this.

Suddenly, Lady Lippet grabbed hold of her arm tightly. "Oh, I was wrong. Here are two very eligible noblemen."

Arabella felt her heart sink as she followed the lady's gaze, but fortunately, one of the two was not Croesus Belmaris.

Sir Richard Blythe, looking more sardonic than ever, stood watching the game, and beside him was Lord Cheddersby, rather oddly dressed. Although he was still bewigged and his broad-brimmed hat beplumed, his dark purple jacket and breeches actually seemed subdued.

"We must speak with the charming Lord Cheddersby! He would do very well for you, Arabella. He's from a fine old family. Their estate is somewhere in Sussex, I believe. Or Essex. Wessex, perhaps." Lady Lippet adjusted her necklace with a coy gesture better suited to one half her age. "Who is that dashingly hand-some fellow with him?"

"Do you not recall him from the theater? That is Sir Richard Blythe."

"Oh, yes, of course!" Lady Lippet lowered her voice. "He is not married, either, but the earl would never approve." She glanced around, then whispered conspiratorially in Arabella's ear, "They say he keeps at least three mistresses at once, all actresses. And one of his former lovers tried to kill herself when their liaison was at an end, or so she claimed. I saw her shortly after, and if she really tried to do it, I am the Empress of Austria. No scar at all!"

A cry went up from the crowd as the king sent the ball sailing back over the rope with a broad stroke. Neville returned it again, this time to the far left of the king.

Charles deftly intercepted it from close to the rope and struck it hard, sending it to the right corner of Neville's part of the floor. With a speed she would have thought impossible, and twisting like a snake, Neville hit the ball and sent it back over the rope.

The king must miss—but no! He ran back and caught the ball with his paddle before it touched the ground. It didn't fly over the rope, but struck the outer wall of the court and ricocheted.

Arabella swiftly looked at Neville—who was

not watching the ball at all. He was staring at her.

The ball was going to strike his face if he didn't move.

"Look out!" she cried.

Neville suddenly came to life and moved out of the way of the king's missile, while at the same time, all the spectators fell silent. Even the spaniels stopped yapping.

Arabella blushed with mortification.

"Arabella!" Lady Lippet chided softly and quite unnecessarily.

"I was . . . I was carried away by the excitement of the game," she explained feebly, keeping her eyes lowered, quite aware that everyone was staring at her, including the king.

"Odd's fish, we believe a penalty might be called for!" the king declared. "What shall it be? A kiss, perhaps?"

Arabella blushed even more.

"Perhaps not," the king said. "Perhaps we shall forfeit a penalty and decree this a tie game, Farrington."

"That would be most generous of you, Majesty, for I did miss the ball."

Although she kept her gaze firmly on the low dividing wall, it was obvious that the players were coming closer.

"But you were beating us before," the king remarked. "Indeed, if we did not think you an honest fellow, we would be tempted to think you were allowing us to win."

"I assure you, Majesty, I always play to win."

Charles laughed, a great, booming, roar of delight. "We appreciate a man who admits it," he declared. Then he lowered his voice and said in a teasing and significant tone, "Although there are some games in which we shall insist upon the royal prerogative."

As Arabella curtsied, she glanced up at Neville and thought his cheerful expression seemed rather strained.

Because he didn't like to lose a tennis game? Or was the significance in the king's tone related to some other kind of sport?

"Ah, Lady Arabella, we are so pleased to see you this morning," King Charles declared.

The genuine pleasure in his voice gave a sort of horrible credence to the duke's remarks last night—and yet he had sounded similarly pleased when he spoke to Neville.

Perhaps everyone was jumping to a conclusion based only upon the king's naturally easy manner.

She would think that, for to believe otherwise was surely vain and foolish, as well as extremely disturbing.

Again she glanced at Neville; she realized he was watching her and quickly looked away.

Before she could speak, Lady Lippet forcefully pushed her aside. "Good day, Your Majesty! Such fine exercise, I'm sure, although you hardly need it."

"You flatter us, Lady Lippet," he graciously replied. "But where is the earl? We understand he had matters of great import he wished to discuss with us."

Here was welcome proof that the king was merely being his gracious self when he spoke to her.

"He is speaking to Mr. Pepys, Your Majesty," Arabella replied with a nod in their direction.

"Ah, yes," he replied, glancing at the two men.

The earl was red in the face, while Mr. Pepys looked rather pale.

"We hope you will again grace us with your presence at Whitehall this evening, ladies."

"Oh, Your Majesty! Nothing would be more delightful, I assure you!" Lady Lippet gasped as she curtsied even lower—so low, in fact, that Arabella feared she might never be able to get up.

"Excellent!" the king replied. "Do you play cribbage, Lady Arabella?"

"No, Your Majesty."

"It is a simple enough game. We shall instruct you ourselves."

"Thank you, Your Majesty."

"You have never wagered before?"

"No, Your Majesty."

The king glanced at Neville. "Stay clear of this fellow, then, for he is a very clever player, who tells us that he always plays to win."

"I shall proceed with care, Your Majesty."

"Excellent! Now if you ladies will excuse your sovereign, we should see what wisdom the earl wishes to impart to us. Will you join us, Farrington?"

"I think not, Your Majesty. My presence would not be conducive to civility on my father's part."

The king's brow furrowed slightly, but that was the only reaction he gave before snapping his fingers at the keeper of his dogs, who led the boisterous animals to their master.

"Until this evening, Lady Lippet, Lady Arabella," the king said.

And then, shockingly, he winked, and not at the still-bent Lady Lippet, either.

Arabella could scarce believe it. The King of England *winked* at her before leaving them.

Oh, surely, surely, this was only more evidence of his easygoing manner or a merry sort of compliment. The king could not mean anything significant by that simple action.

She became aware that Lady Lippet's arm was flailing, indicative of distress. "Arabella, your assistance, if you please!"

Arabella quickly hurried to help. Her ladyship slowly became upright.

"My dear, another invitation from the king!" she cried happily when she was standing, her delighted smile causing the powder on her face to crack.

Arabella suddenly had the impression that Lady Lippet was like a piece of porcelain, liable to shatter at any moment, this time from sheer happiness.

"The king's notice will certainly not go unremarked! I dare say several young men will be wanting to meet you now!"

"I am quite certain of that, too," Neville seconded. "You will be getting famous, although not, perhaps, in a way you would like."

So he believed that the king's attention was of a lascivious nature.

Right now, she wished she could go home to Grantham!

Except that Neville would not be there.

Lady Lippet frowned, more cracks appearing. "I don't understand you at all, Neville. Of course she will be heard of and talked about. That is what we want, if she is to find a proper husband." Suddenly, an expression of alarm came to Lady Lippet's face. "Oh, dear me! Is Lord Cheddersby leaving?"

She abruptly pushed past Arabella and hurried to intercept Lord Cheddersby at the entrance to the court before he could escape.

"I suppose Lady Lippet would consider dear old Foz a suitable marriage candidate."

With a sinking feeling, Arabella mentally agreed.

"What do *you* think of him?"

"I haven't met a nicer man in all of London," she answered honestly.

Neville told himself that he did not particularly want to be considered nice. "Nice" was for old women or elderly gentlemen or little girls. "Nice" was no word to describe a virile, passionate man.

"He is not as rich as Croesus Belmaris, surely another of the many candidates for your hand," he remarked. "You must be very flattered. Is it not every maiden's dream to be surrounded by a bevy of admiring swains—and to count the king among them?"

"You believe the king finds me fascinating?"

Surely she could not be so naive, Neville thought as he struggled not to betray any hint of his jealousy. "I assure you, he would not trouble himself to invite you anywhere if he did not find you very appealing."

She frowned, then gave Neville a look that set his heart beating as it had when he was dashing about the tennis court. "It is not my dream to be chased after and captured like some sort of beast. I dream of finding a man I can love for my husband."

"I am sure my father and Lady Lippet do not subscribe to that particular dream. Unfortunately, the king himself is already married."

She nodded slowly, and he was sure she was being sincere when she seemed displeased by the mention of the king's obvious interest.

"What did you assume the king meant by his invitations?" he asked, genuinely curious.

"I thought he was just being gracious."

He remembered that for all her intelligence and seeming adaptation to London, she was still a Puritan-raised young woman from a sleepy little country village.

A lamb among the wolves.

And he was supposed to be one of the wolves.

"Arabella! Here is Lord Cheddersby!" Lady Lippet called out as she bore down upon them, a red-faced Foz in tow.

Richard, with a damnably smug smile, sauntered along behind them, the look in his eyes telling Neville as clearly as words that he was anticipating being vastly amused, and at somebody else's expense.

"Well played, Neville," Richard remarked, "although I thought you were planning to sacrifice your head to let the king win. Half the female population of London would have gone into mourning at your martyrdom."

"I was just telling Sir Richard Blythe that I have been to every one of his plays," Lady Lippet gushed. "Where do you get such clever ideas for your plots?"

Richard looked around secretively. "When I

was in exile with the king in Europe, a peddler sold me an ancient manuscript full of stories, plays and poems. I confess I simply copy them in my own writing."

Lady Lippet gasped, and Foz gazed, wide-eyed.

"He jests with us, Lady Lippet," Arabella said, her eyes twinkling with mischief as she looked at Richard.

At Richard.

"Of course he writes them himself," she continued. "I'm sure anyone who saw his latest play could have little doubt that it would take a man of his particular talent and temperament to pen such a work."

Richard frowned. "What would you say are my particular talent and temperament, Lady Arabella?"

She shook her head. "If you do not know, I shall not attempt to enlighten you."

"Oh, please do," Neville insisted.

"Yes, do!" Foz cried.

Richard darted a look at both of them. "Really, gentlemen," he protested half-heartedly.

"I am only a girl from the country, sir, as was so kindly noted the first time we met. I can hardly be expected to voice my opinion in such company. You would all ridicule me."

"Not I!" Foz cried immediately, while Richard bowed with a surprisingly elegant flourish. "You must forgive my behavior that night,

Lady Arabella. I fear, like many men, I do not respond well to criticism."

"I recall she thought your play immoral," Neville reminded him.

"I write only what the audience prefers," Richard said, his voice intimately low as he slyly insinuated himself next to Arabella. "Tell me, now that you have been longer in London, do you still think it so very bad?"

Neville knew that tone of voice, and if Richard knew what was good for him, he would cease to use it, or by God, Neville would challenge him to a duel, friend or not.

"Oh, yes," she replied brightly. "It was terrible."

Neville nearly choked as he fought not to laugh at Richard's stunned expression. Foz looked scandalized, while Lady Lippet clearly did not know whether to smile or frown.

"At least the lack of honor and loyalty in the characters was terrible—and that is the pity of it," Arabella explained. "You waste your talents on such frippery. I think, if you were to put your mind to it, you could write something truly splendid and immortal."

"Splendid and immortal?" Neville scoffed. "What, is he Jonson? Or Shakespeare?"

"I said you would ridicule me."

"Zounds, she did, too!" Foz cried. "For shame, Neville!"

Richard Blythe said nothing; he simply

turned on his heel and strode away.

"You've insulted him," Neville observed.

Arabella was not extremely sorry. She was, in fact, rather glad to see him go, for she did not doubt that friends like Richard Blythe had contributed to the change in Neville. If Neville had met other men in London, might he not be different? Might he not have remained as he was?

"You would have done better to keep your Puritan opinions to yourself," Neville said.

"What would you know of Puritans?" she said, challenging him. "He asked for my opinion, and against my better judgement, I gave it."

"Puritans would have us spend the days on our knees in prayerful contemplation of our many sins," Neville countered, "although how they can find the time to sin, I do not know."

"I suppose a person of your vast sophistication would not deign to speak with one and ask."

"She has you there, Neville!" Lord Cheddersby chuckled with evident delight. "You, speak with a Puritan!"

Lady Lippet giggled, too. In a woman of her years, that was not a pleasant sight.

Neville glanced over his shoulder. She followed his gaze and saw his father talking to the king, who petted his dogs and nodded. "The time has come to rescue His Majesty. If

Lady Arabella will be so good as to accompany me, I'm sure she will find a gentle way to disengage my father."

Thinking of Neville's effect on the earl, Arabella said, "Perhaps I should go alone, my lord."

"Although my father will be loath to see me, I think the annoyance of my presence may be necessary to provoke him to leave. Therefore, I suggest that we go together."

"Yes, Arabella, go," Lady Lippet agreed. "I would have some private conversation with Lord Cheddersby."

Lord Cheddersby looked as if he would prefer to refuse; nevertheless, he nodded, and together they went toward one of the benches at the far end of the penthouse.

As she watched them go, Arabella reflected that Lord Cheddersby was unmarried, he was rich, he was a nobleman—in short, he was indeed everything Lord Barrsettshire required in a candidate for her hand.

Interrupting that disturbing thought, Neville took her hand and placed it on his arm. "Come, my dear, let us intervene before my father gets himself thrown into the Tower for treason."

Chapter 13

$\longsim\!\!\!\circ\!\!\!\circ\!\!\!\circ\!\!\!\longsim$

As they walked toward the king and Lord Barrsettshire, Neville gave Arabella a wry, sidelong glance. "Perhaps if you were to intercede, you could save my opinionated father from such a fate, no matter what he said."

She frowned. "I have no influence with the king."

"I have no doubt you could be very influential, if you chose to be."

"I do not."

Did she mean she did not think she could be or that she might but did not wish to exert that influence? "Lady Castlemaine is very influential."

"You would know better than I what that person is capable of," she said with a peevishness he was both glad and sorry to see.

Glad because she did not seem at all eager to wield the kind of power that might tempt a moral woman to become the mistress of a powerful man; sorry because she was still obviously under the impression that he and Lady Castlemaine had an intimate relationship.

"Lady Castlemaine has been the bane of her husband's life, and he was a friend of mine. I am pleased you have no wish to emulate her in any way."

"And I wish everyone would stop comparing us!"

He inclined his head. "I shall never do so again. Nevertheless, do not underestimate yourself. You bested poor old Richard, who will probably spend the next fortnight growling like a bear at anyone who dares to say a word to him."

"If I have succeeded in upsetting your friend," she replied, trying not to be so aware of the sinewy muscle beneath her fingers and not to be jealous of a woman no better than a harlot, "I have no doubt that he will soon recover."

"Thank heavens he is not a Puritan, or he would be despondent for days with the burden of sin you would place upon him."

"I put no burden on him. He does that himself, and I think you should not speak of what you do not know."

Neville halted and turned to face her. "I do know something of the Puritans' beliefs and have read many of their pamphlets. For instance, this fellow John Milton has some very interesting views, although I suspect he cannot find many other Puritans who agree with his favorable opinion on the subject of divorce."

Milton favored divorce? No wonder her father had banned his works from the house and declared that the writer's near-blindness was a judgment from God.

"I simply cannot accept the heavy toll Puritans would exact for the many things they consider sinful," Neville continued. "We are all made of flesh, not some celestial matter."

"Yes, we are," she replied, "but that does not mean we should not attempt to subdue our baser animal natures."

"I will not condemn myself because I enjoy the flesh God gave me."

"God also gave you an immortal soul, my lord. Would you risk that for a few flecting moments of pleasure?"

He took hold of her hand and again placed it on his arm. She wondered if tennis explained his unexpected strength. "I would risk many things for the pleasure of some people's company," he said.

His fingertips subtly caressed her knuckles, just as they had her breasts. Her body reacted just as if he were stroking her, with heat and throbbing, powerful desire.

Wishing she had worn gloves—although even that scant protection would perhaps not have made any difference—she swallowed hard as his dark-eyed gaze grew more intense. "Do not try to kiss me again!" she warned.

She meant what she said about subduing one's baser nature, and she was determined to do just that, no matter how he spoke or looked at her or what his fingers were doing. After all, although she suspected he was a better man than his father gave him credit for, she still lacked undeniable evidence.

Indeed, given his behavior when he was alone with her, she should be of the same mind as the earl.

Neville's lips turned up at the corners. "Kiss you in front of all these people? My dear young woman, what do you take me for?"

The king caught sight of them and called out, "Ah, Lady Arabella! Farrington!"

Grateful for the interruption, Arabella hurried to the king and her guardian. She was pleased to note that the king did not seem annoyed. Perhaps Lord Barrsettshire was capable of diplomacy, after all.

"Your Majesty, my lord," she said, pausing to curtsy.

The king continued to smile, apparently not noticing or choosing not to notice that the earl's expression when he regarded his son was decidedly hostile.

Was Lord Barrsettshire's reaction to Neville justified or not? How could she find out?

A stout man in fine clothing appeared at the entrance to the court, and the king waved at him.

"Here comes Lord Clarendon full of the affairs of state," Charles observed, turning to leave. "Farewell, and thank you for your thoughtful advice, my lord of Barrsettshire. We shall muse upon it. Come!" he called to his dogs, and trailed by his spaniels and their keeper, he hurried off toward Lord Clarendon.

"Well, Father, you have not been arrested," Neville noted dryly. "Since you have not and therefore do not require my assistance, I shall go."

"Of course I haven't been arrested!" the earl replied scornfully. "Why should I be? And yes, go. Go to your degenerate friends."

Arabella watched Neville's broad shoulders as he sauntered away until the earl spoke again. "Arrested? I knew he was a fool, but is he mad?"

"He feared you would be . . . indelicate," Arabella explained, "and the king would take offence."

"His Majesty was very interested in what I had to say," the earl grumbled, pulling his goatee thoughtfully. "Indeed, I begin to believe I may have misjudged the fellow."

Arabella wished the man before her could be so open-minded about his son.

*   *   *

Neville strode into the coffeehouse, barely pausing to toss his hat onto a peg. As he had suspected, Richard was in the corner, staring into his steaming mug, oblivious to everyone around him.

He barely looked up when Neville threw his leg over the bench to join him. "A pox on you, Richard!"

That got the playwright's notice.

"What are you thinking about so studiously?" Neville demanded.

"A new play."

"Liar!"

Richard's expression hardened. "You had better have a good, if misguided, reason for that last remark."

"You are scheming of a way to seduce her."

"Who?"

"Don't treat me like an idiot! Arabella—and she didn't even like your play!"

"That would be an idiotic reason for me to ignore a beautiful woman. But calm yourself, Neville—"

"I am calm!"

Richard smirked before he responded, "I would no more think of seducing her than I would my own sister."

Neville eyed him dubiously.

"I think your father is right," Richard said with apparent sincerity. "Lady Arabella Martin is a genuinely good and virtuous woman. Instead of seducing her, why don't you tell him the truth?"

"I have explained this to you before. He won't believe me. He'll think I'm trying to lie my way into his good graces."

"Then get the bankers to go with you."

"He won't believe anybody where I'm concerned. Even if he did, he would surely insist upon taking charge of his own affairs. The result would be disaster."

"Be that as it may, I cannot countenance your using Lady Arabella in this way."

"Perhaps my plans have changed. Perhaps I would prefer to offer my hand in marriage."

"Your father would never agree, and frankly, I think he would be right."

"*What?*"

"She is too good for you—and for me, too."

"By God, Richard, don't you dare play the hypocrite for me! You want her—and her inheritance, too, no doubt, as well as what is rightfully mine."

"I don't want money as badly as that."

"No? You seem to have conveniently forgotten that this has been the theme of countless conversations between us—how all you need is money, and then you can return to the bucolic paradise of which you were unjustly robbed."

"I would never seduce a woman for money."

"But to satisfy your own selfish desires you

would. 'I only write what the audience prefers,' " he mimicked mockingly. "Meanwhile, you were staring down her dress!"

"Your mind is a cesspool," Richard growled, rising from the bench.

The coffeehouse fell silent as Neville jumped to his feet. "At least I don't put my obscene musings on the stage and call it art!"

"At least I don't plan to seduce innocent young women to get back at my father and even make a wager on my success!"

"Only because your father is dead! And don't bother lying to me. If you could get her into your bed, you would not hesitate a moment."

"Neville," Richard said in a low, determined voice, "give it up. Either tell your father the truth or accept his decision, but leave Lady Arabella out of it."

Neville straightened his shoulders and fought to regain his self-control. "And when I have quit the field, you will gladly step in."

Richard shoved back the bench and came around the table, standing so that his face was inches from Neville's. "If you do seduce her, I will find the fifty pounds to pay for losing the wager to you, and then I will kill you for dishonoring her."

"If you would be her champion, challenge me to a duel now."

For an instant, he thought Richard would.

But then his former friend shook his head, a sardonic smile coming to his face. "No. For old times' sake and because I have faith that you will not succeed, I will not. Please remove your belongings from my lodgings while I am at the theater. Good-bye, Neville."

Neville didn't move as Richard walked away and out of the coffeehouse. He stayed motionless for a long moment as around him, the buzz of gossiping patrons filled the air.

Then he sat heavily on the bench, staring at nothing.

"Oh, Neville, there you are!"

He half turned, not at all pleased to see Foz's befuddled countenance.

"I saw Richard outside, but he was so deep in thought, he didn't hear me calling him."

Foz sat in Richard's vacated place and looked about the place. "Has something happen?" he asked as he took off his hat and absently scratched under his wig. "Everyone seems most excited."

There was no sense in trying to keep what had just passed a secret. "Richard and I quarreled. Loudly, I am ashamed to say."

"A pox!" Foz cried. "Whatever about?"

"Lady Arabella."

Foz's face fell. "About what she said to Richard? Was he very angry? She meant well, I'm sure."

"It was about the wager."

"Oh." He twisted his hat in his hands. "I've been wanting to talk to you about that. I think we should call it off. I shall gladly part with the fifty pounds."

"Because you think she is a virtuous angel?"

"There's that, too," Foz agreed pensively. A most unusually resolute expression came to his face. "Neville," he said, his voice slightly tremulous, "you must give up the notion of seducing Lady Arabella."

Neville's eyes narrowed. "Why?"

Foz looked away and toyed with his hat plume. "Because Lady Lippet has given me to understand that there is a chance . . . that it is not impossible that I . . . that is, that Lady Arabella might consider . . . that although I am far from outstanding, the earl has his heart set on a nobleman and—"

"You think you stand a chance of becoming her husband!"

Foz blinked. "There is no need to sound so angry about it. She could do worse, you know."

That was something Neville could not deny, yet any woman of common intelligence and goodness would do for Foz.

Arabella would be wasted on him. He was no match for her spirit and passion.

But if she married Foz, she could be the making of him. And their children—

Oh, God, he could not bear to think of Arabella in Cheddersby's bed—in any man's bed except his.

"What about my inheritance, Foz?" he asked quietly, willing himself to sound calm.

"Oh, that."

"Yes, that. It is rather important to me."

Foz continued to destroy the plume on his hat. "I could give you money in compensation, I suppose,"

Neville slowly got to his feet. "I am not a whore."

Foz paled and swallowed hard. "Yes, well, you should leave her alone."

"Don't tell me what to do!"

"It's wrong, Neville, and you know it."

"I will do what I must."

With that, Neville left the coffeehouse.

Whatever he thought he was beginning to feel for Arabella, she was destroying his life. First she usurped his inheritance; now she was costing him his friends.

He was alone in the world again, and it was all her fault.

"I think he would be the perfect husband for you, my dear," Lady Lippet confided as she poured Arabella tea that afternoon, while the earl dozed in a chair near the hearth.

The queen loved the new beverage, and so it was becoming popular among those who emulated the ways of the court, Lady Lippet included. "He's a sweet boy, rich as an emperor, and best of all, he's absolutely smitten with you!"

Arabella girded her loins to both swallow the bitter drink and provide some reason why she could not marry Fozbury Cheddersby.

"Lady Lippet, he is indeed a most gentlemanly young man," she began, reaching to take the cup of tea and then setting it on the table before her where the scent could not reach her nostrils. "But I fear you overestimate his feelings . . ."

She let her deferential words trail off in a heavy sigh.

Lady Lippet took a large and audible sip of tea. "Nonsense, my dear," she replied, setting down her cup with a rattle. "I have never seen a young man more smitten in my life! Still, you should waste no time securing him before he changes his mind."

"Is Lord Cheddersby not, perhaps, *completely* smitten, then?" she replied, trying not to sound overly hopeful.

"Oh, he's *madly* in love with you, my dear. Quite besotted, which should content your romantic nature." She made it clear she thought Arabella's nature a serious failing on her part. "But men are such fickle creatures!"

"Given my romantic nature, Lady Lippet, I must point out that I do not desire only that my bridegroom should love me. I must love him in return."

"Perhaps you also require the crown jewels for a wedding present?" Lady Lippet replied with unexpected bitterness.

As Arabella regarded Lady Lippet with obvious surprise, the older woman took another sip of tea, adjusted her skirt and smiled. "Love will come with time, my dear. Or not, as the case may be. And in that case, a woman would be wise to choose a man who seems . . . moldable."

"Moldable?"

"I mean kind and gentle, and not driven to always have his own way with things. Lord Cheddersby may not cut the most dashing of figures, but he will never be a domestic tyrant, either."

"I cannot disagree," Arabella confessed. "And yet . . ."

"And yet, what?"

Arabella shrugged her shoulders. "He is not very . . . exciting."

"Exciting?" Lady Lippet exclaimed.

The earl snorted, and both ladies turned to look at him, but he only shifted, still sleeping.

"The earl is in favor of this marriage, I suppose," Arabella ventured.

Lady Lippet leaned a little closer. "I haven't told him yet, but I'm sure he would approve."

"I confess I am surprised you have not mentioned this to him," Arabella said, feeling a surge of hope.

"I wanted to know how you felt about it first," Lady Lippet confessed. "If you were absolutely opposed, I would keep silent."

"You would?"

Lady Lippet gave a short, decided nod. "Yes, I would. Lord Cheddersby is not the only eligible man in London."

Arabella thought of Neville Farrington. Then Croesus Belmaris.

"As for the lack of excitement you fear, once you bear your husband a son, there will be plenty of time for excitement."

"I don't know what you mean."

Lady Lippet looked genuinely surprised. "Surely you are not that naive?"

"Apparently I am."

Lady Lippet took a gulp of her tea, and Arabella wasn't sure if that explained why her face turned so red or not. "Once you provide a legitimate heir, then it is time to think of yourself and . . . well, think of yourself."

Arabella recalled *The Country Cuckold* and the many bits of gossip she had heard since, most of it from Lady Lippet. "Take a lover, you mean?"

"Yes," Lady Lippet replied with unusual brevity.

"Even if my husband is a lord?"

Lady Lippet colored a little more. "Perhaps

especially under those circumstances, for I dare say he would have a mistress by then anyway."

"Even a husband as devoted as Lord Cheddersby professes to be?"

"He may be faithful longer than most," Lady Lippet said eagerly, as if this was a great point in his favor.

Arabella was more inclined to believe that this whole topic proved that no man from the upper class could make her happy. "Surely my husband will be angry if he finds out?"

"It won't matter as long as the heir is legitimate."

Arabella gave her companion a sidelong glance. "Did you do that?"

Lady Lippet reached for her tea with very great dignity. "That is not an appropriate question."

Considering how few questions Lady Lippet thought inappropriate, Arabella believed she had her answer, hard though it was to believe.

Then Lady Lippet glanced at the earl and Arabella nearly spit out her tea. Was it possible that Lady Lippet and Neville's father—no, surely not! He was so stern, so moral—

He was a nobleman.

Did Neville believe that? Did that explain their mutual hostility?

"Well, should I speak with the earl about Lord Cheddersby?"

"Lady Lippet, this is all coming upon me so suddenly," Arabella demurred, "and so many exciting things have happened since I arrived in London, would you mind delaying a little?"

Instead of being upset, Lady Lippet grinned slyly. "Other irons may be in the fire, eh?" she whispered with a wink. "Very well. I shall say no more just yet."

Arabella wasn't sure what other irons Lady Lippet referred to, whether Lord Belmaris or some other young nobleman at Whitehall; nevertheless, it seemed such possibilities would keep her companion silent on the subject of Lord Cheddersby.

And for that, Arabella was grateful.

Chapter 14

“**Y**ou have won again!” the king declared cheerfully.

“I have?” Arabella stared at the playing cards in her hand, then at the gold-embossed cribbage board, the silver markers gleaming in the candlelight illuminating the Banqueting House. Around her, many other people were playing different card games, and with different degrees of success, to judge by the sighs, cries and moans they made.

Smiling, Lady Lippet clapped excitedly, as if she were the winner. “Well done, my dear!”

Arabella smiled wanly, for she had the distinct feeling that the king should not have lost; however, to say more would imply that he had cheated for her benefit.

She looked about again and noted that the earl was still deep in conversation with Lord Cheddersby. Or rather, the earl was holding forth on his many opinions. The young noble-man didn't appear to be attentive, for he continually watched *her* while he chewed on the end of his wig.

And Neville was nowhere to be seen.

With a smile, Charles pushed the pile of coins toward her. "Here, now, take your winnings like a good girl."

"I cannot take the money," she replied. "You stood me, so you should have it."

"We only gave you a small sum to start. All the rest you won, and we insist you take it," the king said, and there was a look in his eye that told her she would not be wise to contradict him.

"Very well, Your Majesty," she acquiesced, deciding she would give it to charity. "Shall we play another hand?"

In the gallery, court musicians began to play.

The king shook his head, then rose. "We think not, for the music for dancing is begun. We have promised a dance to Frances Stewart."

Arabella half rose as the king strolled away, then sat again, contemplating how she would carry away her winnings and wondering why Neville was not at Whitehall tonight.

A shadow suddenly loomed over the table, sending a chill down her spine. In the next instant, the Duke of Buckingham insinuated himself into the king's vacated chair. "Good evening, Lady Arabella. How lovely you look this evening. That shade of blue is very becoming on you."

"If you will excuse me, Your Grace," she said, standing, "I should join the earl."

"Not yet," the duke said softly, laying his cool, damp hand over hers. "I wish to speak with you."

"I—"

"It is very important to you and to Neville Farrington, too, I should think."

Arabella sat down.

"I am delighted to know you can be reasonable," the duke said, mercifully taking his hand from hers to shuffle the cards. "We shall play a hand or two, shall we?" He gave her a leering smile. "Winner take all."

"I would rather not play with you, Your Grace. I am too new to these courtly games."

"We shall have to change that, won't we?"

"Your Grace—" she began with a hint of her annoyance.

"Lady Arabella," he interrupted, his cold, reptilian eyes narrowing, "you would be wise to listen to what I have to say. Surely you cannot be so naive that you do not appreciate the compliment a man's attention implies. And you have caught the attention of a very important man."

Arabella knew the duke was vain, but to hear him speak of himself with such arrogant pride was really too much. "If the man is married, he should keep his attention on his wife."

"How provincial," the duke retorted. "We are at court, not some little country village."

"Should not the court provide the example of morality? Or," she said, frowning, "do the courtiers mean to lead by providing examples of how *not* to behave? If so, Your Grace, I fear your lessons are quite lost on simple folk like myself."

The duke scowled. "You have no idea what is being offered to you."

"Perhaps I have too good an idea—and so must reject it," she retorted. Then she looked past the duke. "Oh, Your Grace—here is Mrs. Hankerton."

With a low curse, Villiers turned to look over his shoulder. That whore had no business coming here!

He surveyed the crowd of card players but couldn't see Mrs. Hankerton.

When he turned back, Arabella Martin was nowhere to be seen.

Some time later, as she made her weary way upstairs in the earl's townhouse behind Jarvis, Arabella sighed deeply.

It had been a very trying evening, looking for Neville without being obvious, listening to the earl mutter complaints and disparaging remarks about the court and everybody in it, her growing awareness that Lord Cheddersby seemed to be the husbandly choice of the moment and avoiding the Duke of Buckingham. Now, safely home, she was utterly exhausted and wanted nothing more than to go to bed and sleep. With that in mind, she had dismissed the yawning maid who had awaited her return.

At the threshold of her bedchamber, Jarvis handed her the rushlight, bowed and departed. With another sigh, Arabella entered, set down the light and removed her cloak. She laid it on the chair. As she reached for the laces at the back of her bodice, she saw her bed curtains make a sudden, unexpected movement.

The window was not open, there was no draft.

"Who's there?" she demanded in a whisper.

Then she saw him.

Neville stood in the shadows of the bed curtains. His hair and clothing were disheveled, and he held a bottle in his right hand. He was not so much in the dark that she could not see his devilishly sinful grin.

Her heart, already racing, seemed to beat even faster. She felt a trickle of perspiration run down her side. "What are you doing here?"

Neville put his finger to his lips.

"Hush, hush, Arabella," he said in a sing-song voice. "No need to be so upset. My father forgot to send some of my belongings, so I came for them tonight. If you make a hubbub, Jarvis will suffer for allowing me in the house. You wouldn't want Jarvis to suffer, would you?"

She went to the opposite side of the bed. "That does not explain what you are doing in *my* bedchamber."

"I made a mistake, and then I saw the light. I didn't want to have yet another tedious argument with my father, so I sought refuge here."

"Now your father is safely in his room, so you must leave!" she ordered in a stern whisper, pointing at the door.

"Leave, she orders me," he muttered. "In my own house, too."

"It is not your house. It is your father's. Please get out, or . . . or . . ."

"Or what?" he inquired. "Or you'll call my father?" He gestured widely with the bottle in the direction of the other bedchambers. "Go ahead. Let him toss me into the street. He'll need Jarvis to help him, though. Or *you*."

He dropped the bottle, which hit the floor with a dull thud, then splayed his hands on the bed and leaned toward her. "Would you do that, dear, sweet Arabella? Are you so hardhearted a wench you would throw me out into the streets like the contents of a chamber pot?"

"I will if you do not go, and quickly," she declared firmly.

He climbed on the bed, and she moved back from it as he lay on his side, holding his head in one hand while he smiled at her. "I don't want to leave."

"Why do you not visit your friends? They may find your antics amusing."

Neville rolled onto his back and stared upward. "I don't have any friends. Not anymore."

"I find it hard to believe that a man of your many attributes is left completely friendless," she said, sidling toward the door.

He turned his head and grinned. "Do you like my attributes?"

"You are not unattractive, my lord, but I dare say you know that well enough without hearing it from me."

He sat up. "I could never tire of hearing my praises sung from your lovely lips. I'faith, I could never tire of anything from your lovely lips. I think I would find curses delightful if they fell from your lovely lips."

He must be in his cups to spout such nonsense.

She was nearly at the door. "Surely there are ladies who would be your friend."

He was off the bed and at the door before she quite knew what was happening. "As you would be the king's friend?"

"I don't know what you mean."

"I'm only a little drunk and not at all stupid," he said, leaning against the door. "The whole court is buzzing with the news of your conquest, although I think the king an easy continent to claim."

"The whole court is wrong," she retorted, eyeing him warily. "Please go!"

"Where? Where would you have me go? You have taken my place here."

"Surely Sir Richard—"

"Would probably offer to meet me in a duel if I showed my face at the theater tonight."

She moved away from him, across the room. "Why?"

"We have quarreled."

"What about?"

"You."

"Me?" she cried softly, putting her hand to her breast in surprise.

Not taking his gaze from her, Neville nodded slowly. "He's going to try to seduce you. It's quite obvious, really. Even a countrified miss should be able to tell."

She frowned, but continued to regard him just as steadily. "Then it would seem he is very like every other man in London."

"Not every man."

"No," she agreed. "Lord Cheddersby is the soul of propriety."

"That puppy!"

"Ah!"

"There you are again with that ejaculation. Why "ah" now, Lady?"

"Because I think you have quarreled with Lord Cheddersby as well. Why?"

Unexpectedly, his gaze faltered. "Perhaps because he would presume to marry you."

Of all the explanations he might have given, she had not expected this one.

Then, just as suddenly and unexpectedly, he lunged for her and pulled her against his hard chest so that the breath was nearly knocked from her. He captured her mouth in a fiery, passionate kiss that again unleashed an incredible burning, fierce desire within her.

This was not weakness. This was a strength she didn't know she possessed, a yearning so potent, it must and would dominate her.

"You want me as much as I want you," he murmured, pressing heated kisses upon her temples, her cheeks.

As he gently nibbled on her earlobe, her arms encircled him, seemingly of their own volition. His arm tightened about her, holding her like a band of iron, leaving his other hand free to stroke and caress her.

She moaned softly as he cupped her breast and his thumb brushed across her nipple. It was so tempting to give herself over to the passionate excitement sweeping through her body, to yield completely until she knew the fulfillment of release from this thrilling tension building within her.

To surrender, even though she knew it was wrong.

If they did not stop immediately, she would do what every lustful particle of her body was urging her to do. She would weaken and go up in the flame of passion like so much tinder—and risk her soul for sin.

She summoned all that remained of her righteous resolution and placed her hands against his broad chest to push him away. "Stop," she murmured.

"That is your Puritan father speaking," he muttered as his lips trailed across her collarbone.

He ground his hips against hers in a primitive, lascivious action that had nothing to do with love or affection but only lust.

"No, it is Arabella."

He stopped and stepped back, his gaze hardening. "I perceive I have underestimated you, Arabella."

"I . . . I don't know what you mean."

"You are very clever, my coy and teasing lady. You spur me on one moment only to withdraw the next, knowing that to do so only whets my appetite. Is this the strategy you would use upon the king?"

"I am not being clever! You surprised me!"

"It amazes me that you can always be caught so unaware. But I forget—it is time for the virtuous virgin to appear upon the stage," he said scornfully. "This wench who kisses with such blatant desire is all righteous indignation now."

"I am not a wanton!"

"You enjoy my kisses."

"No doubt that is how you think every woman reacts to your embraces," she replied defensively.

"If they do, they do not dissemble. What is it you hope to gain by this?"

"Gain?"

"My devotion? You had that, for tonight at least."

"I do not want anything from you!"

A smirk twisted his face. "Apparently not. Or at least, not for the moment. I have to wonder if this is but a feint that I am supposed to parry." He sighed dramatically. "To think I was beginning to believe you were the innocent you seemed! You belong upon the stage. You would be a great success—in many ways."

"I think you would be better, for you feign sincerity so well."

"I feign sincerity?" he scoffed with a laugh. "What about you? I see full well how you manage my father and poor dim Foz. I wonder what they would have thought had they ventured into this room a few moments ago. Their countenances would surely have been amusing."

"There would have been nothing amusing about it."

"Really? Then you do not have the sense of humor I credited you with. I'faith, I more than half believed that is what led you to entertain thoughts of marrying Foz. Either that or greed. Tell me, does my father know of your propensity for entertaining visitors in your bedchamber like my lady Castlemaine and others of her sort?"

"You invade my privacy and then think to criticize me?"

"You are hardly the embodiment of virtue my father thinks, and I have the proof."

"Why?" she demanded. "Why would you seek to destroy me in your father's estimation?"

"Oh, please, Arabella, no more of this coyness!"

"I do not understand."

"Then perhaps your stupidity explains why you had such difficulties interpreting your father's silences."

She gasped as if he had stabbed her. Tears started in her eyes. "Get out and never speak to me again!" she ordered, her voice quavering slightly.

"Arabella, I'm sorry!" he cried softly, meaning it as much as he had ever meant anything in his life. "Forgive me! I should not have said that."

More, he knew he should not have acted as he had, alone here with her. He had behaved like a despicable cad, a rake, a libertine—like Buckingham and Sedley and their ilk. He, who always prided himself on his self-control, had been no better than the most selfish brute, because he wanted her so very, very much. Just being alone with her robbed him of his self-control.

She remained motionless, glaring at him. She looked like an avenging angel standing there, her curling hair a halo in the moonlight. "You sneak into my bedchamber, press your kiss upon me, and now you request my forgiveness?"

"Yes."

"Since I am a Christian, you have it." She pointed imperiously at the door. "Now get out and never seek to come near me again."

He held out his hands in a placating gesture. "Please, Arabella, do not send me away before I can explain."

"There can be no good explanation for your conduct in this room tonight."

"Except a little too much wine and a great deal of human frailty."

"Or madness," she proposed harshly.

"All three, perhaps."

"Then truly, my lord, you do not belong here. You should be in Bedlam."

He walked toward her cautiously. "Perhaps

I am in Bedlam. I think I have been half mad ever since you arrived, or perhaps Bedlam has expanded its boundaries to encompass me.''

"My lord, I—"

"It is your fault, Arabella.''

"Mine?"

"For being so beautiful that you make every man desire you.''

"I cannot help how I look.''

"As I cannot help how I feel. Please do not marry Foz.''

"Who told you I was going to marry him?"

"My father and Lady Lippet approve, do they not?''

She did not respond, and he knew he was right. "You don't love him, do you?"

She stared at the floor, still silent.

"Do you no longer wish to marry for love?"

"I have been given to understand that is no longer the fashion,'' she murmured.

"You told me once that if you could not have love from your parents, it was your dearest wish to have a husband's love.''

She raised her eyes, which seemed to glow in the moonlight like the North Star guiding a lost soul home. "You do remember!''

"You were very certain then.''

"We were both younger then.''

"Yet when I first saw you here, you did not seem so very different.''

"You did. What happened to you, Neville?"

"I grew into a man and came to London."

She sighed softly. "I wish you had not."

He turned away and went to the window. "I had little choice about coming to London. Life with my father was unbearable."

"Because he criticized you?"

He turned to face her, the moonlight casting a long shadow. "Constantly. Unendingly. Nothing I do or have ever done has earned me one good word from him.

"But I am not a peevish child, Arabella. There is more amiss between my father and me than those apparent faults he declares so loudly and so often. Another reason he could not bear my presence, and one that I can never amend."

She took a step closer. "What is it?"

"I am like my mother." He swiped a hand over his perspiring brow as he turned to look out the window again.

He was reacting like a fool. He wanted—required—her to believe herself in love with him, and if painful revelations were necessary to accomplish that, he would make them.

But that was the only reason he would speak of these things. "She liked music and dancing and games. She craved amusement and joyful things. You have seen my father. You can guess that they did not exactly suit."

"Yet your father took me to the theater," Arabella said. "He has gone to Whitehall and, indeed, seems to enjoy himself there."

Neville sighed. "Well, I suppose they might have managed well enough, or as well as plenty of other noble couples do. But then came Cromwell and his Roundheads. When the king was executed, my father would not leave England, and she would not stay.

"By then, of course, I had been born and I had lived. The succession was secure.

"So also by then," he continued, hostility creeping into his voice, "they each had a lover. My mother went to France with hers, my father stayed in England with his—and his child, who resembled his absent wife in feature, voice and disposition."

"She left you?" Arabella asked, her voice full of pity, her heart aching for him. "How terrible. But it must have been difficult for her, too. I'm sure she felt she had no other choice."

He turned around and cocked his head. "As much as I would like to believe that, I know it is not true. She was being what she always was—selfish. Her lover would not welcome me, so she left me behind."

"How do you know this? Your father—"

"Never spoke of her again for good or ill. I found her in France a few years ago, and she told me this herself in her own charming way, shedding the falsest tears I ever beheld. Then she asked me to leave. She was expecting a man—her latest lover, without doubt—and

didn't want him to think she was being un-
faithful.''

Then he laughed, but it was the most
ghastly, unnatural laugh Arabella had ever
heard. "Have I not been blessed in my parents?
Honor thy father and thy mother, indeed!''

"Neville, I am so sorry!''

"You need not be," he replied, and this time,
she heard the bitter pain beneath his flippant
tone. "All you need do is understand that there
is more than childish petulance where my father and I are concerned. He hates me.'' He
straightened his shoulders and resumed his
cavalier air. "I should be glad his hatred and
resentment got me out of Grantham.''

"Don't!'' she cried softly, hurrying to him.

"Don't what?''

She put her arms around him in a gentle,
loving embrace. "Don't talk that way! It is not
you!''

He stood as stiff as a sentry. "What, pray tell,
is me?''

"You are yet the boy in the garden!''

He glanced down at her. "By the world, you
would have time stand still?''

"I am certain you are not so completely
changed. You have built a wall of flippant composure around yourself, but the Neville I knew
is there, hidden behind it.''

Her arms went around his neck, and then
she kissed him tenderly. Lovingly.

A kiss of affection, not lust. Of a love he had never known before. Of a love he never wanted to lose.

His embrace tightened about her as their kiss deepened. He would keep nothing back but would give her all his love.

Tonight and for the rest of his life. For as long as his heart continued to beat, it would be hers.

Moaning softly, she opened her mouth, and with heady delight he plunged his tongue inside its welcoming warmth.

How the languorous dance of her lips over his aroused him! And her fingers—each light brush of their tips seemed to set him aflame.

He needed her so much!

Still kissing her, he stripped off his jacket and let it fall to the ground. She tugged his shirt from his breeches and put her hands under it, slowly moving them upward over his naked flesh.

"Oh, sweet heaven," he groaned as he pulled off his shirt.

She leaned forward and kissed his bare shoulder, then lower, until she took his nipple in her mouth.

With fumbling fingers, he untied her satin-soft hair so that it fell freely about her smooth shoulders. He took her chin in his hand and lifted her face to press another passionate kiss upon her succulent lips.

He would love her as he had never loved a woman, he vowed. He would love her with his heart and soul as well as his body.

Now. Here. At once.

He lifted Arabella in his arms and strode to the bed, laying her upon it, gently sliding his hands from beneath her lovely, eager, willing body.

She looked up at him, her disheveled curls upon the pillow, her face slightly flushed, her lips parted.

He knew what he saw in her luminous eyes. He had seen that look in a woman's eyes too often not to know what it meant.

She trusted him. She thought she was in love with him. He could do with her what he willed with no promise given, no pledge of obligation exacted.

And be the lascivious, derelict scoundrel his father thought he was.

Without a word, Neville grabbed his discarded clothing and strode from the room.

If the walls had crumbled about her, Arabella could not have felt more stunned, shocked and dismayed.

For a long moment, she did nothing. Then, slowly, she got off the bed and knelt on the floor beside it, regardless of the hard wood beneath her knees.

Clasping her hands, she began to pray. She prayed for strength, because she was as full of sin and lust as her father had always said. She prayed for forgiveness, because as she had lain on the bed, looking at Neville, she had been every bit as weak and tempted as Eve. She prayed that the earl would see his son's merit, for Neville's righteous strength had saved them both from a terrible sin.

Evidence of his worth?

Neville had just provided all she would ever need by not taking what she had so wantonly offered.

Chapter 15

⌒◯◯⌒

Four nights later, warbling the chorus of a particularly bawdy ditty, Neville lurched drunkenly through the darkened streets of Bankside as he vainly searched for his new lodgings or at least another tavern.

He had been cracking a bottle ever since he had left Arabella and had every intention of continuing for as long as his limited funds lasted. If his father thought him a drunkard, he would be a drunkard. And a wastrel. And a rogue.

By leaving Arabella without making love with her, he had, of course, abandoned all hope of his inheritance and even the fifty pounds of the wager.

His last virtuous act might very well be his final virtuous act, and he was going to have to find some way to earn a living.

Maybe he could emulate Richard.

"Or perhaps I should become a highway-man," he mumbled philosophically, address-ing a shop sign. "Everyone thinks I will be hanged anyway."

A movement in the shadows of a nearby alley caught his eye, and he drew his sword. Brandishing it, he moved toward the narrow opening between two decrepit wooden build-ings. The smell of rotting vegetables and other refuse grew stronger.

Then he heard the sound of running feet.

"Ha!" he exclaimed triumphantly, swaying like a seaman on the heaving deck of a ship in rough seas.

Even drunk, no one would dare to attack him. His father, who did not love him, should see *that*!

Arabella thought she loved him. He had seen that in her beautiful eyes.

She was too young and inexperienced to truly love, to feel that heady mixture of respect, admiration and desire that overwhelmed you until you could think of little else except Ara-bella . . .

He shook his head as if he could shake her memory from his brain. She probably just lusted after him, as other women had, he told himself as he staggered onward. They saw him only as an attractive, amusing fellow able to entertain them in bed and out, nothing more.

What was love, anyway, but a jest? Some-

thing for poets to wax poetic about and playwrights to take literary jabs at.

He would not love anybody, especially not
Arabella.

What could he give her? No fortune or hope
of one. No position. No home.

His pride would never allow him to live on
his wife's money, so he had only a title to offer.
Nothing more.

For a moment he leaned against a rough wall
as if he needed the support. Then, raising his
head, he took a deep breath. He straightened
his shoulders and pressed his lips together
while he ran his hand through his tangled hair.

He was Lord Farrington, whom most men
admired and women desired.

"I'faith, I *could* be a poet!" he muttered with
an attempt at his usual jocund manner.

He nearly collided with a low-hanging shop
sign. He stared at the three balls indicating a
pawnshop. "A pox! I'm home!"

A door at the side of the pawnshop opened
onto rickety stairs. He made his way up the
dark, narrow, half-rotten steps toward the gar-
ret, shoved open his door—and then nearly
threw up when he saw who stood in his bare,
dank room, now illuminated by what had to
be his whole store of rushlights.

Fortunately, he was not ill. Instead, he immediately went down on one knee. "Your Majesty!"

"We think in these humble surroundings, 'Charles' will do."

His head still lowered, Neville tried to look and sound sober. "You come here alone, sire?"

Bankside was hardly safe, even for the king, even though he came here with some frequency attired in what was, for him, plain clothing and accoutrements. Despite his garb, however, Charles was an unmistakable figure.

"We have men nearby, Farrington, but your concern does you credit," Charles said. "Please rise."

"Yes, Maj—"

The king cocked his head. "Charles."

Neville gestured feebly at the battered stool. Besides the fetid bed, this was the only article of furniture in the room. "Charles, please, won't you sit?"

The king glanced at the stool dismissively. "We think not."

"I confess I am stunned to find you in my humble lodgings, Your—Charles."

"As we are stunned by the poverty of your lodgings, Farrington," the king replied. "And we are most displeased to see you in such a state."

Neville tugged on the bottom of his jacket, then gave up any effort to make himself presentable, for he knew it would be hopeless. At least he was feeling somewhat less inebriated.

From the shock, no doubt.

"We understand you are no longer living in your father's house. That you have had the misfortune to be . . . how shall we put this?"

"Cast out describes it, Maj—Charles."

"Indeed," the king concurred with a slight inclination of his head. "You have been cast out. And you have not been at court for some days."

"Given what my father has done, sire, and that he is often at Whitehall, I thought it best to stay away."

"We wondered if your absence had something to do with a certain young lady."

Neville stiffened. "Majesty?"

The king raised the royal eyebrows expectantly.

"Charles," Neville corrected himself.

"We speak of the delightful Lady Arabella, who currently resides in your father's house."

"What of her, sire?"

"She intrigues us, Farrington."

Neville had suspected this from the first, but the king's fascination did not explain what Charles was doing here talking about it, unless this was part of some heavenly plan to punish him. "The king is known for his discerning eye."

Charles chuckled. "Well, we like a pretty woman and we do not trouble ourselves to hide it. Nor, my Lord Farrington, do you."

Neville's mouth went slightly dry.

The king laughed again. "Come, man, that is no serious failing! Indeed, spare us from a man who keeps too close counsel, for that way leads to deceit."

"I am glad you think me an honest fellow."

"Not *too* honest, we hope," the king replied with somewhat less levity, "considering what we would have you do."

"What is that, Majesty?"

"Can you not guess?"

"That might not be prudent."

Charles smiled. "Indeed, it might not. However, it concerns this young lady of whom we speak. As you know, Lady Castlemaine has a furious temper when she is annoyed. She has, unfortunately, discovered that we fancy Lady Arabella and so is extremely annoyed."

"A most inconvenient state of affairs, I imagine."

"Inconvenient does not begin to capture the effect of one of my lady's moods," the king muttered before he smiled again. "We hope for your assistance in our desire, which is to have peace with my lady Castlemaine, and Lady Arabella in the royal bed."

Neville's nausea returned. "What would you have me do?"

"We would have you appear to be wooing Lady Arabella without actually seducing her, all the while convincing her that her place is elsewhere."

"I am to woo her into your arms?"

"Precisely. Make it clear to her that her king is a good-hearted, generous man. She shall have apartments in Whitehall, albeit far from Barbara's, clothing, horses, jewels, whatever she desires."

"Do such things not fall into the Duke of Buckingham's province or Sir Charles Berkeley's?" Neville asked, fighting to maintain his composure. "Buckingham has been most diligent in the matter of La Belle Stewart, I believe."

"And we both know how he has failed there," Charles replied. "We are even more determined this time, and Lady Arabella shies from Buckingham like a nervous mare. As for Berkeley, there are, as we are sure you are aware, other reasons we would not wish to enlist his aid.

"You, on the other hand, Lord Farrington, may be the very fellow we require for this delicate business. She does not seem to shy away from *you*."

"I must remind you, sire, that I am not welcome in my father's house, so my contact with the lady is somewhat curtailed."

"What is a family squabble to the king's interest?" Charles replied with a hard look in his dark eyes that reminded Neville he was speaking to the ruler of a nation. "We trust a man of your abilities will find a way." He paused a moment, then smiled again. "You obviously have some pecuniary difficulties as well, Farrington. Naturally, you will be amply rewarded: titles, commissions, estates and so forth. We can be very generous to our friends."

A thrill of excitement ran through Neville. The king's reward might finally make his father consider him worthy of respect. No, he would be free of his father and rich. Influential. Important.

All he had to do was give up any hope of Arabella and sacrifice her to the king's pleasure.

"I appreciate your generosity, sire," he replied slowly. "However, I should tell you that there is a chance her scruples will render her compliance impossible."

"Perhaps you do not comprehend us fully," the king said. "It is your task to overcome any scruples. She seems an intelligent young woman capable of understanding what will be to her advantage."

"There is also the matter of her possible betrothal to Lord Cheddersby."

"Fozbury Cheddersby?" the king cried as if vastly amused. "Foolish Fozbury wants to marry her?"

"More important, Majesty, I believe my father will think the match a most agreeable one."

"For Cheddersby, certainly," Charles agreed. "And for her it is good, too, for he will be the most easily managed husband in the kingdom."

"No doubt."

"Has anything been definitely decided?"

"I do not think so, Majesty."

The king grinned as he rubbed his gloved and jeweled hands together with satisfaction. "Odd's fish, then, man, the point is moot. Besides, the fellow will hardly think himself ill used if I provide a suitable estate and a title or two in compensation, should he still want to marry her afterward."

Neville was not so certain that Foz, for all his simple good nature, would think so, yet he remained silent. He had enough with which to concern himself without protecting Foz's interests, too. "I think it would be wise to say nothing to him until matters are more in hand."

"In hand? Precisely," the king replied with a laugh. "We very much wish to have Lady Arabella in our hands and count on you to insure it!"

Neville bowed as the king started toward the door.

His Majesty paused before leaving, looking around at the stained and filthy walls. "These buildings are truly disgusting. It is tempting to have them all torn down and replaced, but I fear the people would never concur. We shall have to count upon God to do it for us, eh?"

The next evening, Lady Lippet's sigh spoke of exasperation and fatigue. "I cannot see Lord Cheddersby! Where can he be?"

"I do not know," Arabella replied with considerably less concern. "He will appear soon enough. The Banqueting House is so crowded tonight, he might be close by and yet out of sight."

Arabella had not seen Neville, either, although she continually searched the boisterous gathering.

She had not seen him since he had left her four days ago. It was as if he had disappeared completely.

She would have been very worried had not Lord Cheddersby told her he had been spotted about the city.

Why, then, had he not tried to see her?

Lady Lippet's fan moved rapidly. "I have never seen so many people here before! No doubt the rumors are true and Lady Castlemaine plans on making an appearance, although there is no hiding the fact she is *enceinte*, and perhaps not by the king."

It was clear it was Lady Castlemaine's decision to appear in public that was cause for Lady Lippet's displeased tone, not the questionable identity of the husband of her child.

"Do you see the earl anywhere?" she demanded.

"No, and he has only been absent these few moments looking for Sir Thomas."

Arabella moved back as a pair of women pushed past them, trying to make their way through the crowd.

"What is this commotion? Oh, this is too aggravating," Lady Lippet whined, turning this way and that without really pausing to see anything.

"Why, Lady Arabella, what a pleasure!" a deep, familiar, thrilling voice whispered in her ear.

With a gasp, she turned to find Neville at her side, slightly behind her.

Surely there was no man his equal in all the court or all of England, either. Although he was attired simply in black, his natural grace and bearing amply compensated for any lack of luxury in his clothes.

Then she got a good look at his face. Glancing at Lady Lippet, who was as yet oblivious to his arrival, Arabella moved back slightly to stand beside him. "Have you been ill?"

"I am merely tired."

She gave him a quizzical look. He sounded just as he had on her first day in London.

Could illness be the explanation for his pale, drawn features and his bloodshot eyes—or was it something else? Lord Cheddersby had not said where Neville had been seen; at the moment, Bankside came to mind. "Where have you been?"

"Here, there, about the town," he replied.

A loud roar of approval went up from the crowd. Ignoring them, he took hold of her hand, the grip of his fingers strong as he gently pulled her back through the crowd, away from Lady Lippet.

"They are playing blindman's buff," he explained in that flippant drawl. "It amuses Frances Stewart. That and other childish games, like building houses of cards. As you know, the rest of the sophisticates of the court prefer other sport. Well, perhaps not Lady Castlemaine. When she plays blindman's buff, she is forever running her hands over someone without being able to guess who they are, apparently."

Now at the back of the mob, he began moving around the outside, yet drawing closer to the most boisterous group.

She wanted to be alone with him again, yet although he had detached her from Lady Lippet, he seemed intent on keeping her among the revelers. "I would rather not play."

"The king himself requested that I summon you to the game."

"Do you think I should play?" she asked, completely confused by his absence, his demeanor and his actions.

It was as if the memorable events of the other night had been a dream instead of reality. Or as if he wanted to forget what had happened.

"Most women would be flattered to have their presence requested by His Majesty."

"I did not say I was not flattered," she replied truthfully. "I have never played blindman's buff before and don't wish to look foolish."

"I don't think you will."

"Neville, I—"

Lady Castlemaine suddenly appeared directly in front of them, making something of an impediment, given the fullness of her satin skirts. It was no secret she was with child, either.

"There you are, Lord Farrington," she purred, running a dismissive glance over Arabella.

Who barely refrained from curling her lip. This woman was surely the boldest, most immoral hussy at court, if not in all of England.

"Lady Castlemaine, may I present Lady Arabella Martin, my father's ward and the daughter of the late Duke of Bellhurst."

Lady Castlemaine's eyes widened a little, and a patronizing smile appeared on her face. "So this is the country-bred beauty of whom I have heard."

Arabella suddenly felt like a badly dressed, homely rustic.

The king's mistress gave Neville an arch look. "You did not say she was so charmingly lovely. No doubt you want to keep her all to yourself. And here I intended to invite you to play cribbage with me, my lord."

"Charles Berkeley is otherwise engaged? And Henry Jermyn?"

Lady Castlemaine's smile disappeared. "I do not wish to play with them."

"I do not know how to play your favorite games," Neville replied lightly.

Her eyes narrowed, and Arabella realized she was quite forgotten by the woman before them. "I could teach you."

"I know you are very skilled," he answered. "Alas, I fear I am a slow study. Would you not agree, Lady Arabella?" He continued before either the now hostile Lady Castlemaine or Arabella could answer, "So good evening, my lady, and good luck in finding a partner." He made a courteous bow.

Lady Castlemaine scowled as she turned and strode away.

Suddenly, the crowd in front of them parted like the Red Sea before Moses. King Charles, resplendent in purple and gold and with a white linen blindfold across his eyes, groped his way toward them.

Neville's grip tightened.

"Come," he growled, tugging her backward. Without a word, and ignoring the smiles, smirks and surprised expressions of those around them, Neville led Arabella away from the king and into the Privy Garden.

Chapter 16

~~~OO~~~

Glad to be rid of Lady Castlemaine, Neville led Arabella toward a secluded portion of the garden where they would be undisturbed and where, hopefully, even the king's own servants wouldn't find them, should Charles send them searching.

He wondered what the king would make of their sudden defection, for Neville had not done what he was supposed to do. He was to take Arabella toward the king, who would "find" her. Touch her. Run his hands over her under the pretense of trying to discover who she was by touch alone.

What was that compared to what the king really wanted to do? What were those impertinent smirks from the other courtiers compared to Arabella's possible fate after the king was done with her?

The king's order was more important than

his mistress's request, so he would do as the king commanded and present Arabella with the opportunity to be the king's lover. If questioned, he would explain that he had gone with her into the garden for that very purpose.

He glanced at the lovely woman at his side. Tonight Arabella wore a heavy velvet and satin gown of dark green. Her hair was dressed in curls and ribbons, and her face remained free of cosmetics, her own lovely complexion requiring no assistance.

The warm spring air carried a hundred subtle scents: of blooming flowers, the shrubbery damp from an afternoon's shower, the river, Arabella's perfume. The silvery moonlight made the paths a ghostly white, and the shadows odd and unfamiliar. She kept looking at him uncertainly, with that same mixture of confusion and concern as when she had first seen him this evening.

"What is it, Neville?" she asked anxiously when he halted near a particularly ugly statue. "You *have* been ill, haven't you? You still look far from well."

"I have merely been imbibing in Bankside."

"Why?"

"I do not have to explain anything I do to you."

She looked away, obviously hurt.

Good. She should not care about him, just as he must not care about her. Therefore, he would ignore his own pain, because of what he now had to do. "Arabella, I congratulate you."

"Congratulate me? Why? What have I done?"

"You have attracted the notice of a very important man."

"If you refer to the Duke of Buckingham, I regret that I have." Her expression brightened. "Unless you mean the notice of another man who is much more important to me?"

He wanted to groan with dismay as she looked at him with guarded hopefulness. "I do not mean the duke, but I do not refer to myself, either. Vain I may be, but not so vain as to account myself very important."

"Oh."

"I daresay an 'oh' has to be better than your 'ahs' have been, yet you do not sound very enthusiastic."

"I am not."

"Perhaps it will increase your pleasure when you learn who this very important person is."

She took his hands in hers. "There is only one man I care about."

Her tender touch, combined with her heartfelt words, nearly overwhelmed him. "Have you not yet realized I am speaking of the king?" he asked dutifully.

She smiled her beguiling smile. "Everyone keeps mistaking the king's kindness for something more."

"You are too modest."

"He is flirtatious, as are most courtiers, I have discovered. However, the king has never said anything at all to me to indicate that he has any such base desire."

"He has to others—to me."

"To you?"

"Yes."

"To be any man's mistress is to be sinful and immoral," she said firmly. "The Bible does not say, Do not commit adultery unless you are the king."

"An excellent point," Neville observed, "and one rarely thought of in these debauched days."

"Besides, there is only one man I love."

Neville might have felt worse if someone had stuck a knife through his ribs and twisted. He might have.

"I have seen so-called love die too many times to have much faith in it," he observed.

"Love always dies?" she asked softly.

"It has been my experience thus far."

She contemplated his answer, then fixed her shrewd gaze upon him. "Thus far," she noted. "You leave room for hope."

"A man must always live in hope. But why talk of these things, Arabella? What do you know of love between men and women, of desire and passion?"

"That I have not yet shared a man's bed does

not mean I am ignorant of physical desire. Indeed, I have felt much more than merely that."

"What more need there be than passionate desire?"

"Love, my lord. True, lasting, devoted love."

"Many women have claimed to love me," he said, taking refuge behind his light-hearted mask once more, although his heart throbbed as if it would burst through his ribs. "And sworn their eternal devotion, too. Regrettably, their notion of eternity apparently comprised a month or two."

"Then they did not love," Arabella replied, not acknowledging his attempt to make sport of this subject. "Neville, although I am young, I know whereof I speak, and it is of a love that fills your heart with joy. That makes long, dark days brighter. That brings happiness in the midst of pain, hope when all seems hopeless. A love that sees beyond apparent change." Her hands tightened around his. "A love I have known since a summer's afternoon in the Earl of Barrsettshire's garden."

Holding up his hand as if it was something rare and precious, she tenderly kissed his palm. How soft and gentle were her womanly lips against his tougher masculine flesh! How shining were her eyes when she raised them to look at him with love and faith and compassion!

Then she turned his hand over and nearly unmanned him when she pressed her lips to the mark that still remained where she had burned him. The place was seared anew.

Yet the anguish he felt now was nothing compared to that burn, and he was sure his aching heart would never heal.

He wanted to moan with despair, for the love he felt for her could not be. It must not be.

One last kiss, his heart begged. One last embrace to last him a lifetime.

To feel her lips upon his just once more and for the last time to sense a passionate desire that matched and enflamed his own. To know a kiss that spoke both of possession and surrender.

Instead, with more effort than it would have taken him to lift one of the king's statues, he tugged his hand away. "I'faith, pretty Arabella, I thought you had learned some sophistication since your arrival in London. Are you such a simpleton that you are insensible to the honor the king does you by desiring you and the rewards he could offer you?"

Her brow furrowed as she frowned, yet he continued inexorably, "His mistresses are housed, clothed, and honored with titles and estates. If they bear him children, the children are also given titles and estates. They will be able to marry into the first families of England."

Arabella didn't know what to make of his

words. What was he doing? What was happening? What was he really saying? "So that means they are expensive whores, but they are whores nonetheless."

"Or merely practical."

"Better to starve than demean oneself."

"You have never starved."

"I told you my father believed in fasting."

"I take it that is a refusal."

"Of course!"

"Very well. I shall inform His Majesty that you do not wish to play blindman's buff or any other game."

"Please do."

He turned to go. She grabbed his arm to make him halt, and he glanced back, one eyebrow raised questioningly.

"Neville, do you not care for me at all?" she asked, her eyes pleading with him to tell the truth.

It took every ounce of determination he had to lift her hand from his arm. "I found your naiveté amusing for a time, and you are an undeniably lovely woman—but love? That is for fools."

Then he marched back to the Banqueting House, abandoning her, unable to tell her why she must not love him.

Although he was not as lax and disgraceful as his father believed, somewhere within him there was a great flaw or failing.

It must be so, for even his own mother had not been able to love him.

And he could not abide the thought that Arabella would one day find it.

Lady Lippet, in obvious high dudgeon, exited the Banqueting House. She marched down the main path of the Privy Garden, then spotted Arabella standing so motionless beside a statue that she might have been one herself.

"There you are!" Lady Lippet cried. "What is the meaning of this?"

"Of what?" Arabella replied flatly.

"Of leaving the Banqueting House with . . . that man! And just as the king was about to speak to you."

"I do not think the king intended to speak to me."

"Well, notice you, then!" Lady Lippet peered at the shrubbery. "Is he still here, hiding in the bushes like the scoundrel he is?"

"Who?"

"Neville, of course!"

"He has gone inside."

"What did he want with you? Nothing improper, I hope?"

"He came as a representative of the king, who apparently wants me to become his mistress."

Lady Lippet gasped. "What did you reply?"

"I refused."

"Then you are a *fool*!" Lady Lippet cried angrily, her silly manner and mincing affectations suddenly gone. "It is a great compliment—and a great opportunity."

Was no one in London what they seemed? "I believe I must be a fool."

Lady Lippet frowned. "Your father never should have been allowed to raise you."

"At one time, I might have agreed with you. But you cannot disagree that the king's desire is immoral."

"I could understand if it were Belmaris or Cheddersby. But this is the king!"

"I do not want to share the king's bed."

"You stupid, stubborn girl!" Lady Lippet snarled, grabbing her arm so hard that Arabella cried out in pain. "You already have beauty and the admiration of many men. You do not have to settle for whoever will take you. Yet you are so vain you would deny your king?"

"It isn't vanity that makes me refuse him," Arabella retorted, twisting away. "What he asks is shameful, and I know it. You should, too." Her eyes narrowed as she rubbed her sore arm. "I wonder if the earl would share your opinion of the king's proposal."

Lady Lippet made a dismissive gesture. "It doesn't matter what the earl thinks. You are being given a chance for power and riches that most women only dream of. You will be intimate with the King of England!"

"Will the King of England love me?" Arabella demanded. "Will he care about me outside his bed?"

"He might."

"And if he doesn't, what will I have sacrificed for nothing?"

"But he is the king!" Lady Lippet repeated, as if that was all that mattered.

He is not Neville! Arabella wanted to shout.

Then she wanted to cry, because Neville didn't love her. Her emotions raw, she struggled for control. "Tell me, my lady, were you ever a man's mistress?"

"We are not speaking of me!"

"Were you Lord Barrsettshire's mistress?"

"No!"

As Arabella watched Lady Lippet's face, she had a moment of illumination. "But not for lack of trying."

Lady Lippet stared at her. "How did you—?" She paused, then straightened her shoulders. "I am going to find the earl. We are leaving!"

"For a man who professes to hate the court and everybody in it, he certainly finds ample excuse to spend time here. But then, I gather every aristocrat is a hypocrite," Arabella said coldly.

Lady Lippet's only answer was a disdainful

sniff as she turned on her high heel and marched away.

As Arabella watched her go, she resolved to ask Lord Barrsettshire to take her home to Grantham. He still denounced London frequently, although not with the ferocity of before, but hopefully he would not require much of an explanation.

If he did, she would tell him about the king.

She would not say one word about Neville.

"All alone, are we?"

Arabella raised her eyes to find herself facing the Duke of Buckingham.

Another figure moved in the shadows. Sedley, she thought. Like wolves, Villiers and his friends would travel in a pack.

Her stomach knotted with dread.

"We missed you at the game. So did the king."

"I did not want to play. Now, if you will excuse me—" she said, trying to move past him.

"She says she does not want to play," Villiers noted in a singsong voice.

"She says she does not want to play," Sedley repeated.

"She says she does not want to play," Buckhurst mocked.

"You do know *how* to play, do you not?" Villiers inquired. "We cover up your eyes and you must guess who we are." His expression grew into a lascivious leer and he lowered his voice. "By touch."

"Leave me alone!" she cried.

Suddenly, a hand grabbed her roughly from behind, hauling her backward. The duke came closer as she struggled in the man's arms and opened her mouth to call for help.

"Say a word and I'll slit your throat," the man holding her muttered.

It was Lord Buckhurst. She felt the prick of a knife in her neck.

"No need for blindman's buff, eh, my friends?" Villiers said as he boldly caressed her. "You really do have such a lot to learn, my dear, the first lesson being humility. You should not presume to think yourself too good for any man in this court. Not the king. Not me. Not any of my friends. Not even Belmaris or Cheddersby."

Other mirthless male laughter joined with the duke's. "The second lesson is of a more intimate nature."

Gripping her arms, Buckhurst shoved her forward.

Where were they taking her in this maze of buildings? Away from the Banqueting House, that much was certain.

What were they planning to do to her?

Arabella forced her mind away from that. Instead, she concentrated on thinking of a way to escape the strong hands of the man who held her.

A scent different from the heavy perfume of the man holding her reached her nostrils. The river. From there they could take her anywhere.

A figure stepped out of the shadows, and they halted.

"Wilmot?" the duke queried.

The man drew his sword. "Sadly for you, Wilmot is drunk as a drowned mouse."

Arabella nearly fainted with relief at the sound of Neville's voice.

"You should not let Wilmot listen when you make your sordid little plans. He has not nearly the capacity for keeping confidences as he does for wine, which is to say, none at all."

"Put up your sword," Villiers said with a joviality that was blatantly artificial. "There is no need for it."

"When I come upon a fellow and his knaves dragging off a defenseless woman, I must, perforce, think otherwise."

"We were not dragging her anywhere," Sedley protested.

Neville sauntered closer. "Why, good evening, Lady Arabella. I must say I am not at all impressed by the company you are keeping, and apparently in preference to me."

"I—" She felt the prick of the knife again.

Neville's eyes narrowed ever so slightly before he turned to Buckingham. "I must also confess myself surprised that she has fallen into some sort of stupor that renders her incapable of speech, although that might also explain her odd lapse of judgment."

"Let us pass, Farrington," Villiers commanded, drawing his sword, while Arabella looked on helplessly. She heard the soft sounds of swords being drawn from their sheaths.

"Go back to the king, since you are the new favorite," the duke finished.

"What, I?" Neville said, putting his free hand to his breast in a gesture of surprise. "It is Lady Arabella who is to be the favorite."

"Perhaps I should rephrase. You who are Lady Castlemaine's new favorite."

"Jealous?"

"Never of you."

"Alas, you quite crush me," Neville replied. "Nevertheless, I feel duty-bound to point out that the king will not be pleased when he hears that you attempted to abduct Lady Arabella for some end that is, I fear, only too easy to guess."

"I should think you, of all people, would be the last to champion her. Everyone knows about your father's plans."

"You really mustn't try to think, Villiers," Neville replied sympathetically. "You aren't good at it, as your conclusion demonstrates."

The Duke of Buckingham approached Neville warily, obviously mindful of the still-drawn sword.

"Why not join us in teaching Lady Arabella her place?" he suggested. "You like a choice bit of tail."

Neville raised his sword so that it nearly touched Villiers's chest. "Although you may take your pleasure any way you can, Buckingham, I like my women willing."

"You dare to criticize me?" the duke demanded.

"I do, and if you do not order Buckhurst to let her go, I will do my criticizing with my blade."

"We are three to your one, Farrington."

"Three to one. Not bad odds. Of course, one of you must keep hold of Lady Arabella, lest she scamper away, so that means two to one."

"Then two to one it shall be!" Buckingham cried as he lunged for Neville.

As he did so, Arabella sensed that Buckhurst had let down his guard and she quickly pulled away from him. Free, she lifted her heavy skirts and started to run away.

"Let her go!" she heard Buckingham shout.

She halted confusedly. Neville was in peril because of her. For whatever reasons, he had come to her aid.

She could not abandon him now. Yet what could she do? She had no weapon. She could try to find a guard, but who could say how long that might take in this place? By the time she returned with help, it could be too late.

Chewing her lip, she scanned the surrounding area, the sound of the sword fight and cursing clearly audible.

She spotted a piece of wood, dropped from a workman's bundle, perhaps. It was about two feet long, squared and looked like oak, the hardest wood in England.

She grabbed it up and went back the way she had come. Before she reached the fighting men, however, she heard the sound of running feet. She pressed back into a shadowed alcove, her legs weak and trembling as she tried to stay still. Three men ran by—Buckingham and the others.

Where was Neville? If anything had happened to him . . . !

Then Neville came charging down the narrow way, his expression so fierce that he was almost unrecognizable.

"Neville!" she cried out softly.

He halted. "Thank God!" he whispered.

She ran to him, throwing her arms around him and laying her face against his chest. His rapidly beating heart throbbed in her ear, and his chest rose and fell with his ragged breathing.

"Thank God and you." She pressed a grateful kiss to the base of his throat, and his breath caught.

He did not put his arm around her. Instead, he gently disengaged himself, and his gaze faltered as he sheathed his sword. "Did they hurt you?"

"No."

"I am very glad of that."

"I am very glad you appeared to help me," she said, her voice quivering slightly.

Neville began to examine his left sleeve.

"Are you wounded?" she asked, chastising herself for not thinking of this sooner. "Did they hurt you?"

"Only a ripped sleeve," he said, fingering the sides of a long tear.

"But you are not hurt?"

"No."

"You must be a fine swordsman," she said.

He left his sleeve alone and looked at her. "The day I cannot defeat those three in a sword fight is the day I retire to the country and take up sheep farming. Come, I'll take you back to the Banqueting House."

"I want to go home," she declared, sounding like a child even to herself. "I have no wish to see Buckingham or anyone else from the court tonight."

"What about Lady Lippet? Or my delightful father?"

"Your father is probably engrossed in cards. I would rather not have to listen to Lady Lippet for a while."

"I could escort you home, if you would like, and we can send word to my father that you have gone."

She nodded her agreement. "Please, Neville, take me home."

Chapter 17

"**W**e should find a boat at the Privy Stair," Neville said, trying to maintain his composure. "Buckingham had one waiting. Sadly, he will have to find another way home."

"How do you know all this?" Arabella asked as she followed him toward the river.

"I happened upon young Wilmot at a propitious moment," he replied, commanding himself not to notice the subtle scent of her perfume wafting over him. Or to remember how she had clung to him. He marveled, too, at her matter-of-fact questions and self-possession. Other women would be weeping and helpless with fright.

Yet despite her outward calm, he heard the slight tremor in her voice, and he wanted to kiss away her distress, yet feared that would be only self-indulgence.

276

"Apparently Buckingham saw me return without you from the garden and suspected you would be there alone," he explained. "He told Wilmot his plans, and the sot was too delighted by the fortuitous circumstance to keep quiet or to notice I was standing behind him."

"I am glad Wilmot wasn't with them."

"Do you think an additional sword would have enabled them to triumph over me?" Neville demanded as if mightily offended, and in truth, he was a little insulted by her evident doubt.

"It would have been four to one."

"The one was skilled and sober, and the four drunken louts."

"I did not mean to offend you. Indeed, I am very grateful that you are skilled and sober." She gave him a sidelong glance. "You *are* sober, my lord?"

"Much more so than Wilmot. He was too drunk to stand, which is why he remained behind."

"Then I thank heaven the king provides plenty of wine."

He chuckled softly and allowed his hand to squeeze hers a little tighter, telling himself that liberty was not too much to take, considering he had just saved her honor.

The scent of the river was strong now, and he could hear the wavelets striking the stone stairs. He was almost sorry they had reached the river, and now must leave the dark confines of the walk, but being alone with her was less important than getting her home to his father's house, where she would be safe.

And forever out of his reach.

As he had predicted, there was a boat waiting. It was powered by one man and illuminated by lamps in the bow and stern. There was a wide, cushioned seat in the bow, covered with a canopy, so that it was like a small tent.

The seat was as big as a bed, Neville realized, his rancor returning as he thought of what Buckingham might have done to Arabella there. The lone oarsman would never have dared to interfere.

"Ho, there, boatman!" he called out, leading her down the slick and slippery stairs and onto the boat.

The short, scruffy man in the stern of the small vessel scrutinized him. "Ye're not the duke."

"No. He has sent me on ahead with the lady." Before the boatman could say more, Neville handed him his last florin and gave him directions to the stairs closest to the earl's townhouse.

As the boatman unshipped his oars, Neville ducked beneath the tentlike canvas where Arabella waited.

"May I?" he asked before sitting beside her. She nodded her assent, but when he went to do so, the boat bumped into the steps, sending him tumbling into her lap. She gasped and shoved him away.

"I assure you, Arabella, I am not attempting to copy the duke," he said contritely as he moved, making the boat rock a little. He decided it might be wise to keep as much distance between them as possible.

"I know. I . . . I was startled."

"Still, you seem to have recovered quickly," he noted as the boat went out onto the river.

"Perhaps." She wrapped her arms about herself. "I wonder what your father will say?"

Neville wished he dared to take her into his embrace—only because he wanted to offer her warmth and comfort. "You intend to tell him?"

"Of course! Why not?"

"He will likely never let you leave the house again."

"I want to go home to Grantham anyway."

She sounded very determined, as if returning to Grantham were the dearest wish of her heart. He told himself he should be glad of that. "What of Cheddersby?"

"I'm sure he will recover from his infatuation."

"You think his feelings only infatuation?" A hope he should not have felt began to grow, as the embers of a blacksmith's forge glowed brighter from the bellows. He moved a little closer and caught the scent of her light perfume.

Roses. She smelled of roses. From now on, whenever he smelled roses, he would always think of her.

"Don't you?"

He smiled. "Yes. And I should warn you, Lady Arabella, that you are not the first to capture his heart."

"I thought not," she replied evenly.

"You do not sound particularly devastated. I thought you considered him a fine prospect."

"He is better than most," she replied, suddenly regarding him steadily with her disconcerting eyes. "What did the duke mean when he spoke of your father's plans?"

Neville considered what he should tell her.

If she went back to Grantham, this could well be the last time he would ever see her.

Why not tell her the truth? his heart prompted. *Allow yourself this one thing: that she knows how you saved your father from his own extravagant ways.*

For once, Neville listened to his heart. "When you marry, he is going to bequeath the bulk of his estate to you and your husband, whoever he may be."

She inched closer to him, her gaze anxiously searching his face. "That cannot be!"

He tried to ignore her tempting proximity. "I assure you, it is."

"He . . . he cannot. He would not."

"He ought not, but he can and he would, for he thinks I am going to waste it on gambling and drinking and women."

"Would you?"

"No," he replied with quiet gravity. "Not when I created it."

"*You* created it?"

"Yes." He was set on the path to the truth now; he would not turn back. "When I first arrived in London, I was immediately visited by my father's bankers. They brought me proof he had been overspending his income for some time and was deeply in debt. Whenever they wrote to him, he replied that they had to be mistaken. He said it was not possible that his funds could be so limited, or if it was, it was their fault and he would have them arrested. They wanted me to urge him to take out a mortgage on the estate before his creditors compelled them to declare him insolvent. I knew they must be speaking the truth about my father's reaction to their pleas." Neville's voice grew bitter. "He is the most stubborn man in England, and he would never believe his estate could be taken from him by bankers or creditors, seeing that he had held on to it during the Interregnum."

"He always said he was so respected that even Cromwell would not touch him," Arabella said.

Neville laughed sardonically as he watched other boats, lantern-lit, on the river. "That wasn't what kept him safe. Cromwell didn't know whether he was friend or foe. My father is very adept at grumbling and complaining in private, then being smooth as honey to a man's face. Did you not wonder why the king didn't look more annoyed when my father confronted him at the tennis court?"

Arabella stared at him in amazement.

"Nevertheless, I was still relieved he was not removed to the Tower, for there was no telling what he might actually say."

"So what did you say to the bankers?" she prompted.

"Something had to be done, or my father would be bankrupt. And I, too, of course," he added. "Therefore, I suggested to the bankers that they should loan me a sum of money. Fortunately, they agreed."

Arabella envisioned Neville attempting to persuade a group of middle-aged men to loan him money, his only collateral his own attributes. It was not so difficult to believe they would.

"Taking that capital, I . . . invested it."

"In what?"

His smile grew rueful. "Cards and dice, and some on a ship bound for the New World. Fortunately, all three ventures prospered, enough to stave off the creditors and pay some off completely. Then I invested in two more ships and a third that is still at sea. So you see, that part of my reputation—that I gamble—is not unearned."

"What of the other parts?"

"Lady Arabella, you astonish me. Would you know all my secrets?"

"I knew your bad reputation was undeserved!"

His low chuckle seemed to mock her. "That depends upon what one means by 'bad.'"

"Why did you not tell your father this?"

"Because he would have interfered, and that would have been disastrous for both of us. In the meantime, my father was secretly put on an allowance, and I was held accountable for the lack of forthcoming money."

He reclined upon the cushions and stared at the canvas covering. "I knew he would blame me and not question the bankers or his steward further."

"That is a great pity, Neville," she said softly. "You should have told him what you have done for him when he revealed his plans regarding his will to you."

"He most certainly would not have believed me. He would have claimed I was lying to protect my own interests."

"Perhaps he will listen to the bankers."

"Probably he would not believe them, either. He would still hate me. Yet he is no more of a

saint than I, Arabella, and very much a hypocrite. For all his criticism of me, did he ever tell
you of his mistresses? As strange as it may
seem, Lady Lippet was one of them.''

''She denies it.''

''She is a liar.''

Arabella found that easy to believe, too. ''She
thought I was a fool to refuse the king.''

''So would most people.''

Neville raised himself on his elbows to regard her, and she was surprised by the resolve
in his face. ''You will say nothing of what I
have told you to anyone.''

''But Neville—!''

He sat up and shifted his body close beside
her. Reaching out, he placed his finger against
her lips. ''Not a single word. To anybody.''

He did not move away immediately. Instead,
he traced her parted lips with his fingertip, his
own so very, very close. Instinctively, she
sucked his finger into her mouth.

With a low exhalation, he slowly withdrew
it.

''I'm . . . I'm sorry,'' she whispered, embarrassed and unsure what had prompted her to
do that.

''There is no need to apologize,'' he muttered, moving away from her. ''It is merely that
this time, Lady Arabella, *you* have surprised
me.''

The boat brushed up against a set of wide

stone steps going up from the river. "Here we are, then, sir," the boatman declared.

Arabella gasped. "We never sent word to your father or Lady Lippet that I was leaving!"

"They may not have missed you yet," Neville replied placatingly. "I will tell them where you are when I return to Whitehall."

She nodded her head in agreement.

Neville helped her onto the steps, then held her hand to lead her. He would rather have put his arm around her slender waist, but he was not sure he would have been able to prevent himself from kissing her if he had done that.

It was but a short distance from the Thames to the earl's townhouse, and neither spoke as they hurried through the dark, quiet streets.

When they reached the house, the door swung open to reveal Jarvis. When he spied Neville on the threshold, he stared with obvious surprise. "My lord!"

Neville stepped inside, followed by Arabella, and he closed the door. "I have brought Lady Arabella home. She was most anxious to leave Whitehall. Unfortunately, we could not find my father or Lady Lippet, so they may not yet be aware that she is safely home." He hesitated for a moment. "Go to the Banqueting House, Jarvis, find them and tell them she is here."

Arabella opened her mouth to protest. It would be wrong of Neville to stay. And yet she did not speak.

"What, my lord, now?" Jarvis asked.

"At once," Neville replied firmly.

"Who'll let them in if they've come away already?"

"I will man the door," Neville answered. "The earl is probably playing piquet in one of the rooms. Give him Lady Arabella's apologies and say she will explain in the morning. If you see Lady Lippet, tell her the same thing."

Although he made no attempt to hide his reluctance to leave or his surprise at Neville's presence, Jarvis obeyed.

"Won't you come into the withdrawing room?" Arabella asked when Jarvis had gone.

"Since it will be a little while yet before my father can arrive, I see no harm in it," Neville replied.

Only a little while, and then he would likely be parted from her forever.

A few moments more. That was all he wanted.

Once in the withdrawing room, Arabella lit a candle. The pool of golden light spread out around her and illuminated the room, which looked very different.

It took but a moment for him to realize why.

It was clean. From the hearth to the corners of the ceiling, everything had been dusted and polished and scrubbed until it was as if he was in another house.

"Someone has been busy," he remarked, trying to lessen the tension that seemed to suffuse the room like the candlelight. "I detect a Puritan's influence."

Ignoring his comment, she clasped her hands and regarded him steadily, agony in her eyes. "Neville, did you *ever* love me?"

She had not intended to ask that. She had not planned to say anything at all of feelings. Of emotions. Of love.

Yet she knew, as she stood there, that this might be the last time she would be with him, and she had to know if he had ever cared for her the way she had for him. The way she still did.

She waited for what seemed an eternity, trying to see his downcast face.

When he still did not answer, she told herself she had her answer and began to leave.

If he let her go now without a word, he would rue it for the rest of his life. "Arabella!" he whispered in a strangled voice as he raised his head to regard her with burning anguish. "I love you. I have loved you since that day in the garden. You have always had a special place in my heart, walled up and kept secret, but always, always there."

"Truly?" she asked, hope and joy dawning in her lovely eyes as she went slowly toward him.

It was as if he had been long absent from home and suddenly, in one great and glorious instant, had been transported there again, to find it eternal and permanent in a constantly changing world. "Truly."

"Why didn't you tell me before?"

He spread his hands in a gesture of hopelessness. "Because I do not deserve your love."

She halted before him. "Why not?"

"Because perhaps I am disgraceful blackguard, a sinful wretch, a wastrel—"

She shook her head. "A disgraceful blackguard or sinful wretch would not have left me that night when he could have so easily made love with me. A wastrel would not save his father's fortune in secret." She placed her hands on his shoulders and looked up into his doubtful, questioning face. "I see a man who is good and honorable. Who is worthy in every way of a woman's love. I see the man I love and will always love." She smiled gloriously. "No matter how much he tries to dissuade me."

"Arabella," he whispered doubtfully, as if he still could not quite believe her.

"I love you, Neville. I promise I will never stop loving you."

For so long he had told himself that love was a lie or a jest of God, if it existed at all.

But that was wrong. He loved Arabella, and she loved him. Now it no longer mattered what anyone else in the world thought of him, not even his father.

Complete at last, he drew her into his arms and kissed her.

Yearning for his touch, Arabella reveled in his burning, blatant desire, which set her own heart beating wildly.

Her hands moved up his strong back as she pressed against him, while his came to cradle her face.

"Oh, Arabella," he murmured as his lips dragged along her cheek toward her ear. "I want you so much."

"I want you, too," she whispered, arching, letting her head go back as he continued to trail his mouth lower and lower yet.

Then slowly, without a word of suggestion, their bodies commanding, they slowly knelt upon the floor.

Arabella did not consider where she was or the morality of what she was doing. She did not wonder what the earl or anyone else might think.

All she knew and cared about was this man whose kiss inflamed her and who returned her love. They would marry and be happy for the rest of their lives.

So she did not protest as his hands fumbled with the laces of her bodice, loosening them. When his hand slipped inside her gown, she welcomed his caress. Then he broke the kiss and she sighed as he gently eased her bodice down to expose her breasts to his lips and tongue.

She clutched at his shoulders and gasped. She had not known . . . She could never have guessed . . .

Wanting to pleasure him in some similar way, she opened her eyes, for a moment caught by the dark desire in his eyes as an animal can be startled by sudden sunlight.

And then she smiled, for this was right and good. Being here with him, feeling as she did, knowing that he loved her, too, could be no sin.

With trembling fingers, she pushed aside his jacket and opened his fine white shirt. His eyes closed as she ran her hands over the hard muscles of his chest. Learning from him, she leaned forward to gently tug his nipple into her mouth, letting her tongue swirl around the hardened nub of flesh.

Breathing rapidly, he groaned softly and clutched her upper arms as if he would collapse if he let go. "Don't stop," he sighed as she trailed her lips across his chest to capture the other nipple. "Oh, sweet heaven, don't stop."

"Only for this," she whispered. And she lifted her face to kiss him deeply.

As they kissed, he sloughed off his jacket. Turning away for a moment, he quickly bundled it up and laid it beside him. Then, taking her by the shoulders, he laid her down so that his jacket became her pillow.

She boldly pulled him down beside her for another passionate kiss. Desire burned hot and eager in her, inflamed even more as he began to stroke and caress her, his hands moving over her as if she were made of some soft and valuable material, velvet or satin or silk.

At his gentle prodding, she parted her legs, and he rolled so that his body was over her, his legs between hers. His hands continued their exciting, maddening exploration of her body while his mouth again took possession of hers.

Another instinct came into play, one of rhythm called forth by the hot blood throbbing through her veins. She began to move her hips to this primitive beat, not knowing or caring why or wanting to stop it.

Slowly, his lips again parted from hers to slide along her chin and the tender flesh of her neck, past her collarbone to her naked breasts.

She panted softly, awash with the sensation of his tongue flicking across her pebbled nipples while his hand made leisurely progress along her leg, pushing her skirt upward.

He stopped where the throbbing was most intense, resting his hand for a moment before pressing gently, that slight and subtle motion making her cry out softly.

His hand left her body and her eyes flew

open, for she felt suddenly abandoned.

She would not be alone or lonely ever again.

Emboldened by her desire, she ran her hands over his body. He caught his lip with his teeth and his eyes shut tight as she felt lower until she found what she sought.

Now it was his turn to be stroked and caressed. She watched his face, saw the growing tension there, matching the building need within her.

"I am yours, Neville," she whispered. "I will be yours forever."

His eyes opened, his passionate gaze intense as, with a low growl, he tore at her drawers, ripping the thin fabric from her body.

She didn't care, for with equally eager fingers she struggled to undo his breeches.

In another moment, he was free. Placing both hands beside her and raising himself, never taking his dark piercing gaze from her face, he slowly pushed inside her.

There was one moment of doubt. One instant of knowledge that they were not married. That this union would be condemned in the eyes of God and man.

One moment, and then it was gone, because she was his and he was hers, and they must join completely.

Her rhythm became his as their hips moved in perfect unison. Their breathing, too, was synchronized as with each passing moment, the desire and need and tension built in glorious agony.

And then, as he uttered a strangled cry, the tension within her shattered as a stone shatters the calm surface of a still pool, sending wave after wave to the farthest edge.

"Good God!" Lord Barrsettshire cried.

Chapter 18

A rabella jerked her head around to stare at the enraged man standing in the doorway, hands clutching the sides of the frame.

Lady Lippet was behind the red-faced nobleman, staring open-mouthed like a fish in Billingsgate market.

At once, Neville withdrew. Fumbling with the ties of his breeches, he rose swiftly.

The realization of what she had just done assailing her, Arabella quickly pulled her bodice back into place with one hand and shoved her raised skirt down with the other.

"I . . . I believe I shall go home," Lady Lippet mumbled through the handkerchief she pressed to her mouth, as if she needed to block the stench of sin.

"By all means, please go," Neville agreed with iron in his words. "Jarvis, my father and

I will have no more need of you, so you may show Lady Lippet out.''

Jarvis waited for Lady Lippet to exit, then followed her, closing the door behind him.

''You!'' the earl roared, glaring at his son. ''You . . . you despoiler of women! How could you?''

Arabella waited with bated breath for Neville to explain that there was no need for such wrath, to tell the earl that although what they had done was wrong and a sin, there was no cause for such animosity, because they would be married.

Neville slowly turned to look at her.

Say it, she urged silently. *Say you love me. Say we will be married.*

The silence seemed to stretch forever.

Neville raised one quizzical eyebrow and looked at his father while he calmly finished tying his breeches.

''How could I?'' he repeated with a sardonic little smile. ''It was quite easy, really.''

Arabella felt as if Neville had knocked her to the ground.

''She is ruined!'' the earl roared. ''Utterly ruined! Though you are my son, I should kill you for what you've done!''

Arabella got slowly to her feet, shame and dismay warring within her.

Quite easy. Making love with her was quite

easy, and she had quite easily let him.

She had made love to a man to whom she was not married or even formally betrothed. She had told him how she felt and he had said he loved her, yet now he stood there as if what they had done was nothing to him at all.

"I am to blame for her ruin, am I?" Neville inquired.

"Who else?" the earl demanded. "I see no other man in this room."

"Did it not occur to you, Father, that she could be responsible? That she might have tempted me into sin?"

"Me?" Arabella gasped. "Tempt you?"

"Don't be ridiculous!" Lord Barrsettshire bellowed.

"You still think her a moral, virtuous woman deserving of my inheritance?"

Neville raised an eyebrow as he slowly turned to regard her. "Fortunately, I have just proved that she is no more virtuous than I. I'faith, considering she is a woman, her sin is all the greater, is it not?"

The import of Neville's words struck Arabella like another blow.

"You seduced me only to prove that I am not worthy of your father's trust?" she whispered. "You would sink that low?"

She had made the most horrendous, shameful mistake of her life. She had believed Neville

Farrington's smooth words and apparent sincerity.

She had been a lustful, naive fool, a sinner unable to resist temptation, who should have known better than to trust in men's words or smiles or kisses.

Even his.

Especially his.

Neville didn't meet her gaze.

He would not look at her anymore.

She had not said one word in his defense, even though she had been as eager to make love as he. After all her declarations of love, she had not refuted the accusation that he had ruthlessly seduced her. She had not accepted any responsibility for what they *both* had done. She would let him take all the blame.

What kind of love was that, that would abandon him to his father's poor opinion?

As his mother had all those years ago.

"Good God, you are beyond redemption!" his father growled. "I am ashamed to be your father!'

Neville regarded him as he might a flea he had picked off his clothing. "I have merely done what I set out to do. I have proved that even Lady Arabella is capable of sin, like any other mortal, and so not worthy to usurp my inheritance."

"I do not want your inheritance!"

"You miscalculated, boy!" his father replied,

ignoring her. "You have only proved your complete unworthiness."

"She sinned as much as I"

"She is but a weak woman."

"I *was* weak," Arabella began, "but I—"

"The same could be said of Eve, and God made no allowance for her weakness, as you would make no allowance for mine," Neville retorted.

"Don't you dare to speak of the Bible to me!" the earl snarled. "It is a wonder you are not struck dead!"

"That would please you, wouldn't it? Your rogue of a son conveniently dead in an instant. But then who would look after your money, Father? You would be bankrupt in a year!"

"You've gone mad! Since when have you done anything but spend my money?"

"Since I first arrived in London and your bankers came to see me. Tell me, Father, did you not find it odd that after years of pestering you regarding your debts and loans, they suddenly fell silent?"

"They understood that I was not to be bothered with such minor irritations. There was no need for me to know every small detail of the business of my estate."

"You know *nothing* of the business of your estate, and you never have, because you prefer to ignore it. If I had not taken charge, you would be penniless now."

"That's a lie!"

"Is it? Ask Mr. Pettigrew. Or Mr. Hutchins. They can confirm all this."

"Do you mean to tell me they have given you free rein with my money? I will have their heads on London Bridge if that is true!"

Neville ground his teeth in frustration. It was useless. His father would never believe he owed his prosperity to his son. He was glad Arabella was here, so that she would see why he had kept silent—

She was gone. At some point when he had been arguing with his father, she had left the room.

Just as his mother had left him without a word of farewell.

Convinced that love was nothing but a delusion after all, he strode to the door, threw it open and marched out, determined never to set foot there again.

The next morning, Arabella sat alone in her bedchamber, staring out the window as she had for the whole of the night. Before dawn a thick fog had drifted up from the Thames, so that all she could see was a soft, dull gray beyond the droplets on the panes of glass.

Her eyes burning, she twisted a handkerchief in her fingers and thought that soon she would begin to pack. Soon, when she was in command of herself again. When she could stop thinking of her terrible, shameful mistake and the horrible argument she had not been able to endure.

When she could think of Neville Farrington without feeling like a naive simpleton. When the tears would finally come to wash away her pain.

There was a soft tapping at the door. Jarvis, she assumed, and bade him enter.

She looked up when the door opened, to see Lady Lippet standing on the threshold.

She was plainly dressed, her large, black hat and black gown trimmed with only a few inches of scarlet ribbon. She wore little powder and not a single patch.

She looked as if she might be in mourning.

"May I, my dear?" she asked, her sepulchral tone matching her clothing.

"If you wish," Arabella replied, rising and gesturing at her vacated chair.

While Lady Lippet sat and arranged her skirts, Arabella inwardly prepared herself for the denunciations to come, which she fully deserved.

"You look so tired!"

"I did not sleep last night."

"No, no, of course not. Such a to-do! I'm afraid we all got rather upset."

With good cause. "Yes, we did."

Lady Lippet leaned closer, a conspiratorial

look on her face. "There is no use in weeping over it."

"I have not."

"No, no, I can see that you haven't," Lady Lippet replied, adjusting her hat and clearing her throat delicately. "So now you must carry on as best you can. This business will not matter to certain people. Certain important people. Certain *royal* people."

Arabella folded her arms over her chest. "I want to go home to Grantham."

"Oh." Lady Lippet frowned. "This is not a hopeless tragedy, my dear. You are not the first woman to find her affections misplaced, you know." The older woman's eyes turned hard and cold as marble. "We give our love, and it renders us weak and capable of being used and discarded. You have little cause to think yourself more ill used than most, for you are luckier than most. You have beauty. If you feel the need for pity, save it for women who have none."

Again Arabella heard that note of bitterness, but a remnant of her pride made her speak. "I did not ask to be beautiful."

Lady Lippet smiled sympathetically. "No, no, of course not. And fortunately, the king will not mind if you are ... experienced. So, you see, there is no need for you to go running back to Grantham."

"I want to go home, Lady Lippet."

"That would be the very worst thing to do!"

"I do not think so."

"Arabella, in London what you have done is not the sin it is in Grantham," Lady Lippet explained, as if Arabella was a particularly dim scholar. "And if you run away, who has won then?"

"This is not a game to me, my lady," Arabella replied. "I have no wish to stay in London. I have my inheritance. That is more than enough to live on."

"Do you?" Lady Lippet asked pointedly.

"What do you mean? The earl told me my father bequeathed me ten thousand pounds."

Lady Lippet was all pity and commiseration as she slowly shook her head. "He told you that—and me and Sir Thomas and everyone else he met in London—to attract the right sort of husband. But your father left all that he had to the church."

"That cannot be!"

If she had money, she could manage, perhaps even be able to overcome the scandal, if she was generous enough. But penniless? Or beholden to the earl, whose son had ruined her? The earl should have protected her better from Buckingham and the king and Neville, too.

Lady Lippet's smile grew. "So you see, my dear, the king's offer is most fortuitous."

"But my lack of fortune would surely have

been discovered when it came time for a marriage settlement to be drawn up."

"Well, my dear, Wattles planned to use some of his own money and claim all the rest was in investments. Once you were married, he would have explained to your husband that the dowry wasn't terribly important, because the earl was bequeathing him a fortune."

"That fortune should be Neville's."

"To fritter away? Oh, no. Wattles is quite right, you know. He is the wastrel son of a selfish, spoiled mother. Neville would simply spend it all to amuse himself."

Arabella heard the outer door open downstairs and then her guardian's familiar, if slightly muted, voice. At once she hurried to the hall.

"Arabella!" Lady Lippet called after her, but she did not stop.

She ran down the steps and into the withdrawing room, slamming the door behind her as she confronted the earl. "My lord, is it true that I have no inheritance from my father?"

"Where did you hear that?" he demanded.

"Lady Lippet has just told me."

The earl flushed. "She should not have. Is she still here? Where the devil is she?"

Arabella would not be distracted. "Is it true?"

"Your father, good man though he may have

been in some respects, was a fool with his money."

"If he was, he was not the only one."

"What does that mean?"

"Did my father leave his money to the church?"

"Yes," he replied with obvious reluctance.

"Nothing at all for me?"

"He left you a little money."

"How much?"

He cleared his throat. "You've spent it."

"*I? I* have spent it? On what?"

"The gowns, the maid, the ribbons."

"Because I thought I had ten thousand pounds! Oh, how could you have lied to me like that?" Her eyes narrowed accusingly. "Indeed, you are not like your son, for at least he saved your fortune and did not encourage someone in his care to spend theirs!"

"He did not save my fortune! That is a lie, and he has persuaded the bankers to lie, too! He can twist people around his fingers like yarn, as you should know! His mother was the same." He struck his hands together, as if his anger must find physical release. "I have been seriously deceived in my bankers—but no more! They will not get another penny out of me!"

"You have been to see them?"

"Of course! Neville told me some nonsense last night about saving my estate. I've never heard anything more ridiculous! He lives to spend my money!"

"What did they say? Are you in serious arrears because of your son?"

"That is not the point! They did not have my permission to give Neville anything." He scowled darkly. "Are you some kind of inquisitor that you would question me in this manner? I think not!"

She flushed but would not be silenced. "He told me that when he arrived in London, you were nearly bankrupt. That your bankers were suggesting mortgages and retrenchment. Is that so?"

"They made a few suggestions, but I—"

"Then the suggestions stopped?"

"Maybe they learned how to do their job better."

"Or perhaps because it was no longer necessary. Is it so impossible that Neville could and would do everything in his power to keep you solvent?"

"If I were bankrupt, he would have nothing, too."

"He could marry well," she said, and not without some bitterness.

The earl began to pace. "He is a spendthrift. A wastrel. All of London knows of his decadent habits. He would not help me unless there was gain in it for himself. He hates me." He halted and turned a suspicious eye on her.

"Why do you now rush to his defense, after what he has done to you?"

Arabella straightened her shoulders. "I only seek to know the truth. Can't you see that if he has saved your fortune, it gives him more cause to want to destroy me? I'faith, my lord, if he didn't hate you before that, he would have hated you after hearing of your plan, and he would despise me, too."

"If I had not said what I did, you would not have had a chance of catching a courtier."

"Can you not understand, my lord?" she demanded. "I did not *want* a courtier. I wanted a man who loved me! Now no honorable man will have me after my disgrace."

The earl seemed to shrink a little. "I have done nothing wrong. He can't have saved my fortune."

"Why do you find this so hard to believe? Why do you hate him so?"

"Because he is just like his mother! Everything he does reminds me of her. His looks, his expressions, his words—I can scarce stand to be in the same room with him. I tried to curb the qualities in him that were like her, but I might as well have tried to hold back a flood or stop the sun from rising."

"No, he is not like anyone else in the world. And she abandoned him, too, my lord."

"I know that better than you!"

"You loved her very much, didn't you?" Arabella asked after a moment of heavy silence.

The earl stared at her, then shook his head. "No, I did not."

"Why else would you hate her so when she betrayed you? And I think you feared that Neville would betray you, too. Better to force him away and save yourself from heartache."

The old man felt for a chair and sat heavily.

"He would have offered you comfort if you had not driven him away. Yet despite all this, he was your dutiful son, for when he found out how things were, he did not leave you to suffer deprivation. Indeed, my lord, he was a better son than you a father."

"You speak your mind very decidedly for a woman, and a young one at that. Although he has stolen your honor, you defend him."

"Would you tell me I am wrong?"

The earl's gaze faltered, and suddenly, he seemed very old and very tired. "You loved him, as I loved his mother," he muttered.

"Yes, I loved him. I trusted him. But if I have cause for regret, it is because *I* was weak and immoral. He could not have shamed me if I had not chosen to be with him. I must bear responsibility for my act, and so I will. I shall make my own way in the world without you or your son."

"Surely you cannot be serious!"

"I have never been more so." *Except when I told Neville I loved him.*

"As your guardian, I forbid it!"

"As my guardian, you have failed," she said bitterly. "As I have. Do not trouble yourself over my fate, my lord. I choose it, just as I chose to be with your son."

"You cannot live on your own! It would be scandalous!"

She turned to leave the room. "I did not say I would be living on my own."

She opened the door, to find Lady Lippet anxiously pacing outside it.

"Nettie, talk to this chit!" Lord Barrsettshire commanded from the withdrawing room. "She says she will live alone in London."

"Utter nonsense! You must both stay here, at least for the present," Lady Lippet said. "Sit down, the pair of you. I declare I am disgusted with you both."

"I don't know what the world is coming to," the earl snarled, "or women, for that matter. How can she stay here? She is disgraced, thanks to my son, but no one in Grantham need know—"

"Sit *down*, Wattles!"

The earl grudgingly did as he was bid.

"If you will pardon me, Lady Lippet—" Arabella began.

"No, I don't pardon you," the older woman said. "Sit!"

Arabella felt she had no choice but to obey or else the whole household would hear them.

She closed the door firmly before taking a seat.

"So, Wattles, you think she should go back to Grantham in disgrace?"

"Yes."

"I thought you wanted her to marry a courtier. How will she be able to do that in Grantham?"

The earl continued to scowl.

"Now, Wattles, we have got to think of Arabella's future. I think perhaps the best thing would be for her to come and stay with me."

"With you?" the earl demanded.

Arabella did not feel any more pleased with this plan than he did.

Lady Lippet nodded and fixed a steady gaze on the earl. "She should be seen to be parted from you and therefore from your son. Otherwise, people might think you were encouraging Neville with an eye to obtaining Arabella's inheritance."

"Good God, I had not thought of that."

"I told you spreading that tale was a mistake."

"But I don't have an inheritance," Arabella observed.

"This is not the time to tell people!" Lady Lippet cried. "Good heavens, most certainly not the time."

"I should continue living this lie, then?"

"Don't be such a little fool! Of course you must. And you must come home with me directly. Then tonight, we shall go to Whitehall just as if nothing at all had happened."

"I will not."

Lady Lippet clenched her teeth. "You must, or Neville will have everything *his* way. He can say what he will, and there will be no one there to contradict him."

"Nettie, I think we should go back to Grantham."

"*You* think," Lady Lippet said sarcastically. "It is your thinking that has got us all into this mess."

The earl rose in outraged majesty. "This is *my* house, and I will not be spoken to in such a manner."

"Please, do not quarrel!" Arabella exclaimed, tired of the bickering. Tired of everything.

"I will not be party to anything dishonorable," the earl warned.

"Wattles, stop being so selfish."

"Selfish? If that is how you are going to speak to me, there is the door."

Lady Lippet rose haughtily. "You are the most stubborn man I have ever met. If Arabella stays with you, she *will* be ruined. Come along, my dear, we are leaving."

"Arabella, if you leave this house now, don't think you can come back."

Arabella regarded her former guardian coldly. "I don't want to come back. Do for me as you did for your son. Send my things to my new abode."

Then she left the earl standing alone in his withdrawing room and followed Lady Lippet out the door.

With a beaming smile on her homely face, Lady Lippet watched as Arabella sat down on the cushioned seat opposite her in her coach. "I am so glad you are being sensible about this, my dear. There is no reason at all to treat last night's adventure as the end of the world. I assure you, it is not."

Lady Lippet might believe that, Arabella thought as the coach lurched into motion, but her world, the world she knew and the world she had dreamed of with Neville, was completely destroyed.

She could only hope she had the courage to make her way in a new one and forget everything about honor and morality she had ever been taught.

And she would pray that God would forgive her for being so weak that even now, she loved the man who had so callously seduced her.

Chapter 19

‹‹❧❧››

"Neville? Neville, is that you?"
Neville raised his head about five inches off the battered table in the tavern and squinted his bleary eyes as he tried to see who dared disturb him. Three empty bottles of sack blocked his view, and he slowly shoved them out of his way. One fell to the ground and shattered, making him wince. His reaction had nothing to do with the loss of the bottle; the sound made his head ache more.

Or maybe it was the sunlight streaming in through the window behind him.

He decided he didn't care who was calling him, so he laid his head down on his arms again and mumbled, "Go away."

"Zounds, it *is* Neville!" Richard declared incredulously. "I thought that red-haired Irishman was seeing things."

"Now we know he's not dead in an alley, so

312

let's do as he says and leave him alone," Foz said nervously.

"I don't think leaving him here, tempting though it may be, would be a wise idea," Richard said, surveying the wharf-side tavern filled with some of the most unsavory characters Richard had ever seen—and he had seen many in his time. "Half these men look as if they would gladly do murder for his jacket."

"I suppose you're right," Foz replied. "For old times' sake, we should assist him."

"Help me get him up."

Richard came around the table while Foz went to Neville's other side. They put their shoulders under Neville's arms and hauled him to his feet.

"I said go away!" Neville growled. "I wanna stay here. More wine!"

"Zounds, Neville, what's got into you?" Richard demanded. "How long have you been here?"

"What's got into me?" he slurred, lifting his head as if it weighed a hundred pounds. "Nothing's got into me—but I got into her!" He grinned stupidly. "That's right! You both owe me fifty pounds!"

Richard and Foz looked at each other.

"I had her last night. The virtuous angel. And it was angelic—but never mind about that. I want my hundred pounds."

"Then you must come with us to get it," Richard said grimly.

"Oh?" He frowned petulantly. "Do you want to ask her? Very well, then, we shall. But let's have a little drink first, shall we? A toast to the fair Arabella—may she rot!"

"Neville!" Foz cried, aghast.

"Sorry, sorry, old son," he apologized. "I forgot you want to marry her."

" 'Ere, now, then!" His hands on his hips, a heavy man in an apron as filthy as his face blocked their progress. "What's all this, eh?"

"We are taking my friend home," Richard replied evenly.

"He hasn't paid up."

"If you are the proprietor, my good man, I shall be happy to—" Foz muttered, reaching for his purse while still trying to help hold up Neville. "How much does he owe?"

"Two guineas."

"You must be mistaken," Richard said.

"Oh, beware the fair Arabella, she's after any young fella!" Neville caroled drunkenly.

"It doesn't matter, Richard," Foz hastened to say, ignoring Neville's tuneless effort. "I've got two guineas."

"If all we're paying for is those three bottles, Neville cannot owe two guineas."

"She'll get you stiff, that little miss," Neville warbled. "Oooooh!"

"I says he owes two guineas."

"Sorry, Foz," Richard suddenly declared, pushing all Neville's weight onto Foz.

In the next instant, Richard's sword was at the tavern-keeper's throat.

Those patrons who had been watching the confrontation suddenly seemed mindful of their own concerns.

"Odd's bodikins!" Foz cried as he staggered and tried to hold Neville.

His hat and wig slipped seriously askew, almost covering his eyes, but he could not push them back without letting go of Neville.

Who finished his song with a loud, maniacal flourish. "Beware the fair Aaa-raaa-bella!"

"It would be rather unwise of you to persist," Richard remarked, ignoring everything except the man in front of him. "Two shillings is more like the true price, is it not?"

His eyes on the sword blade, the man nodded.

"Foz, give the man two shillings."

"I—I can't," Foz panted. "He'll fall."

"Oh, no, I won't!" Neville declared. "I'll never fall in love. She can try all she wants with her smiles and kisses and sweet body, but I won't."

"Hush, Neville!" Foz urged, struggling to hold him upright.

With a flick of his sword, Richard cut the strings holding Foz's purse to his belt. When it hit the ground with a metallic clink, every eye in the tavern turned to them, drawn to the sound as a hawk to the lure.

Smiling, Richard sheathed his sword, scooped up the purse and found two shillings. He tossed them into the damp, filthy sawdust on the floor.

"There you are, my good man." He returned to Neville's other side. "Come, Foz, let us away. The stench in here is making my eyes water."

Foz sighed with relief as his burden grew lighter.

"Why, Richard, what an unexpected pleasure!" Neville cried, as if he had only just arrived. "Are you joining me for a drink?"

"Be quiet and come with us," Richard muttered, and together the three men made their way to the door.

Once out of the fetid atmosphere of the tavern, Neville seemed to revive a little. "Where are we going?"

"We'll take you to my lodgings, where you can sleep this off," Richard said.

"I don't want to sleep," Neville complained drowsily. "I want to have another drink. A celebratory dram." He raised his hand in a mockery of his usual elegant grace. "A salute to my conquest, and you both must join me."

Richard glanced at Foz and saw the concern on his friend's face. "He's too drunk to know what he's saying."

"I hope so," Foz said breathlessly. "Can we not get a coach?"

"Excellent suggestion."

They half carried, half dragged Neville to a wider thoroughfare and soon caught sight of a hackney coach. In another few moments, they had managed to get Neville inside. Before they had even a chance to sit down, he was snoring.

"Odd's bodikins," Foz said with a sigh as he straightened his hat and wig. "I do not know whether it was a lucky circumstance that brought Jarvis to us or not."

"We couldn't leave him with those cut-throats."

"No, no, I suppose not."

"Foz!"

"Well," Foz answered with a peevish pout, "you heard what he said about Lady Arabella. If it's not true, it was very insulting, and if it is true . . . Do you suppose it's true?"

"I hardly know what to think," Richard answered honestly. "But it could only be wishful thinking, you know," he continued when he saw Foz's woebegone expression. "Unfortunately, we shall have to wait awhile before he can tell us the truth."

"What do you mean by disturbing me at this ungodly hour?" the Duke of Buckingham demanded of his manservant from the depths of his large and ornately gilded bed.

Every article of the furnishings in the duke's large bedchamber was likewise ornate and gilded and upholstered in deep-red velvet. An expensive carpet covered the floor of inlaid wood, and the draperies at the tall windows were of thick, red silk brocade. At present, they were shut, keeping out the bright sunlight of midmorning and muffling the sounds of the city.

"It is nearly noon, Your Grace," the manservant noted calmly, quite used to his master's arrogant responses, especially when the duke had spent the night without companionship of one sort.

Or another.

"As I said, how dare you disturb me so early!"

"If Your Grace pleases, Sir Charles is here, and Lord Buckhurst."

"Your Grace doesn't please to see them. They had the audacity to win two hundred pounds from me last night. Tell them I am indisposed."

The servant nodded. "Your Grace, there is also a lady who wishes to speak with you."

The duke shifted a little. "A lady? What lady?"

"She gives her name as Lady Lippet."

"Tell her I'm indisposed, too."

"She seems most agitated, Your Grace, and says she will not leave until you see her."

"Very well, I'll see her. Send her in."

The servant bowed and left the room.

The duke got out of his bed and pulled on his robe. He put on his wig and sat in his chair, his manner not unlike that of a king upon his throne, as the horribly ugly Lady Lippet came charging into his bedchamber as if it were a public hall. She wore a ghastly black gown that made her look like an old buzzard.

"Well, this is a pretty to-do!" she declared.

"My lady?"

"I gave you every opportunity!" she cried, punctuating her exclamations with a jab of her bony finger in his general direction. "Every opportunity. And you failed! How many times did I leave her alone—and where were you? Off gambling or drinking, no doubt! Well, I will have my money, even if Neville Farrington has had her first!"

Villiers' hands clasped the slender arm of his chair so tightly that his knuckles went white. "What do you mean?"

"You know very well! He's made love to her!"

"How do you know this?"

"I saw them with my own eyes. They did it right in the earl's withdrawing room! How could you fail, after all I did to help you?"

The duke rose from his chair. "Woman, have you forgotten to whom you are speaking?"

Lady Lippet blinked and colored.

The duke gestured to another chair and resumed his seat. "If you want your money, you will sit."

Chastised, Lady Lippet did as he commanded, then leaned forward. "I thought the earl was going to fall into a fit when he saw them."

"Will he make them marry?"

Lady Lippet shook her head. "No. Neville's completely estranged from his father now, I am pleased to say. Which is just what he deserves!"

"Spare me your condemnations of sons of your former rivals. What does Lord Barrsettshire intend to do? Spirit his dishonored ward back to the country in disgrace?"

"Of course not! Am I a fool?"

The duke didn't answer.

"The earl suggested it, and Arabella wanted to go, but it is not to be. And," she added triumphantly, "Arabella has left the earl's protection and come to stay with me."

"For how long?"

"I think that depends on you, Your Grace, and what offers you care to make."

"I dare say you will expect a reward for that, too."

Lady Lippet smiled. "Now that Arabella is a fallen angel, she will not be so stubbornly high-minded, and so you may seize your chance."

"Her virginity was part of her allure," he mused.

Lady Lippet's lip curled. "But she is still so very beautiful, so now I will have my money."

The duke smiled coldly. "Money? What money?"

Lady Lippet's face flushed. "The two hundred pounds you offered me if I would look the other way."

"And so you did. But it was Neville who took advantage of your willing blindness, not me. Ask him for the two hundred pounds."

"You gave me your word!"

"How much did Neville bribe you to keep the earl away last night?"

"Nothing! You know he doesn't have any money."

"I don't believe you—and neither will any of my friends. Either he paid for your cooperation, or you have been sorrowfully remiss in your responsibility toward your young charge, as some have already noted.

"When they hear of this, and they will," he added with another cold grin, "they will either fault you or think you conspired with Farrington."

"Everyone knows I would never do such a thing!"

He raised his eyebrows.

"Not for him! Not for *her* son! I would

sooner hang myself. And how can they fault me? I am no relation to her!"

"You were seen to be acting as her chaperon. Of course, I have considerable influence of my own, and I could always champion you—if Arabella Martin comes willingly to my bed. Otherwise, Lady Lippet, you would be wise to plead illness and retire to the country."

The older woman turned pale. "You rogue! After all I've done for you—"

"A rogue who will always survive, Lady Lippet, no matter how many men try to bring me down. If you wish to retain my good regard, you will encourage Arabella to look upon me with favor. Otherwise . . ."

He didn't have to finish his threat.

Her limbs trembling as if she had been stricken with palsy, Lady Lippet got to her feet. "Very well, Your Grace, I shall do my best, but you may have to wait your turn to get between those lovely young legs—until the king has had his pleasure of her!"

With that, she marched from the room with as much dignity as she could muster, hating him and all men.

Because not a one of them had ever looked on her with desire.

Neville groaned softly, rolled on his side and opened his eyes.

His head ached and his mouth was as dry as

chaff. He had never felt worse. Yet it was not the wine he had imbibed that made him feel so terrible.

He slowly realized he was in Richard's lodgings. He recognized the battered table covered with bits of old candle wax near the foot of the bed. One was lit now, for it appeared to be twilight outside. Or maybe it was merely foggy.

How many hours had they spent talking here in the past? And drinking? And wenching?

Before a woman came between them.

Then he encountered the severe, condemning gaze of Richard himself, sitting on a chair beside the bed.

Neville closed his eyes and shifted onto his back. He had seen enough condemnation in a person's eyes to last him a lifetime.

"Is it true?" Richard demanded.

Neville threw his arm over his eyes. "Go away and leave me in peace."

"Is it true? Did you seduce Lady Arabella?"

Of all subjects, he wanted to avoid this one the most. "Who says I did?"

"You did," came the harsh response. "I am hoping you were too drunk to be speaking the truth."

"You are wise to be doubtful, for I am a great liar. Ask my father and the lady if you would like confirmation of that fact."

"Neville," Richard said, suddenly lunging from his chair to grab his shoulder so roughly that Neville feared he intended to drag him from the bed. *"Did you seduce her?"*

Neville regarded the man who had been his friend since his first days in London. That friendship was surely lost to him now.

But what was that compared to the king's ire when he discovered what Neville had done? He would probably be thrown into the Tower; without doubt, he would be exiled from court, left to fend for himself. "You owe me fifty pounds."

Richard leaped to his feet, scowling darkly. "A pox on you, Farrington!"

Neville put his feet on the floor and heaved himself upright. "I'm leaving. Send me the money later. And tell Foz, too. If it is any comfort to you, I will need the winnings because, despite the evidence of his own eyes, my father will give Arabella my inheritance yet."

"We would have done better to leave you in that filthy tavern to get your throat slit."

"I did not ask you for any assistance," Neville replied as he began to straighten his disheveled clothing. "Nor do I regret what I did," he lied. "There was the glory of being her first."

"You disgusting scoundrel!"

"Oh, how you hurt me!" Neville replied sardonically. "As if I have not been called that a hundred times. Nay, a thousand! And a wastrel and lecher and gamester, too." He suddenly grabbed his friend's jabot and pulled him close. "Will you next tell me I am like my mother?"

"Who would you say you are like?" Richard retorted, slapping his hand away. "Buckingham, perhaps? He would be as proud as you are for what you've done. I suppose you bragged of it in that tavern and every place else you went last night. By now, you and your conquest will be quite famous, and Arabella's reputation utterly destroyed."

Neville shoved Richard away. "You are angry only because I beat you to her!" He spotted the pile of papers on Richard's writing desk. "Odes to her beauty, no doubt," he sneered, grabbing the top one. His smile grew as he read it. "*The Virtuous Lady: A Tragedy of Love.* What drivel is this?"

"Drivel I doubt you would ever understand," Richard said, snatching the paper away.

"She inspired you, eh?"

They heard a commotion on the stairs, a sound Neville knew heralded Foz's approach.

Foz, who wanted to marry Arabella.

Then the hapless Foz appeared on the threshold, his gaze darting between the two men. "It's true what he said. About last night. I went to his father's house and—"

"Did *she* tell you?" Neville demanded.

Foz shook his head. "Jarvis. Everyone in the household knows about it."

"How much did that information cost you?" Neville asked sarcastically.

His foolish friend regarded him not with anger or hatred but a sort of weary sorrow that was anything but foolish.

Neville blushed, then commanded himself not to be such an idiot. She was as much to blame for what had happened as he, deny it though she might. "And has my father and his delicious ward gone scurrying back to Grantham?"

"No, they have not. Well, not yet. That is, the earl is planning to go home. There was an argument, and Arabella has left the house."

"Left the house?" Neville repeated, taken aback. "Where did she go?"

Who did she know in London that she could go to for help and comfort?

"She's going to stay at Lady Lippet's, Jarvis said."

Neville stared at him. Then he stumbled out the door.

Lady Lippet started and turned from her mirror as someone abruptly entered her boudoir without so much as a knock. "Neville!" she cried, falling back in her chair with surprise.

"Where is she?" he demanded, his eyes

bloodshot, his face deathly pale and his bearing as aggressive as a ruffian from the docks.

"Who?" Lady Lippet stammered.

"A pox! You know who! Arabella. Where is she?"

Leaning on her vanity table for support, Lady Lippet slowly got to her feet. "Where are my footmen? How did you get in here?"

"They were wise enough to let me pass. Now, where is Arabella, for I will not leave without her."

"Do you think she will want to go with you? You've dishonored her, and the whole city knows it. I have seen to that!" Lady Lippet had waited a long time for this moment, and so she smiled with evil relish as Cordelia's son suffered for his sin and his mother's, too. "Now all of London knows you are as base, deceitful and lustful as your whore of a mother, and so does Arabella."

With a bellow of rage, Neville lunged for her, grabbing her by her scrawny throat.

"Are you going to kill me?" Lady Lippet gasped. "You would add murder to your list of crimes?"

His eyes still burning with menacing wrath, Neville let go and stepped back. "You are disgusting," he growled. "Perhaps I *should* kill you before you corrupt any more innocent women."

Lady Lippet rubbed her sore throat. "You

are hardly in a position to talk of corrupting women. Besides, your father was her guardian, not I."

"I should have warned her about you, but I thought her own good judgment, with his influence and protection, would keep her safe from you. I curse myself for being wrong. And now I will take Arabella away from you."

"I cannot allow that."

"You? You cannot allow it?"

Suddenly—and Neville never did know how—a pistol appeared in Lady Lippet's hand, perhaps from the wig box kept on her vanity. "Get out right now, or I will shoot you down like the dog you are and claim you were trying to rape me."

There was no denying that she meant every word she said.

"I won't leave without Arabella."

"Fool! Do you think she wants to see you after you humiliated her?" Lady Lippet's eyes glowed with sly triumph. "You can see her again, you know. She will be at Whitehall this evening. Of course, she will not want to speak with you. She will have so many other men to talk to. The Duke of Buckingham is very anxious to offer her a shoulder to cry on."

"You're despicable!"

"No, my handsome young man. I am only a silly, harmless, ugly old woman. Isn't that what everybody thinks? Now, shall I shoot you, or will you go?"

As he stared at her for a long moment, she thought she might really have to shoot him, which would make a terrible bloodstain on her new Turkey carpet.

Fortunately, however, he finally turned on his heel and left.

With trembling hands, Lady Lippet set down the pistol and sank heavily into her chair. Her heart pounded, her legs felt weak—she suddenly felt most unwell.

And her left arm was most curiously numb, although she had been holding the pistol in her right hand.

Chapter 20

Neville would sooner have gone to hell than meet the king in St. James's Park; unfortunately, he had little choice but to obey a royal summons.

After he left Lady Lippet, he marched home, trying to decide what to do, and discovered the king's page waiting with a note ordering him to meet Charles in the park at once. Masking his dismay, anger and dread, and ignoring the page's scornful reaction to his lodgings, Neville had tidied himself up and dutifully followed the young man to St. James's.

All too soon, the king appeared, strolling about with ease and nodding graciously to all and sundry.

When Neville thought of this seemingly kind-hearted, friendly man's lascivious plans for Arabella, he wanted to denounce him for a base scoundrel.

330

But he could not, for he was no better.

"Ah, Farrington," the king cried when he spotted him.

Neville smiled and bowed. "Majesty."

Charles gestured for him to come closer, then led him a little away from the page, his other attendants and his ever-present spaniels. "We have heard some very disturbing rumors about you and Lady Arabella."

"Rumors, Majesty?"

The royal brows furrowed. "Do not play us for a fool, Farrington. Is it true that you deflowered her?"

So Lady Lippet hadn't lied. The story was already all over the city. "Lady Arabella's virtue was an impediment to Your Majesty's pleasure, at least in her countrified mind. Now that is gone."

"Ah, Farrington, for king and country, eh? We knew there would be a suitable explanation," the king replied, and still with apparent good humor. "Was she as delectable as she looks?"

"A gentleman never reveals the details of his *amours*, as you know, Majesty. I will only say that it was not a particularly onerous duty."

"And then you quarreled?"

"Yes, sire, so now she will have nothing more to do with me."

The king chuckled. "Bravo, my lord! Bravo! We feared you had forgotten your duty to your sovereign and are delighted to find it is not so. And this argument heralds the complete end to your liaison?"

"Yes, Majesty."

"Well done!"

"Thank you, Majesty."

"And you will have ample proof of our pleasure, we assure you."

"Again I thank you, sire."

"We have also heard she has left your father's protection."

"So I understand, Majesty."

"A pity about Lady Lippet, but that is better for our plans."

Puzzled, Neville said, "What of Lady Lippet, Your Majesty?"

"The woman is dead."

"Dead?" Neville asked with wide-eyed disbelief. "I saw her only a short time ago—" He halted in confusion when he realized the king was regarding him shrewdly.

"We heard of this, too, and that you also quarreled with Lady Lippet."

Neville nodded once. "Yes, Majesty."

"You did not kill her."

"No. When I left her, she was alive and apparently well."

"We know. The physician says it was apoplexy or her heart. We never had a thought of charging you with murder."

Neville couldn't quite subdue a sigh of relief.

"But what of Lady Arabella, Majesty? She has nowhere to go in London, no friend—"

He fell silent as the king slowly smiled.

Of course. The king would be her "friend."

Neville felt sick and ashamed. But he would not blame himself. He had not sinned alone, and she had been willing.

"She has already sent us a most welcome message, Farrington. Tonight we shall have great cause for celebration at Whitehall." Then the king held out a purse full of coins. "As promised."

Judas.

The name rang in Neville's ears as he stared at the purse.

"Well, take it, man. Payment for a job well done."

Unable to think of a reason to refuse that would not insult the king, Neville obeyed.

"Since you have proved to be so adept at these proceedings, we trust we can count on your assistance in the future, should a similar case arise?"

Neville bowed.

The king ran his gaze over Neville. "The first thing we would do with such a sum is purchase some new clothes. We would have all our courtiers look their best, Farrington."

"Yes, Majesty."

"We expect to see you at Whitehall this evening, too."

Neville bowed, then watched the king saunter away.

That night, Neville forced himself to keep his gaze on George Villiers as they stood together in the Banqueting House, and not scan the gathering for Arabella.

He knew that several of the courtiers were watching them. Perhaps they thought they might witness the precursor to a duel; perhaps some of the women wondered if they could take Arabella's place. Perhaps they were all admiring his new clothes, bought with the money the king had given him.

Neville didn't care a whit what any of them thought.

"You don't have to tell me everything," Villiers said. "I know it is true."

"I suppose some men might be tempted to brag of having conquered such a virtuous and lovely lady, but that has never been my way."

"You have won this battle, and I acknowledge that," the duke replied with an insincere smile. "I am offering my congratulations."

Neville regarded him stonily. "Never one to lose an opportunity to be obsequious, eh, Villiers?"

The duke stiffened. "I also wanted to ascertain if you intend to continue conquering her?"

"Once the battle is won and the prize given, I see no necessity for repeating the process—

especially when the battle is fought for some-one else."

"You wooed in proxy? What fool would set you in pursuit of the object of his desire? Any-one familiar with you would guess how it would end."

"I would not call the king a fool, Bucking-ham, unless you relish a sojourn in the Tower."

The duke colored. "The king?"

"After she has lost her virtue, a young woman will be more amenable to sharing her charms with others, do you not agree?"

"That was my thought, too, when you came upon us on the way to the river."

Neville's jaw clenched. That anything he might do should be comparable to an action of this man . . . !

He was no better than this man.

"No wonder Lady Castlemaine was in a tem-per today. Berkeley is still with her, offering his own particular brand of comfort." The duke clapped a hand on Neville's shoulder, and it was all Neville could do not to shrug it off. "But beware, my friend, beware. Charles is the most capricious of men, as I have cause to know. One minute, one is in favor, the next out."

In Buckingham's case, Neville thought, he had only himself and his inability to see how his actions might reflect poorly on the king to blame for that.

"I wish you better luck in keeping in his good graces than I have had."

"I shall endeavor to do so."

The duke leaned yet closer, so that the wine on his breath was nearly overpowering. "And when the king has had his fill of her, will you reclaim your prize?"

With that question, Neville envisioned Arabella passed from man to man until she ended her days as a sick, bedraggled wharfside whore or beggar.

His seduction would be to blame.

No, she was willing. She was as guilty of her fate as he.

Yet if he had not been so determined to seduce her in the beginning . . .

"I am done with her," he replied when he realized that the duke was still looking at him intently. "Or perhaps not. And perhaps the king will not tire of her."

The Duke of Buckingham laughed. "Maybe you are right, but I hope not. Otherwise, I might have to abduct her again, eh?"

"I would not do anything so foolish, if I were you," Neville said evenly, yet with a tone of underlying ferocity.

The duke backed away. "If I did not know you, Farrington, I would say you cared about her."

"If you think I care about her beyond being a means to gain my sovereign's thanks, i'faith,

Your Grace, you do not know me. Now, if you will excuse me, Buckingham, I believe I see La Belle Stewart."

"You will try your charms on her next, will you? For whom—yourself, or the king?"

Neville didn't answer but walked away.

For it was not Frances Stewart who had caught his eye.

It was Arabella.

She was alone, dressed in a gown of deep-blue velvet trimmed with gold and silver, her hair very elaborately dressed with gold ribbons, her face powdered and with a patch near the corner of her eye and another on her chin.

As she made her way through the courtiers, she looked as if nothing at all had happened to upset her.

To judge by her smiles and nods to those who greeted her, she was the happiest woman in the world, not at all ashamed to have lost her virginity, or dismayed by the fact that everyone in this room probably knew it.

One might even think she was happily rid of an impediment to her plans.

Could it be that she had tricked them all?

Everyone knew what she had done.

The moment Arabella entered the Banqueting House, she was certain of it. A hush fell over the milling crowd. Then came leering, speculative looks on the men's faces and smug satisfaction on the women's.

Never in her life had Arabella felt more like hiking up her skirts and running away. So must Daniel have felt that first moment in the lions' den, and Eve when she first faced Adam after the expulsion from Eden.

But what else could she do? She had no home or any place else to go. As upsetting as it had been to leave the earl, it had, of course, been many more times upsetting to hear Lady Lippet's maid screaming, then to be told that the woman was dead.

Arabella had not liked Lady Lippet, but she was sorry for the woman's death and even more sorry when Lady Lippet's lawyers had arrived and told her she had no business staying in the house.

Who else could she appeal to but the king? So she had, even though she knew exactly what that meant.

She scanned the room. Immediately she saw Neville, wearing fine new clothes of rich black satin and velvet. Then she realized to whom he was talking: the odious Duke of Buckingham. Again she wanted to run away, but she would not compound her sin with cowardice.

She was going to belong to this world, and therefore she would get the worst over with at once.

Lifting her chin with its fashionable patch,

she made her way through the gathering toward the man responsible for her presence here. She ignored the stares, whispers and smirks, and intercepted him as he moved away from Villiers. "Good evening, Lord Farrington."

The moment Neville looked at her, she realized her mistake. She had not yet had time for her anger and remorse to quench her desire completely. Her heart started to pound, and she had to struggle to maintain her composure—while he was able to regard her as if she were a complete stranger.

"Lady Arabella, your servant," he said with a bow.

He took her hand and pressed a kiss upon her knuckles that, despite everything, made her whole body flush. "I am sorry to hear of your loss."

She raised one eyebrow questioningly.

"I refer, of course, to the recent demise of Lady Lippet. I am delighted to see you are not prostrate with grief, although I must confess myself surprised to see you here, and in such finery, too. Not a speck of mourning, I note."

"No, my lord, no mourning for me. And why should I not come here? I would think you would be the first to say this is where I belong."

He glanced at the people near them, then, regardless of possible speculation, drew her away to the side of the room, where it was less crowded.

"I assumed you would be too ashamed and guilt-ridden to show your face," he said.

"You are not. Why should I be?"

"Your father must be turning in his grave."

"Perhaps. *Your* father has fled the city. Surely a man of your sophistication understands why I am here," she continued, allowing a hint of her bitterness into her voice. "Did you not tell me yourself that the king wished me in his bed? I'faith, was I not to be honored by that proposition? Therefore, I am come to be the king's toy, to give him a few moments of pleasure. To be used and discarded at whim, perhaps married off afterward, or perhaps not."

"You don't—"

"I do. I have no other choice."

"And that is all my fault, like your supposed ruin?"

"Supposed ruin? What else would you call it?"

"Arabella, you were willing! Very willing! One might even think your virginity was something you were glad to be rid of, you are so quick to leap from my arms to the king's bed."

"What choice do I have, since you have taken my honor and my reputation?"

"I did not take it."

"It's true I *gave* it—and that makes your sin all the blacker."

"Arabella," he said, his tone half frustrated, half desperate. "I will not deny that I wanted to make love with you. I am not ashamed of that. Nor do I regret what we did together."

"Why should you? You will not suffer for it."

"I will and I am." He took her hands in his. "Arabella, I regret that I didn't take you somewhere private, where we would not be interrupted. I regret that once again, my father intruded where he was not wanted. I regret that I was so angry."

She pulled away. "That I should live to hear you express any regret at all! I am honored by your confidence, my lord."

"You should be."

"As for these supposed regrets, no doubt you are sorry to have revealed your base motive so quickly. Who knows how long I might have gone on allowing you liberties before I discovered how insincere your motives really were?"

"This sardonic manner does not become you, Arabella," he said, finally moving away a little, yet not so far as to render her even remotely comfortable. "Perhaps I should not attempt to be sincere, since you persist in responding so flippantly."

"Of all men I thought you would appreciate

flippancy, sarcasm and mockery. Do I not sound just like you?"

"Yes, and I would you did not."

"This is the mode of speech among the courtiers, and if I must be among the court, I should do my best to emulate them."

"Go home, Arabella. Go back to Grantham."

"What, after ruining my reputation, you will presume to dictate the course of my life?"

He scowled darkly. "If you will not listen to me, I see no point in continuing this discussion."

"I was not aware we were having a discussion. I thought you were lecturing me."

"Oh, no, my lady, I would never presume to teach you anything. Like my father, you would never listen."

This was not fair, and she felt the injustice of his words keenly. "I did listen—much good did it do me! I listened to you and believed your lies, and now I must suffer for it."

"You do not appear to find your alleged suffering particularly contemptible."

"While you again blame your father for your behavior," she said. "You are a grown man, my lord, and you have no one to blame but yourself for what you do."

"I do not blame him for enraging me. That was your fault."

"Mine!" she cried. "How so? I was the ruined party, not you!"

"You let him and everyone else think the worst of me. You didn't tell him that you were as eager to make love as I. You acted the aggrieved party to perfection."

"I was—am!—the aggrieved party! You tricked me with your lies and soft words. You made me think you loved me. I thought you were going to marry me. I was eager, shamefully so, and I must live with that terrible knowledge forever. I was a fool, a weak, stupid fool to listen to a word you said. Did you honestly expect me to lose what little pride I still possessed by acknowledging that in front of your father, especially in such circumstances?"

"So you were surprised and embarrassed— so was I!" he retorted. "If one of us was a fool, it was I, for waiting for you to tell my father that I was not a despicable cad. But no—your pride must win out over the truth. Let my father despise and disown me. He hates me already, or so I'm sure you reasoned. Let everyone think me the lowest form of lecher, so all will pity you.

"And then, after utterly destroying me in my father's eyes, salvage what you can from the alleged ruin of your pride by becoming the king's mistress, which is such a terrible punishment that you could not wait to come here dressed like a harlot."

"I want no one's pity!" she cried. "And if it is pride that brings me here, it is only the tattered remnants of it. You obliterated the rest."

"You should have told them the truth. Instead, you gave my father the confirmation of every bad thing he has ever thought of me."

"Would you rather I boasted of my shame, as you bragged of your triumph?"

"I didn't!" he retorted, and yet she saw the blush spread upon his cheeks.

"Liar! Your own face reveals the truth."

"I didn't boast!"

"What then?"

"I got drunk in a tavern, and I might have said some things," he muttered.

"You got drunk," she repeated with scorn.

"That is what a man does when he is angry."

"Getting drunk is what men do when they are celebrating, and you had cause for that at my expense."

He suddenly grabbed her by the shoulders. "You don't understand anything, do you?"

She met his gaze boldly. "Tell me, then. Explain to me why you seduced me and then saw fit to brag of your despicable conduct in a public tavern. Convince me that what you did was good and honorable and noble. Make me believe that your motive was of the highest caliber, and not based on selfishness and lust and greed."

"Arabella—"

He was interrupted by the yipping of dogs not far away.

Simultaneously, they turned to see the king striding toward them, accompanied by liveried servants. Two carried candleholders, one a goblet and another lead several of the king's spaniels. "Lady Arabella, how lovely you look tonight!"

"You are too kind, Your Majesty."

"Will you join us for a small private supper, Lady Arabella?" the king inquired.

As he reached out to take her hand, Arabella knew he was not merely asking her to eat with him.

If the sight of the king, for all his magnificence and charm and ease of manner, did not stir her at all, it was because she was wiser. Never again would a man's outward appearance tempt her.

She glanced at Neville. For an instant, there was a look in his eyes—yet it was quickly gone, and he remained silent.

"I would be honored, Your Majesty."

Chapter 21

At the start of the corridor leading to the royal apartments, Charles dismissed his grinning courtiers, sent his dogs away with their keeper and smiled at Arabella.

They were alone—or as alone as anyone with the king ever got, for servants stood in position at several places along the corridor. Once they saw the king and Arabella, however, they turned toward the wall and lowered their heads, as if this would render them deaf and blind.

"We are so delighted you are supping with us."

"It is a pleasure, Your Majesty."

"Soon enough, you will have rooms here of your own, if you so wish. Or a house in the city, if you prefer."

She managed an answering smile. "I think I would prefer to live elsewhere, Majesty." She gave him a sidelong glance. "I did not see the queen in the Banqueting House."

"She is resting in her chambers today."

"Or Lady Castlemaine."

He made a wry grin. "She is entertaining in her own apartments, I expect. As I am not exclusive, neither is she. Neither must . . . anyone . . . be."

He was referring to her, obviously.

Arabella had not believed that a man could be so blasé about his lover having lovers, but obviously Charles did not particularly care what Lady Castlemaine did when she was not with him.

This was the depraved world she was going to be part of. Where Neville had put her.

Where she had put herself.

"You shiver, my dear. Are you cold?"

"I merely felt a draft, Your Majesty."

"You will be warmer soon," he promised softly.

Arabella swallowed hard.

"Now, these apartments here belong to the Lord Keeper, and next comes the Treasury, where we shall have to find some suitable jewels for you, eh?"

"That won't be necessary, Your Majesty."

"We do not speak of necessities, Arabella," he said in a slightly sterner tone. "It will be our pleasure."

"Thank you, Your Majesty."

"This is my laboratory," he said, gesturing toward another gilded door. "We live in a fascinating age, Arabella. An age of discovery. Of science."

"Yes, Majesty."

His voice lowered. "As well as an age of love." He halted and gently tugged her into his arms. "My dear, you may call me Charles."

Then he kissed her, his lips moving over hers with sureness and confidence.

She felt nothing except revulsion. But that must not be. It must not!

His hands made leisurely progress over her back, and she felt him caress her breasts.

How was it she could find that so delightful when it was Neville and feel the opposite when it was the king?

Yet she should act as if she enjoyed this . . . this pawing, so she made a few sounds as if she were pleased and excited.

Her ruse must have worked, for he continued, his caresses growing bolder as he shoved his tongue into her mouth.

She was sickened and wanted to tell him to stop—but then what would happen to her?

Fortunately, he ceased of his own volition.

"Majesty, you overwhelm me," she panted, hoping to prevent him from comprehending her true feelings, which had to be subdued.

"And you intoxicate me with your beauty," he said smoothly.

Indeed, he said the words so blithely that she rather suspected he had said these very words many times before.

He started to walk again, and she was glad of that. "These next rooms are for Lord Arlington, and so we come at last to the Stone Gallery."

He led her through more of Whitehall. Finally he opened a door and revealed a set of rooms of great, gilded magnificence well lit with so many candles that it seemed as if the walls glowed with molten gold.

They were his apartments, obviously, for the liveried servants looked as if they expected him. The first room was something of an anteroom, and the king divested himself of his stately coat.

"There, now, that is better," he said with a cheerful smile, rolling his shoulders. "Odd's fish, that must weigh five pounds. Come, Arabella."

He brought her further inside to another room, where there was a table of polished mahogany set with fine crystal banded with silver. Also set out on the exquisite linen were silver plates. A large crystal bowl held oranges, apples and what Arabella supposed must be a pineapple, a fruit from the New World she had heard of. Confectionery dainties also stood upon the table in smaller silver dishes.

So he did mean that they should eat before . . . before . . .

The king escorted her to the table, where two statuelike servants stood at the two chairs. "Please, sit."

Surely the king should sit first. She glanced at the servants, wondering if they would see her uncertainty and give her a sign.

They remained unhelpfully inscrutable.

The king prepared to sit, and at that same moment, the servant closest to her went behind her chair and pushed it forward. Taking a cue, she sat at the same time as the king.

"We shall have no more need of you this evening," Charles said to the servants.

They bowed and left as quietly as if they were spirits instead of mortals.

"Is this not pleasant?" the king asked after the servants had departed. "Just the two of us here together?"

Arabella looked at the face of the man opposite her. Lust lurked below the affable surface of his expression, and it was a lust that had more in common with that of Buckingham than the desire in Neville's eyes.

It had nothing in common with the desire in Neville's eyes or the love she had seen there.

The love that had still been there the last time he had looked at her.

Suddenly, despite the words they had said and the anger she had felt, she knew she loved him yet and was just as sure he loved her.

Arabella abruptly shoved back her chair and faced the surprised monarch. "Your Majesty, I must beg your forgiveness. I have made a terrible mistake."

His brows lowered ominously. "A mistake?"

"Yes, Your Majesty," she said, her knees beginning to tremble as she thought of the Tower. But she would—she must—continue. "A mistake. I should not have come here."

The king leaned back in his gilded chair and regarded her with a slightly puzzled air that lessened her dread somewhat. "Why not?"

"I—I cannot love you."

"I do not want your love," Charles replied with a smile. "Your affection would be enough, and we shall . . . divert each other."

"I do not want to be diverted!" she said desperately.

He toyed with a silver fork. "Do you want a title or a house or some such thing first?"

"No, Your Majesty. Thank you, but no."

"Sit down, Lady Arabella."

It was, as much as anything she had ever heard the king say, a royal command. "Your Majesty, please—"

"Sit down!"

She obeyed.

"Do you not appreciate the honor we do you?"

"Yes, Your Majesty."

"Yet you would refuse your king?"

"Yes, Your Majesty."

"It's Farrington, isn't it?"

Suddenly Arabella thought she might have been wiser to submit. Now she might have put Neville in jeopardy. "Majesty, please—"

"Do you deny that there is another man in your heart?"

"I . . . I cannot, sire."

"And it is Farrington."

She could not deny that, either.

"So even though Farrington has caused your fall from grace, you think you love him."

"My fall was not his fault, Majesty, and I do not *think* I love him. I know I do."

"He told me you had quarreled."

She twisted her fingers together. "I was upset and angry with him, Majesty—but I still love him."

"We take it, then, that he is forgiven for seducing you?"

"He didn't seduce me."

The king straightened. "Then we have been grievously misinformed!"

"I welcomed his embrace, because I love him."

Simple words, and suddenly so easily said.

"Odd's fish, we do believe you do."

Charles sighed softly, then smiled wryly. "As we know from our own experience with

Lady Castlemaine, love and anger are often two sides of the same coin."

"I am sorry I misled you, Your Majesty."

His smile grew rueful. "As much as we think we would both have enjoyed ourselves immensely, we shall confess that our primary objective in pursuing you was to make Lady Castlemaine realize she was not the only apple on the tree.

"And we are now very sure of Neville Farrington's loyalty, for we believe he reciprocates your feelings and appreciate that he was willing to sacrifice that love for his sovereign."

"You think *what*?" she asked, not taking her gaze from Charles and quite forgetting she was addressing the monarch. "How do you know he loves me? Did he tell you?"

"We do not have to be told everything," Charles said with a slightly aggrieved air. "We have eyes."

He picked up the fork and began to tap his chin. "He is a good fellow, Farrington. Not like his father, thank goodness. What a pompous bore that man is!"

"So you used me to test his loyalty to you?" Arabella asked. Then she pressed her lips together. Otherwise, she would undoubtedly have said more, and perhaps something treasonous. But ruler or not, Charles should not have used them in such a cavalier fashion.

"We must be sure of the people around us,

Lady Arabella, lest our fate mirror that of our illustrious father.''

After his rueful remark, she could agree with the king's need, if not his method. ''Yes, Your Majesty.''

Charles fixed a speculative eye on her. ''Do you wish to marry Neville Farrington?''

''Majesty!''

''Come, come, this is hardly the time to dissemble! We can command it, if you like.'' Charles smiled as if vastly amused. ''Or put him in the Tower until he swears undying devotion, eh?''

''Your Majesty, please, I would rather he married me because he loves me than because the king commands it.''

The king put down his fork. ''You are a romantic, I see. So is your sovereign.''

Arabella fought to keep any skepticism from her face.

''Therefore, it is our royal decree that this love story have a happy ending.''

''Majesty?''

''We waited a long time to be king, and sometimes, we enjoy it mightily.''

A troop of the king's guards marched into the Banqueting House. At the sight of them, the courtiers fell silent, and the Duke of Buckingham discreetly sought the exit.

Neville watched the soldiers for a moment

until another, more shocking sight met his eye.

His father.

He should have been well out of London by now.

"Lord Farrington?"

Neville started and turned to the sergeant-at-arms. "Yes."

"Come with us."

Neville was vaguely aware that his father was coming closer but had to be more concerned with the soldier before him. "Why? Am I under arrest?"

"I have a warrant for your arrest, signed by the king," the sergeant replied.

"Really? May I see it?"

Neville took the paper the sergeant pulled from his large cuff, immediately noted the royal seal, and opened it. He quickly read the writing, which was, indeed, in the king's own hand. "It does not say with what crime I am charged."

The sergeant shrugged. "You are to come with us."

"Delighted," he replied.

"Neville, what is the meaning of this?" his father demanded, pushing his way through the courtiers.

"I'faith, Father, what brings you here? I thought you would be far away by now."

"I came for Arabella."

"Then you are too late. She is with the king."

"What have you done? Why are you under arrest?"

"Does it matter? Perhaps I am finally meeting the fate you think I deserve." Neville glanced at the waiting soldiers. "I had no idea she could be so vindictive."

"Who? That bitch Castlemaine? I have heard of your liaison with her!"

"Father, please! You are not in a barnyard speaking of a pack of dogs. And no, I don't mean Lady Castlemaine. Your charming ward, who is about to become the king's latest mistress, is, I fear, responsible for my current dilemma."

"Arabella? You're making a jest—and a bad one, too!"

"I think not."

The sergeant barked the order to march.

"Come, Father, don't look so glum. You always knew I would come to a bad end. Now you can congratulate yourself on your foresight."

The sergeant prodded Neville into motion while Lord Barrsettshire watched helplessly as his only son was led away.

"This is not the way to the Tower," Neville noted almost immediately.

"No, my lord," the sergeant replied gruffly. "We're to take you to the king himself."

She had wasted no time getting her revenge. And to think that for a moment, before she accepted the king's invitation, despite all evidence to the contrary, he had dared to hope . . .

The soldiers came to a halt outside the royal apartments. The sergeant stepped forward, knocked and then spoke softly to the liveried servant who opened the heavily gilded door.

"This way, my lord," the sergeant ordered.

Neville nodded, then took a deep breath before striding in to face his obviously irate sovereign, who sat at a small table in the room directly off the anteroom, his brow lowered in an ominous scowl, the food spread before him untouched.

There was, Neville noted at once, no sign of Arabella. Perhaps she was further inside the king's apartments, maybe waiting in his bed.

Neville bowed. "Majesty."

"We are gravely displeased, Farrington," the king said. "Very gravely displeased."

"I am sorry to hear that, Majesty, yet I confess I had some suspicion, since I have been arrested."

"Don't be flippant with me, you young fool," the king snapped, rising and starting to pace in the ornate room. "We are not a coxcomb from the theater or a woman."

Neville bowed his head. "No, sire."

"We have had a most unpleasant experience this evening, Farrington, and it has been laid at your door."

"Majesty?"

"I am sure you know what we were anticipating." The king paused in his pacing and fastened his gaze on Neville. "Odd's fish, you of all men know what we were anticipating."

"I assume Your Majesty speaks of Lady Arabella."

"Precisely. She has spurned us, Farrington, and we understand this is your fault."

If the ceiling had suddenly opened up to reveal angels singing, Neville couldn't have been more astonished or more hopeful of forgiveness for his sins.

"We do not like having our plans thwarted, especially when they involve a lovely young woman like Lady Arabella, Farrington."

"I am sure you do not."

"We understand that you seduced her to make her more amenable to our proposal, and we know women often mistake the physical act for something far deeper. We are sure it is so in this instance. Therefore, we require that you tell her you do not reciprocate her feelings and that she would be wise to accept all that her king offers her. If you do that, and she proves amenable, we are willing to overlook this little difficulty."

Neville regarded the ruler of his kingdom, the man who should command his absolute loyalty and who had the power to imprison him.

He thought of Arabella and the sordid, unhappy fate that might await her. Even if he had lost her, he could not abandon her to such a future. Not when he loved her with all his heart.

"I regret, Majesty, that I cannot do as you ask."

The king crossed his arms over his chest. "You refuse our direct command? That is perilously close to treason, Farrington. We could let you mull over your impetuous response in the Tower until you see the merit of obedience."

If Neville could not have Arabella in his life, he truly didn't care what happened to him. "Put me in the Tower if you must, Your Majesty, but it will not induce me to change my mind. I do not want her to be your mistress."

"*You* do not want—?" the king demanded incredulously.

"I love her."

Simple words, and suddenly so easily said.

Arabella appeared at the entrance to the inner chamber.

"Neville!" she cried before running across the room and throwing her arms around him.

"Oh, Arabella, forgive me!" he murmured, holding her close. "I love you! I have always loved you."

"And I, you! But I have been foolish and stubborn and too full of wounded pride."

"No, I was the proud and stubborn one, or

I would have declared my feelings for you without waiting for you to speak first. How did I ever think I could live without you?" Neville murmured as he kissed her cheeks, her eyelids, her brow, her forehead.

"I love you," Arabella whispered as she took his hand and fervently pressed her lips to his palm.

Then they kissed, revealing their feelings for each other more passionately than with mere words.

"Reunions are always touching," the king remarked.

Arabella and Neville moved apart yet continued to hold hands. Nor did they stop looking at each other, save for an occasional glance at the most powerful man in England.

"Odd's fish," Charles muttered with a twinkle in his eye, "all this emotion is most unsettling. And you might set a precedent for devotion we would rather avoid. Therefore, we must order you to be wed without delay and leave the court, on pain of . . . separation."

"Gladly!" Arabella replied immediately.

"At once," Neville seconded her.

Suddenly, there was a sound of a great commotion in the corridor outside.

"Good heavens, are we under attack?" the king inquired as he put his hand on the hilt of his sword.

Then the Earl of Barrsettshire burst through the door.

Chapter 22

⟋⟍◦⟋⟍

"Take your hands off me!" the earl roared at the soldiers who tried to restrain him.

"Let him go," the king ordered calmly.

When the soldiers obeyed, Lord Barrsettshire stumbled forward and threw himself on his knees before the king. "Your Majesty, spare him! Spare my son! Whatever he has done, I am sure he didn't mean it! He is an honorable, dutiful—"

The earl halted confusedly when he finally noticed his son standing near the king, his arm around Arabella, and on his face an expression of utter disbelief.

"I thought he was under arrest," the earl stammered.

The king rose, smiling. "A little ruse to get him here, that's all. We had no idea it would upset anyone in this fashion, except perhaps

Farrington, but from what we understand, a little comeuppance was not amiss."

"Then he is not under arrest, sire?"

"No."

The earl sighed, and his stern expression softened as he looked at his son.

"I thought you would be pleased to see me in prison," Neville said.

"No, never! You are a good and loyal Englishman, not a criminal! And if there is anyone who deserves to be punished, it is I. I was a poor father to you, Neville," he admitted. "I set out on the wrong course when your mother left, and I was hurt and angry. I blamed you for what you could not help and pushed you away. Can you ever forgive me?"

He had tried to win his father's love for so long, and with so little success—and he was to forgive all in a moment? "This change of heart is so sudden, so unexpected," Neville said slowly. "I cannot grant absolution in the blink of an eye."

The earl nodded. "Nor can I expect you to." He sighed wearily. "We are both proud and stubborn fools. You are like me that way."

"If you beg Arabella's forgiveness, I might be persuaded," Neville replied. "You've lied to her, Father, with no regard for her welfare or her feelings."

Neville felt Arabella squeeze his hand, and he looked down into her pleading, sympathetic eyes. "It doesn't matter," she murmured.

"Yes, it does. I will find it easier to forgive him when he apologizes to you."

"Arabella," the earl said resolutely, "I am sorry. Can you forgive a foolish, stubborn old man?"

"Yes, my lord, I can, because it seems you recognize your son's merit after all."

Lord Barrsettshire approached his son and smiled wistfully. "Perhaps it would help if I explained why I told you I was going to bequeath my estate to Arabella and her husband."

"Because you were?" Neville suggested.

" I never had any intention of giving my estate to Arabella and her husband unless she married you."

"*What*?" the couple cried simultaneously.

"I believed you were wasting what talents you possessed in this Gomorrah of a city, and when Arabella became my ward, I thought I saw a chance to make you see the error of your ways and reform. You would not listen to me, so I wanted you to marry a woman who would make the perfect wife for a wayward son." He looked at Arabella. "I have long known that Neville craves most what he thinks he cannot have." The earl's expression hardened for a brief instant. "His mother was the same."

They were interrupted by the sudden bark of the king clearing the royal throat.

"We are delighted to see this family squabble ended," Charles said as he sat down and picked up an orange, tossing it lightly in the air. "Lord Barrsettshire, we have commanded that they marry without delay. Obviously, you will offer no objections."

"None at all, Your Majesty."

"Second, we think we must give these two cause to stay away from London." He frowned gravely, although his eyes twinkled merrily. "We would not want to have our failure constantly thrown into our face. Therefore, it pleases us to grant your son an estate in Oxfordshire. Beddington is not a great estate, but could be made into one with proper management.

"We have heard, Farrington," Charles continued with a meaningful glance at Arabella, "that you are very clever in this regard. Let us hope so."

"He is, Your Majesty!" the earl declared. "I have it on the best authority—my bankers, Messrs. Pettigrew and Hutchins!"

"I am honored, Majesty, and promise to do my best," Neville said, still not used to hearing his father sing his praises.

"Good. Now you all may leave us."

Arabella curtsied, Neville and his father bowed and they walked to the door.

"Farrington!" the king called out. "May you have many children."

Smiling, Neville turned back and made another bow. "I shall do my best in that regard, too, Your Majesty."

"Good man!" the king replied with a chuckle. "Odd's fish, from the looks you give each other, I think that will be your first priority, as well it should be. God speed!"

"Farewell, Your Majesty," Arabella said happily, curtsying once more.

Yet despite her own happiness, as she looked at the Merry Monarch, she saw beneath the merriment a loneliness that reminded her that his early years had been most unhappy. Perhaps, for all his dalliance, he had yet to find a woman who truly loved him, and for that she could easily pity him.

The earl likewise turned back. "Majesty, in the matter of the Dutch—"

"Good night, Lord Barrsettshire."

Foz idly toyed with the foot-long plume of his new hat as he watched Richard writing. "It could have been worse, you know."

Richard angrily scratched out what he had just written.

"The audience was all drunk, I think," Foz went on. "And you have always written comedies before, so I suppose it was only natural that they were somewhat surprised that *A Virtuous Lady* wasn't."

Scowling, Richard looked up from the table

where he sat surrounded by papers, ink, quills, a penknife and the stub of a candle that cast a feeble light. "Disappointed? They booed and threw rotten fruit."

"Well, I am *sure* everybody was drunk," Foz repeated helpfully.

Richard went back to his revisions. "They hated it and rightly so. Even *I* hated it. Minette couldn't act that part if I worked with her for a hundred years. The dialogue sounded like pompous twaddle. I never should have tried anything tragic."

Foz watched as his friend's pen moved from ink to page and back to ink. "I didn't think it was so very bad. Truly. I quite liked it."

"I'm glad there was one person who didn't want to throw something at the stage."

"Are you hungry?"

"I can't think of food until I rewrite this play."

Foz nodded, sighed wearily, set his hat down, stood up and paced a little.

Richard muttered to himself, then wrote some more.

Foz sat again and reached for his hat. He tickled his chin with the plume.

"Will you keep still?" Richard growled. "I am trying to think!"

"Yes, of course, well, if you wish," Foz stammered. "I am trying to think, too, you know."

"Can you not think and be still at the same time?"

"I can try."

"Then do so, or I'll have to ask you to leave!"

"I've just arrived," Foz protested.

"Then stay—but be still!"

Foz kept still for a full five minutes, staring out the window. Then he fidgeted, gave his friend a sidelong glance and tentatively whispered, "Where do you suppose Neville is?"

"I don't know and I don't care."

"I thought he might come to the theater."

Richard sighed with resignation and tossed down his quill. "Thank heaven he did not. I can imagine his clever, mocking criticism, and after what he has done, I would probably have challenged him to a duel."

"Truly?"

"Truly."

Foz continued to regard Richard pensively. "That was not a nice wager, and I don't think any of us should have agreed to it."

"At least we had the decency to want to end it."

"Yes," Foz agreed slowly. "But then Neville was in a devil of situation. He was desperate."

"That was no reason to make Lady Arabella suffer."

"No, no, of course not."

Richard yawned. "Is there anything to eat?"

Foz gestured at the basket near the door. "I brought some bread and cheese."

"You are a good friend, Foz," Richard said as he rose and fetched the basket, pulling out a still-warm loaf whose fragrance filled the tiny room. "Is there any wine?"

"Over there."

Foz pointed at the cupboard, and Richard poured himself some in a chipped clay cup.

"I am a goblin," Foz suddenly muttered.

"A what?"

"An imp, perhaps, or a gargoyle. That's what I am."

"A pox on your nonsense! Have you been drinking without me?"

Foz shook his head. "No. I must be moonstruck, then."

"What the devil are you talking about?" Richard demanded before taking a bite of well-aged cheese.

"I would have to be moonstruck to think Lady Arabella would want to marry me."

"Of course, you cannot marry Arabella now. Neville has put an end to that."

"If he had not, I would have."

Richard choked a little, then wiped his mouth with the back of his hand. "Why? I should think you would have been delighted by the prospect of marrying her as much as a man could be about marrying anybody. If you must shackle yourself in wedlock, she would have done quite nicely.''

''She deserves better than me.''

''You're a fine fellow, Foz, and you've got the kindest, truest heart of any man I know.''

Foz's eyes lit up at Richard's sincere words. ''Thank you, Richard.'' He rose and stared down despondently at his luxurious and riotous garments. ''But look at me. She can have any man she wants. Why would she want me?''

Why, indeed? was the first thought that came to Richard's mind, but he would not have voiced it for the world. ''Because you are a good, honest, generous man.''

Foz sat down heavily. ''She would never *choose* me.'' He held up his hand to silence Richard before he could protest. ''I'm a fool in many ways, Richard, but I'm not that much of a fool. I've seen the way she looks at Neville, and I've seen the way Neville looks at her.'' Foz sighed with the sorrow of the ages. ''I suppose they'll be betrothed soon.''

Richard started. ''Zounds, I think you *are* moonstruck. Or mad. Lady Arabella and Neville—betrothed?''

''Of course.''

''But he only wanted to seduce her.''

To Richard's further astonishment, Foz shook his head and firmly said, ''No. It's more than that. We've both seen him with other women. Surely you have noted the difference in the way he looks at her."

"If I did, I thought it was because he saw her as an enemy."

"Or because he wants her more than he can bear to acknowledge?"

Richard stared at Foz. "Foz, you astound me." He ran his hand over his stubbled chin. "But zounds, you may be right. How did you . . . ?"

Foz blushed modestly. "Unrequited love is my particular forte."

"Richard?"

Both men turned toward the door as Neville stuck his head into the room.

"Oh, and Foz, too," he continued with a tentative smile. "May I come in?"

"What do you want? Your money? I don't have it," Richard said coldly.

"I have come to beg your forgiveness, my friends," Neville said contritely as he ventured into the room.

Richard raised an eyebrow. "Can this possibly be Lord Farrington?"

"I have been a fool."

"I am delighted to hear you admit it," Richard replied. "What has brought about this astonishing enlightenment?"

"I am not alone."

Richard and Foz exchanged looks. "Since we must hear the cause of this miraculous revelation, your companion shall be welcome, too."

Neville grinned his irrepressible grin. "Then congratulate me, gentlemen, for I am betrothed to this excellent woman."

Their eyes widened as Arabella entered the room to stand beside him.

"Lady Arabella and Neville!" Foz gave Richard a triumphant look that made Neville furrow his brow with puzzlement. "Didn't I tell you, Richard?"

"How did you know?" Neville asked, dumbfounded. "It only happened a short time ago."

"And before that, everything seemed hopeless," Arabella added, equally confused.

She had been dreading Lord Cheddersby's reaction to the news, given what Lady Lippet had been encouraging, but he seemed genuinely happy.

Richard glanced at the delighted Foz, then gave the baffled couple a wry look. "We have underestimated Lord Cheddersby, Neville. He told me not five minutes ago that this would happen."

"Yes, I did," Foz boasted. "I knew you were in love." Then he frowned. "If only I had thought to make a wager on it, eh, Neville, when I wanted to cancel the other one?"

Neville pressed his lips together and tried to will Richard and Foz to keep silent about their bet.

Richard, however, got a devilish gleam in his

dark, satiric eyes. "I thought when you first arrived that you were come for your fifty
pounds."

"What is he talking about?" Arabella asked
Neville.

"Pay no attention to these fellows. I believe
they have been drinking too much. And Richard, you know, tells lies for a living."

"I write plays, which is not at all the same
thing."

"He's not lying," Foz said gravely. "There
was a wager, which Neville won."

"What kind of wager?" Arabella demanded.

"Richard, Foz, I really don't think—" Neville
began.

"Oh, but I do," Richard interrupted. "He bet
us fifty pounds that he could get you into his
bed within a fortnight."

Neville wished they had never come here
but gone straight home with the earl.

Especially when Arabella slowly turned to
face him. "Is this true?"

He made an apologetic smile. "Arabella," he
began placatingly.

"I see," she interrupted. She smiled, and Neville started to breathe again. "You believe he
won it?"

Richard and Foz gave her a look as incred-
ulous as Neville's. "That's what he said," Foz
answered.

"That is not precisely true. *I* made love to

him. And he did not get me into his bed. We made love on the floor."

The worldly Richard's face turned as red as Lord Cheddersby's.

"If you require further proof, gentlemen," Neville said solemnly, "I will show you my poor bruised knees."

"That will not be necessary," Richard replied gruffly.

"I trust you both are satisfied," Neville said with, truth be told, more than a hint of smug satisfaction.

"While I trust *you* will not make any more wagers," Arabella remarked pointedly.

Neville gave her his best, most innocently charming smile. "Of course not."

"Good."

"Now I shall collect my winnings."

Richard's eyes looked slightly panicked, and Neville let him suffer a little.

After a long, silent moment, he said, "I will not take your money, my friends. The king has given me an estate, and even better, it seems my father has learned to appreciate my merits after all, thanks to Arabella."

"What?" Richard demanded, getting to his feet. "Charles gives you an estate?"

"You do not want *any* estate," Neville reminded him. "You want your family's back. Still, since Charles and I are such good friends," he added virtuously, "I will see what I can do."

Richard scowled darkly until Arabella touched him gently on the arm. "We really will try to help your cause, Richard." She turned to Foz. "I hope you can forgive me for marrying Neville."

"There is nothing to forgive," Foz replied, blushing furiously. "You do not love me. And Neville loves you very much."

Arabella kissed Foz lightly on the cheek.

Neville cleared his throat. "I fear we are getting far too maudlin." He picked up one of Richard's papers. "What mess is this?"

"Regrettably, and despite your betrothed's opinion, my attempt at a tragedy was not successful. Poor Minette is probably still trying to get the stench of rotten apples out of her hair."

"Oh, no!" Arabella cried. "Why didn't they like it?"

"A better question would be, was there anything in the play they did not hate? The trouble began with the prologue, about the third line—"

"We could argue your work all night, Richard," Neville said, taking Arabella's hand, "but my father is waiting in a coach below to take us home. This has been a most fatiguing evening."

"Your father?" Richard said incredulously.

"Have you become reconciled?" Foz asked hopefully.

"Not completely," Neville admitted. "I am not as willing as some to overlook the past." He gave Arabella a winsome smile. "However, I am willing to try.

"And," he continued, looking at his friends, "it seems that I was not the only one deluded as to a family member's activities. Apparently, my father had no intention of disinheriting me, and he wanted me to marry this wonderful woman all along."

Foz had to sit down. "He did?"

"I am so sorry that he misled you," Arabella said.

"He did not, particularly," Foz replied. "It was the late Lady Lippet, really."

"Who won't be misleading anyone anymore," Arabella observed quietly.

"You will take time from your writing to come to our wedding, Richard?" Neville asked, lightening the solemn mood. "And Foz, no celebration would be complete without you."

Richard grinned. "I shall be delighted to attend."

Foz's chest puffed up with proud pleasure. "Absolutely!" he cried, jumping up and bowing with a flourish that nearly sent his wig to the floor. "When is it to be?"

"As soon as possible," Arabella said happily.

Neville gave them his devilish little smile. "Within a fortnight, I should say."

"I might even make a wager upon that myself," Arabella said gravely, but with dancing eyes.

Neville chuckled. "Richard, I believe you may have to reconsider your view of matrimony, for I fear we are going to destroy all your notions that marriage is nothing but a prison. With that thought, I take my leave of you. Good night, my friends."

"Good night," Arabella said softly, her eyes glowing with joy and love as she smiled at her future husband.

Foz watched the happy couple leave, then turned to his friend.

"Richard?"

"What now?" the playwright asked absently as he contemplated his views on marriage, which were—or had been—far from favorable.

"I'll wager fifty pounds they have a child before next spring."

Dear Reader,

I just love Julia Quinn! So I'm so excited that, next month, her latest Avon Romantic Treasure is coming our way. It's called *How to Marry a Marquis*, and it's one of the most perfectly charming, witty and romantic love stories you'll ever read. In it, a delightful heroine stumbles upon a Regency-style version of *The Rules*, and needless to say romance follows.

Contemporary romance fans are in for a tender, heartwarming, wonderful treat as Neesa Hart makes her Avon debut with *Halfway to Paradise*. Single mom Maggie Crandall has faced tragedy and vowed to never love again. But handsome Scott Bishop has some very different ideas. Sprinkle in a touch of magical intervention and you have a love story sure to make you laugh and cry.

Genell Dellin returns to Avon Romance with a fabulous new historical mini-series, *The Renegades* –these are tough men tamed by the women who love them, beginning with *Cole*. He may be a gunslinger with a dangerous past, but he's about to be changed by the love of one very special woman.

Suzanne Enoch returns with *Taming Rafe*, a delightfully sparkling Regency-set Avon Historical Romance from an author whose humor, lively dialogue and sparkling sensuality have made her a reader favorite. Here, a confirmed rake wins a tumbling down manor on a bet...but what he doesn't bet on is also winning the hand of the manor's very beautiful owner.

Until next time,
Enjoy!

Lucia Macro

Lucia Macro
Senior Editor

AEL 0299

Avon Romances—
the best in exceptional authors and unforgettable novels!